COZY WITCH

TORRENT WITCHES COZY MYSTERIES BOOK EIGHT

TESS LAKE

ALSO BY TESS LAKE

Torrent Witches Cozy Mysteries

Butter Witch (Torrent Witches Cozy Mysteries #1)

Treasure Witch (Torrent Witches Cozy Mysteries #2)

Hidden Witch (Torrent Witches Cozy Mysteries #3)

Fabulous Witch (Torrent Witches Cozy Mysteries #4)

Holiday Witch (Torrent Witches Cozy Mysteries #5)

Shadow Witch (Torrent Witches Cozy Mysteries #6)

Love Witch (Torrent Witches Cozy Mysteries #7)

Cozy Witch (Torrent Witches Cozy Mysteries #8)

Lost Witch (Torrent Witches Cozy Mysteries #9)

Wicked Witch (Torrent Witches Cozy Mysteries #10)

Box Sets

Torrent Witches Box Set #1 (Butter Witch, Treasure Witch, Hidden
Witch)

Torrent Witches Box Set #2 (Fabulous Witch, Holiday Witch,
Shadow Witch)

Audiobooks

Butter Witch

Treasure Witch

Hidden Witch

Torrent Witches Box Set #1 (Butter Witch, Treasure Witch, Hidden
Witch)

Fabulous Witch

Holiday Witch

Shadow Witch

Torrent Witches Box Set #2 (Fabulous Witch, Holiday Witch, Shadow Witch)

Love Witch

Cozy Witch

Lost Witch

Wicked Witch

CHAPTER ONE

*V*ampires were lurking at the door again.

"This is *so* the wrong weather for those kinds of clothes," Kira said, unfolding what had to be chair a million.

"It's the wrong weather for anyone except maybe, I dunno, *volcano monsters*, full stop," I said, wiping sweat from my forehead. I set up another chair and then stretched, feeling my lower back muscles protest.

"Hey, I found ice!" Sophira called out, walking into the town hall space, carrying three glasses of water.

We stopped and drank the chilled water. My Goddess it was good. I wish I had a bath full of it I could dive into.

"He's doing an excellent Andreas," Sophira said, nodding to the lead vampire who was peering in through the doors, hoping to catch a glimpse of Bella Shade, superstar author of the *Bitten* vampire series. She hadn't arrived in Harlot Bay yet so all the vampires were really doing was standing in the blazing sun wearing mostly black.

"That Tyra is *a-maz-ing*. She even has the locket Jules gave her in book three," Kira said.

I looked, although I was unaware of who Andreas, Tyra or Jules were. I think the girl in the front in a stunning corset with a gleaming silver locket glinting around her neck must have been the "Tyra" character.

"The girl with the locket is Tyra," Sophira said helpfully.

"Join ussssss, joooooooiiiinnnn ussss," Kira said in her best cult leader voice and poked me in the ribs.

"Hey! I will, I'm going to, I promise! I'm trying to write my own story at the moment and from what I've seen, *Bitten* is a new super addictive drug that will suck me in and I'll wake up months later not knowing what happened."

"What will have happened is love and betrayal and treachery and did I mention love? Heartbreaking love!" Kira said.

"And a curse. Don't forget the curse," Sophira added.

"Are you talking about the one in books one to seven or that one later? Or the... you know... that *other* one," Kira said, wriggling her eyebrows and trying to convey information without spoiling the books for me.

"The guy with the spiky hair one."

"I was so sad I cried for hours," Kira said and then wiped away a tear that had appeared at the sudden memory.

"You're not making it easy for me to *not* read them!" I said, not for the first time. Molly and Luce were deep into *Bitten* too, and every day I was feeling the urge to start reading them myself.

"That's the idea Torrent. Then you can learn what true love is," Kira quipped.

"I know what true love is," I murmured, taking a sip of my water that was now heading to tepid. The vampires were conferring, clearly debating whether to lurk near the door in the blaze of sun or find somewhere else cooler to hang out.

It was Summer, blisteringly hot, sweaty, not a drop of rain, feel like we're living in an oven Summer. Writerpalooza had crept up on the town and then exploded. When the Mayor had announced it months ago, it was meant to run for a week. Authors of all stripes were visiting, there were workshops and talks and symposiums on topics such as "The Clumsy Girl in Modern Fiction."

Then it had unexpectedly grown, more and more authors signing up, bigger names until the biggest name at the moment joined: Bella Shade. Writerpalooza at that point had already expanded to ten days, and Bella announcing she'd be attending blew it out to a full two weeks. Overnight, every hotel, motel and bed-and-breakfast were fully booked. The Torrent Bed-and-Breakfast didn't have a spare room, and the moms were debating offering camping spaces for the flood of tourists and fans who would be in town (this decision was still being debated given we had *some* clear land but it edged on to an area of ruined cottages, empty and full wells, cave openings and Goddess knows what other witchy things there were).

Writerpalooza had grown so big so fast that the state decided to throw money into it, with the idea of making it a yearly fixture that could draw tourists from all over the country. Suddenly, there was serious money involved, and the low-paid, almost-volunteer positions were transformed into well-paying ones.

I'd put down my name on a list for a job, like most of the town who didn't have permanent employment, without much hope of getting one. As Writerpalooza drew nearer, and the positions were quickly filled I was looking at a Summer of part-time waitressing work at *The Cozy Cat Café* (Peta had taken over the *Traveler Café* and rebranded it but more on that later), helping out my cousins at *Traveler*, the moms at the bakery and the bed-and-breakfast and Aunt Cass at the Chili Challenge, as well as my library part-time job that was down to two hours a week and sure to extinguish soon.

I was living the life of many people in small towns: try to put together fifty jobs to match a full-time minimum wage.

Yes, I could make a comment about resilience and go get 'em and all that nonsense, but the fact was that living like this sucked, worse than a vampire.

Ha! See what I did there? Vampires... sucked... okay, forget it.

Then someone had dropped out, Kira had put in a good word for me as a replacement and I was in!

Now, sweating in a giant hall (thanks to broken air conditioning that was being repaired), I wasn't *super* happy with my job, but then I remembered the money and felt much better.

To combat the high levels of youth unemployment (and also keep them off the streets), the town had hired every high-schooler who had wanted a job which is how Kira, Sophira and me had ended up working together.

What had seemed like a lifetime ago, the three of us had ended up in a burning mansion together, would-be victims of crazed arsonist Hendrick Gresso. After that, although Sophira and Kira were friends, I'd barely seen Sophira. Part of it was, yes, she was a teenager and why would we see each other but sometimes, I felt it was the problem that arises when you go through something traumatic and extreme with a person - afterward it's hard to be *normal*, although she seemed okay now so far.

The vampires retreated, and I was left sipping my warming water, staring out at the heat rising up from the road (which, by the way, was *melting* in the hottest part of the day. If you weren't careful when you crossed the road you ended up with black gunk on your shoes.)

Normal, there was a word loaded down with meaning.

Was it *normal* to face murderers and dark entities? Was it *normal* to have a spell (maybe) pushing on you all hours of the day and night?

Was it *normal* to find stones with LOST WITCH TOOK JACK carved on them?

The stones in question were, as far as I knew, down in Aunt Cass's lair. After Jack and I had found them there had been a family meeting to beat all family meetings for emotional displays (I'm not only talking about *me* here either).

Here is the thing about witches: we're not big on doing what, as Aunt Cass might say, "the man" wants. We don't like filling in registration forms, we don't like lists of names, we try to stay under the radar in many ways, some subtle (mail delivered to H. Torrent), some not (mail delivered to Pablo Sanchez (Aunt Cass)).

This meant our family history was a mess.

Beyond Grandma and Aunt Cass's grandmother, we didn't know the rest of the family tree. The unknown Torrent witch I'd seen in a vision was still *unknown*. Her daughter, Rosetta, who had barely survived an encounter with the Shadow Witch couldn't be placed. Was she the grandmother's *mother* or somewhere further back?

We'd put Harlot Bay's top researcher (Ollie) on to the job but even after months of trawling old files, ruined newspapers and other aging records, he was no closer to a good answer.

Back to the emotional displays: Jack had been at the family meeting where Aunt Cass and I had pushed for Will and Ollie to be told about finding the LOST WITCH stones. Molly and Luce had argued against this, saying that, and I quote Molly here "A super strong dose of witchy will guarantee both of us will end up single and Goddess help me if that happens I'll curse all of you and no one will end up with grandchildren!".

Aunt Cass had then whipped a phone out of nowhere, tapped away and said: "It's done, they know, let's move on."

Molly was already planning her next curse.

So the boyfriends knew, the moms knew, Aunt Cass and I knew, and what did this produce? Not much. Sure, we'd Ollie on the case investigating at the library, but contrary to what adventure movies have taught us, it wasn't like he'd opened a book, found the puzzle and then we were racing across the desert to steal the golden jewel. It was mostly Ollie keeping us updated saying "I'm still looking. Maybe I'll find something."

Molly, Luce and I had started training with the moms and then Aunt Cass learning new spells, and if you're thinking training montage let me stop you right there. It certainly wasn't one of those events where we were terrible at the beginning, but then as we struggled we slowly improved until the final frame was us being super fit and ready to take on the world. It was more like going out into the forest, trying to learn a spell, dealing with a few snarky comments from our moms, getting frustrated, getting into arguments, and generally all of us finding ourselves too busy to commit time to it.

I still had my wall of crazy up in my secret lair, which only Jack knew about. I went out there as often as I could, but every time I tried to focus on it I found my mind drifting, which is probably the reason I managed to have written about half of my ghost story. I'd sit down and look at the wall, turn my laptop on and suddenly find myself inspired to write. Sometimes in the back of my mind I realized that it was the spell pushing on me but it had a good outcome so, hey, why not go with it?

"Hello... Torrent?" Kira said.

I came back to the here and now and found the two teenagers watching me.

"Sorry, daydreaming," I muttered and gulped down the last of my water which did absolutely nothing to relieve the temperature in the hall.

"Daydreaming about getting married?" Kira said with a smirk.

"When is Jack going to pop the question may we ask?" Sophira said.

"I was daydreaming about whether there was a spell that turned teenagers into frogs," I replied.

"Definitely thinking about her upcoming wedding," Kira said.

"I wonder if she'll wear white?" Sophira said with a grin.

"Oh really, Sophira, who I have seen down the beach hanging around that van that sells ice creams. I wonder why you could have been down there?" I said.

"No reason. Maybe I wanted an ice cream."

"And Kira, Miss I'm-going-out-to-visit-the-Torrents-on-a-weekend and then it turns out you *didn't* visit the Torrents and isn't it interesting that you would tell your grandmother that you were coming to visit us when in fact you weren't. I wonder where you could have been?"

"Oh gosh, did my Grandma ask you?" Kira said, her face turning pale.

My jaw fell open and I laughed. "My Goddess, I got you so bad! You confessed. No, I haven't spoken Hattie in months but you confessed to me because you thought I had. Didn't me, Molly and Luce teach you anything?"

We continued setting up the chairs, the hall seemed to grow even hotter as we did, trading snarky yet humorous comments back and forth.

I discovered the boy that Sophira had a crush on was named Tony and he was indeed working in the ice cream van over the Summer. He was two years older than her and, according to Kira, had luscious blue eyes that Sophira couldn't help herself gazing into.

Sophira gave as good as she got though, teasing Kira about her boyfriend Fox whom she'd met during the play *The Taming of The Shrew* some months ago.

We worked and sweated and laughed, and yes, it was fun hanging out with the teenagers. Their lives were simultaneously deadly serious but also lighthearted and shallow.

They had problems like everyone else did, but they had a complete absence of problems that everyone else had like, say, trying to pay your rent or buy food or get your ancient car repaired before it broke down for the fiftieth time.

We saw another flock of vampires come and go from the door as we continued to set up chairs.

We were getting close to finished when one of the organizers, Angela, appeared at the end of the hall and came rushing in.

"Oh Harlow, it's so good you're here! You're a writer, right?" she called out as she approached.

We all took this interruption as a chance to take a break, Sophira going off to grab more glasses of chilled water.

"I used to be a journalist and I guess I am sort of writing a book at the moment," I said, feeling incredibly awkward to be confessing to writing a book. I don't know why though. You don't feel awkward telling someone you're baking a cake or cleaning your house. But tell someone you're writing a book? It feels *weird*.

Angela zipped around the end of the chairs and came to a halt in front of me before wiping the sweat from her forehead.

"Wow it's hot in here. I hope that repair gets done soon," she said.

"I think the guy is working on it now," I said, still a bit confused as to why she would ask me if I was a writer.

"I need to know if you want to be the personal assistant to Red Forrest."

"What happened to… was it Meredith?"

"She's dead."

I had that plunging feeling in my stomach and a burst of goosebumps, but then Angela laughed, clapping her hands at her own joke.

"Or she has a broken leg."

"What happened?" I said, still trying to recover my balance.

"She was trying to do that dance move… what was that movie where the young girl goes to the resort and there's the sexy dance guy? Anyway, they tried to do the lift, it didn't work, Meredith broke her leg, her husband Rex fractured his arm, it's a mess. She was going to be PA to Red Forrest, but obviously she can't do that now."

"Who's Red Forrest?"

"She writes cozy mysteries with a detective in them who's called Red as well, has a trench coat and bright red hair. All the books have red in the title like *Red Wine and You*, and *Red is the Color of Murder*. It's an extra hundred dollars a day plus there's a rental car that Meredith has already picked up. It's at her house. You essentially need to guide Red around, make sure she gets to all her events, help her with anything she needs. You're on call. I don't think she's going to be ringing you at two in the morning for muffins or anything… although if she does… make sure you get her muffins because we want Writerpalooza to have a great reputation for treating the writers well and to grow bigger and bigger each year. I figure since you're a writer, you'd get along well with her. Can you do it?"

She touched me on the arm and I almost flinched away

from habit but managed to stop myself at the last moment. Months ago during *The Taming of The Shrew* I had slipped and acquired a power where I would hear sounds associated with a person when I touched them. Sometimes it was benign or even good, such as when Jack touched me. I would sometimes hear him speaking about police matters from the past or hear the sound of wood sawing or hammering from the present. Other times it had been terrible, such as hearing the sounds of poisonous frogs croaking and people shouting Shakespearean insults at each other. That had been the murderer, Viola, who had attempted to poison the theater director and had actually killed an assistant. The strange slip power had only vanished about two weeks ago, much to my relief, but I still wasn't back to normal. I kept holding my arms in at my sides and avoiding touching anyone if I could help it.

"I can do that," I said, trying to think my way through all the possible problems that might arise. The current job I had was essentially a low-level assistant. Hence, I would be setting up chairs, folding up chairs, cleaning, opening doors, checking tickets and things like that. The pay was okay, but the job itself promised to be quite monotonous. Working as a personal assistant to one of the authors sounded much more interesting provided they weren't some crazy horrible person which, knowing my luck, they would be. But still, an extra hundred dollars a day and a new rental car to drive? That sounded *amazing*.

"Excellent, here's an itinerary plus I'll message you a copy as well. You need to go around to Meredith's - her address is on there - to pick up the rental and then you meet Red tomorrow. Let me know during the week if you need any help with anything and I'll check in every now and again to make sure things are going okay."

"Thanks, sounds good."

Sophira had returned with ice-cold glasses of water, bringing a fourth one for Angela as well. She gulped it down in record time, waved goodbye to us and left.

"What was that about?" Sophira asked.

"Torrent got promoted up to the big leagues. She's leaving us behind. We're gonna be setting up chairs and checking tickets and she'll be living the high life as an author's personal assistant," Kira said with a smile.

"It's not Bella Shade is it?" Sophira said.

"No, it's Red Forrest," I said, checking the itinerary and information that Angela had given me.

"What does she write?" Sophira asked, clearly disappointed that I wouldn't have the inside link to her current favorite author.

I rechecked the piece of paper.

"She wrote *Better Red Than Dead, Red My Mind, Red Faced, Red Velvet, Red Wine and You, Seeing Red, Red Riot.* They star a character called Red Herringbone who was a former journalist who ends up solving mysteries...," I said, trailing off at the end.

"At least that's better than setting up chairs in a hot hall," Sophira said.

"Yeah, looks like it could be fun," I said, reading through the itinerary.

One of the events later in the week was a panel discussion on *Writing the Small Town Murder.* Another one was called *Getting Cozy with a Witch.*

Definitely hitting a little too close to home.

There was also a free concert halfway through Writerpalooza that looked like it could be fun.

I was startled out of my reverie by a sudden rapping on the glass door. It was another vampire who I now recognized as Andreas from *Bitten.*

"Is Bella Shade here yet?" he called out.

"Nope," Kira yelled out in return. He nodded and walked away, the hot sun blazing down on his black clothing. Just then we heard an enormous thunk from outside, something that sounded like a jet engine starting up, and then there was a burst of cool air from the ducts up in the ceiling as the air conditioning kicked into gear.

"Yes, cold air," Kira said and gave Sophira high-five.

I grinned at them. A new job, more money, hanging out with a published author, and a rental car to drive around—everything was looking great.

CHAPTER TWO

J awoke ridiculously early on Friday morning, hot
and sweaty, alone in Jack's bed. I rolled over and
rubbed the sleep from my eyes and then smiled at the
friendly sound of bacon and eggs cooking from down in the
kitchen. Thanks to the hot weather, Jack had been getting up
earlier and earlier in the morning to go to work, sometimes
even working through the night rather than through the
hottest part of the day. Since his brother Jonas had obtained
permission to rebuild and develop the Governor's mansion
out on Truer Island, Jack had spent a lot of nights out there
with the rest of the crew restoring the mansion to its former
glory.

It had been to Jonas's great surprise that he'd been finally
approved to take over the development of the Governor's
mansion. He'd been facing off against Sylvester Coldwell, the
slimiest real estate agent in Harlot Bay, and felt he was being
blocked at every step by the corrupt developer.

Approval had unexpectedly come through and Jonas had
immediately hired Jack to oversee the work crew out on
Truer Island.

Jack going to work full-time on the Governor's mansion was certainly good for his bank balance but not so great for the house he'd bought. He'd been working on it for months on end now, knocking down walls, making piles of rubble, and generally ripping out anything old and rundown, which to my eye was around about most of the house. He was actually getting somewhere though. There had been *rubble* everywhere then *piles of rubble* then *piles of rubble carefully arranged*. He seemed recently to have reached some kind of stasis point where he was getting rid of as much rubble as he was creating and now, slowly, the house was beginning to clean up, getting right back to its bare bones. When I had time I was often over there helping him, sanding, and knocking down walls, painting rooms. We did still go on dates and it was always great to go out to Valhalla Viking for a steak and beer or to get some delicious Indian take-out to eat on the beach but many times working on his old wreck of a house side-by-side chatting... it felt as though that was the real beating heart of our relationship. We worked and we talked, the conversation careening all over the place. The past, the present, and yes, sometimes the future.

After Will had proposed to Luce both Jack and Ollie had spent some time playing the same practical joke on Molly and me. Jack's version had involved a lot of bending down on one knee pretending he was picking up something off the ground or tying his shoelaces. Then he'd hold up his hand and say "Harlow Torrent, would you make me the happiest man in the world by... helping me up?"

The boys had obviously known that marriage questions would arrive the moment one of them proposed and they had, the moms becoming very interested in the topic. The jokes, as annoying as they were sometimes, certainly helped to take the pressure off. I wasn't wondering when it was Jack would ask me to marry him. I was happy living my life, or at least trying to, given all the supernatural problems floating around Harlot Bay. See that's the thing with problems. You can't live in that tensed up anxious state all the time. It's not possible. So despite the fact I found some rocks with *Lost Witch Took Jack* carved on them and we had no idea where they came from or what they were referring to, eventually, the fear and terror around that had faded and then one day I found myself with Jack on the beach eating an ice cream and laughing. *Normality* had a weight to it. It would always return, pushing away the darkness.

I got out of bed, pulled a skirt on, and then wandered down to the kitchen. Jack was already dressed in his work gear, which was essentially a very nice and well-fitting pair of tan shorts, a blue shirt, and some heavy work boots. He'd already covered himself in sunscreen to protect himself against the hot weather and so what did I essentially see as I wandered out to the kitchen? A somewhat shiny quite muscular man moving delicious crispy bacon around a frying pan.

In other words, *love.*

"I think the air conditioner's dead for good this time," Jack said by way of greeting.

Where Jack was living was a rental. At some time in the past the owner had renovated half the house and then stopped. So part of it was new and the rest of it was trapped in the 1970s. The aging air conditioner had been keeping up reasonably well as the temperature increased. But as it had been left on through more of the nights it had become less effective. It had broken down, which explained why I woke up to a room that felt like a slowly warming oven.

"How long until your house is move-in ready? Maybe you can buy an air conditioner?" I said and came up beside him to give him a good morning kiss.

He smelled like sunscreen which smelled like the beach

and I had the sudden urge to grab breakfast and head down to the seaside so we could go for a swim.

Jack had already poured me a coffee, knowing my morning routine by heart by now. I took it and went around to the other side of the kitchen bench, taking a seat on one of the stools and sipping my delicious drink.

"Could be a couple of months, it depends. How much rubble do we want to live with?" Jack said.

I was still half asleep and no, I'm not some crazy teenager, but still I felt a slight flutter in my stomach as he said *we*.

Long ago when Jack had bought the house and had taken me there, he'd hauled me up a set of very unsafe stairs into an upstairs room and then mentioned that he thought one day it could be a writing room for me. I had blurted out completely the wrong thing, but then recovered and given him a kiss instead, which is always a good way to cover up when you've said the wrong thing. Jack hadn't asked me to move in with him, nor to marry him, but it was a deep and abiding comfort feeling as though we were on a path and it was heading somewhere very good indeed.

"I could probably live with six piles of rubble, that's about my limit," I said with a smile.

I felt a furry shape brush past my feet and looked down to see Adams had stepped out of the shadow.

"Good morning, Adams," I said, knowing already what it was he was going to say.

"They didn't feed me! I'm starving to death!" he said. He threw himself dramatically on the floor but then started purring and rolling around.

"Both Molly and Luce forgot to feed you? I can't *believe* it. How have you managed?" I said.

My sarcasm went straight over Adams' head.

"I had to survive on the water I found in an old boot and then there was a dead bug. That's all I've had for the past three days," Adams said, clearly forgetting that in fact I'd fed him yesterday morning, and he was never bereft of food.

"You know, I think we should call the media, they need to hear your story," I said.

"Maybe I could have some bacon or do you have any eggs?" he asked.

He stood up and sauntered around to Jack's side of the kitchen bench before dramatically throwing himself on the ground again and beginning to roll around.

"All I need is a few pieces of bacon," Adams moaned.

"How's Butterscotch?" Jack said.

Butterscotch was a beautiful blonde cat with green eyes and thanks to me spending $29.99 at Adams' request, she wore a shimmering diamante collar. She was, as far as we could tell, Adams' girlfriend. It was hard to know with cats. They certainly didn't think the same way we did. Questions about their relationship were often met with a blank stare from Adams. We'd met Butterscotch some months ago, coming back to our end of the mansion to find her and Adams watching a documentary on television together. This surprising development was eclipsed by another a moment later when Butterscotch spoke to us.

I'm not saying I expected to have the only talking cat in the world. I'm sure there were plenty of witches who did. Adams was the only talking cat that I'd ever seen however and then to find another one sitting on our sofa was quite a surprise.

We'd seen Butterscotch on and off, and even tried to have a few conversations with her, but we didn't know where she was from or where she lived when she wasn't at our house. Questions such as "Who is your owner?" were met with a cold stare and Butterscotch saying, "I don't have an owner."

I know this might sound like she was some kind of ice princess, but Adams would say exactly the same thing. Both

17

of them consider themselves practically to be humans in cat form.

I saw the crafty look come across Adams' face as he sat up from the ground and looked at Jack.

"She's starving too! She doesn't get fed at all! Can you give me extra and I'll take it to her?" he said and then rubbed his head against Jack's leg. He pulled back a moment later when the fur on that side of his head slicked down thanks to the sunscreen that was all over Jack's body.

I picked up Jack's phone from the counter and used it to craft a lie from my devious cat.

"Molly and Luce say that you were fed this morning and last night, so I don't think you need any more breakfast," I said, pretending to be reading a message from Jack's phone.

Adams frowned at me and then stuck his tongue out.

"Fine, you'll be sad when I starve to death," he said in a huff. He walked away from Jack around the end of the bench but then didn't emerge, disappearing off to wherever it was he felt like going—likely our house and the sofa.

Jack was serving up breakfast when his phone buzzed in my hand and a message appeared. *Coming for a surprise visit! Be there in two days. We'll rent a hotel when we arrive XX J & J.*

"What does the message say?" Jack said, carefully shuffling bacon onto a plate.

I've never seen Jack panic. He used to be a police officer and even in the face of some fairly hairy situations like being trapped in a magical room and me throwing a fireball, he still remained calm. But as soon as I read out the message he fumbled the bacon, dropped the spatula, and burned his hand in his effort to get the frying pan back on the stove before he grabbed the phone from me.

"What is it, what's going on?" I said, somewhat alarmed at what he was doing and also that a piece of bacon had gone shooting off the plate and halfway across the bench.

"My parents are coming!" Jack said, tapping buttons on the phone.

It rang in his hand.

"Not me!" he said as he answered it.

I heard someone say something back and then Jack let out a breath and pinched the bridge of his nose between his fingers.

"You have way more room at your place," Jack said, obviously as a final defense but it was clear that he was losing whatever the conversation was.

"Okay, fine. They can stay here," Jack said.

He hung up and then smiled across at me.

"Surprise… my parents are coming to visit," he said.

"Didn't the message say they were going to stay in a hotel?" I asked, eyeing the piece of bacon sitting in the middle of the bench. Despite the impending arrival of parental figures who I knew I would have to meet, my stomach was getting the better of me.

"They *did* say that, and as per every other time they do this they're going to discover when they get to their destination that there are no hotels to stay at and they have to rely on the kindness of strangers, or their sons in this case," Jack said.

He passed me my breakfast and some cutlery, retrieving the piece of bacon off the bench and passing it to me. I took a bite. It was salty and delicious. Mmmm bacon.

"What are your parents like?" I asked.

Despite the fact we'd been together for a while now this was one topic of conversation that hadn't come up. I knew Jack's parents lived back in Canada and were both American.

Jonas and Jack were half-brothers, sharing the same father, but different mothers. Jack was the oldest brother from the first marriage and Jonas from the second. There weren't many years difference between them so it seemed that first marriage had collapsed quickly before the second had begun.

"They're fine, great even," Jack said, cutting into his eggs and taking a large bite. "You know how it is with parents—you love them. But you love them *even more* at a distance. Say, where they can't just drive and turn up on a whim."

"Do they know... about me?" I asked.

It was only after I asked that I realized there was somewhat of a double meaning in it. Jack caught on to what I was inquiring about, however.

"They know you exist, yes, but not that you're a witch, of course," Jack said.

He stopped with his coffee cup halfway to his lips and then let out a low whistle.

"Oh... we're going to have to introduce them to your family."

I'd still been feeling somewhat calm about his parents arriving but then this new development made me stop like Jack did.

"The mansion's full to the brim of people who have been coming down for dinner as well, so I think we might be able to avoid a big family dinner if we play our cards right," I said.

"Maybe we could take them to Valhalla Viking and invite the family along. Crowded place, lots of witnesses," he said, as though we were discussing a kidnapping victim being handed over rather than a dinner with my witchy family.

"If it's full, there are still all those tables up in the forest behind the mansion left over from Aunt Ro's wedding. I'm sure we could work out something there," I said.

We finished our breakfast, moving as fast as we could off the topic of parents and on to other less anxiety-inducing topics such as my excitement over being an author's personal assistant and my combined dread and hope that she wouldn't be a terrible person. Soon we'd finished our breakfast and Jack kissed me goodbye before rushing out. It was still early, but the heat was already rising and he was anxious to get out to the ferry to get across to Truer Island to begin work as soon as possible so he could finish early in the afternoon.

I was left sitting at the kitchen bench, sipping away on my second cup of coffee. I was idly musing over a few things when I looked down at the notepad Jack had on the bench next to an unpaid utility bill. On it, Jack had written down the twenty-four variations of the four words carved in the stones that we'd found.

Lost witch took Jack.
Lost witch Jack took.
Lost took Jack witch.
Took lost Jack witch.

...

He'd gone through all the variations but none of them made the message any better at all. Probably the least scary was *Jack took lost witch* or possibly *Lost Jack took witch*.

I read through the combinations before I closed the notepad and put it back where I'd found it. We'd all had our own methods for dealing with the odd and supernatural. I now had a wall of crazy up in a hidden lair, and I guess Jack was doing his own quiet investigation on the side. Not so much a wall of crazy as maybe a *notepad of crazy* or *carefully arranged folder of crazy*.

I checked the time—it was still early, but I needed to get moving. Since I'd been promoted yesterday, I now had an unexpected morning off because Red Forrest wasn't due to arrive until the afternoon and I had been relieved of my chair unfolding duties. I was planning to return to my lair to work on my story but that plan got crushed into the dirt, or rather cinnamon sugar, a second later when Mom rang.

"...he can have three dozen and no more. Oh good,

Harlow, I've been trying to get hold of you, can you come into work at the bakery?" Mom said.

As usual, she was halfway through a conversation when she rang me and again doing that thing where she pretended that she'd tried everything else to get in touch, such as sending a homing pigeon, smoke signals, a telegram, and just *now* was the first time I'd managed to speak with her.

"Why? What's happening?" I said warily. I only briefly talked with Mom last night, telling her of my promotion to personal assistant and so it wasn't a surprise to me that the next day I would be drafted. I cursed myself for revealing that I had any free time at all.

"There is some dance thing coming up and Susanna twisted her ankle rehearsing and now she can't come in. I don't know what she was doing but I need you from now until after lunch rush, and I know you aren't working today," Mom said in a breathless rush. Behind her I could hear Aunt Freya shouting out something about the buns that were in the oven. I presumed she was talking about *literal* buns and not metaphoric ones. It would be a little too far for even a witchy mom to bring up babies on an early morning phone call.

"Okay, I can help but I need to go right after the lunch rush," I said.

"Come as soon as you can," Mom said and then hung up without saying goodbye.

I got into rushing mode then, gulping down my coffee and running down to the bedroom to get ready.

It was great news that the bakery was busy. Since the original Big Pie had burnt down the moms had struggled for a while with home delivery before finding a new location and reopening. This was the peak tourist season so between the new reopened bakery and the Torrent Mansion bed-and-breakfast they were making quite a bit of money. So were

Molly and Luce, *Traveler* being packed every day even with *The Magic Bean* taking half their business. Peta's new café *The Cozy Cat* was full most days too. I'd even done some waitressing there before this new job working for Writerpalooza had come up.

I had a heart-stopping moment in my car when the engine refused to turn over but after praying for a moment to whatever magical forces might be around, holding my breath and pumping the gas a few times, my car finally started and I raced, as fast as you can race in a car that is on its last legs, into town.

I drove around to the rear of the Big Pie Bakery and found a spot to park. Even at this time of day there were tourists out on the streets and every car space would soon fill up. I had to wedge my old car between some trashcans and a larger dumpster, which was not the most glamorous of locations. I rushed inside where Aunt Ro immediately handed me an apron and told me to wash my hands. It wasn't yet seven, but they were already open and there was a horde of people out the front buying bread and other baked goods as fast as they could. Aunt Ro and Mom were still at the back frantically kneading dough and moving all kinds of things in and out of the ovens in a steady flow. Aunt Freya was up at the mansion on breakfast duty for all the guests.

Once I got myself ready, I rushed out the front and started serving customers.

There was something quite enjoyable about the sheer frantic speed of it. The bakery was cinnamon sweet, the delicious scent of freshly baked bread entwined with all the desserts and delicacies that the moms created. The whole place was saturated with a low level of magic as well. The moms would never admit to using magic in their baking, but you could feel there was certainly something magical happening there.

Three hours passed in the blink of an eye before the crazed morning rush decreased and I had a chance to take a breath. The air conditioners in the bakery were working overtime but with all the customers coming and going and opening the front door, it was incredibly warm. I managed to get away from the front counter and grab a bottle of ice-cold water in the fridge out the back, which I gulped down before returning to the counter. When I returned, it was to the most unusual sight. There was a man wearing a bright green top hat in a multicolored jacket with shimmery gloves holding a ukulele and talking to three stunned children and their parents who'd gathered in the bakery. My mind went blank for a moment before throwing up a name: Harry Sparkle, children's author and also performer. He wrote funny, quirky books, but also performed songs and dances at his concerts.

"I like your shoes," a little girl said to him and pointed to the enormous pair of green glittery shoes he was wearing.

"I like your shoes too!" Harry said then he straightened up, strummed his ukulele and began to sing "Shoes for me, shoes for you, what could a magical pair of shoes do?" He sang an impromptu rhyme as the children watched, breathless. When he finished, they clapped and cheered along with the parents, and I did too. He was such a joyous character! You could feel that he loved what he did and loved the children that he entertained. His performance finished, he bowed to the children, held out his hand so they could give him high-fives and then he came to the counter and grinned at me. I felt like one of those stunned children myself. His eyes glittered green and he looked like a mischievous elf.

"One loaf of your finest bread and also a magical custard bun, please," he said.

I retrieved his bread and a custard bun in a kind of breathless silence. He winked at me and then waved goodbye to everyone in the bakery before heading out the front door to a waiting car that was painted blue and yellow in stripes that looked like a beetle. Printed on the door with a star around it was *Harry Sparkle*. The crowd of children watched him as he tooted his horn and drove away.

"I met Harry sparkle!" the little girl said to me as she and her mom reached the front counter.

"Me too!" I said.

I looked out through the door and saw a few vampires walking by. Not far behind them was a man dressed in a futuristic robot suit. Writerpalooza wasn't officially kicking off until tomorrow but people in the town had certainly got into the spirit of things. I served the little girl and her mother and then the lull was over as the crowds began to stream in, drawn by the delicious food that the moms baked.

Somewhere in that flood of people I realized I was grinning, skipping about the place, my heart filled with joy.

CHAPTER THREE

I gave the moms as much time as I could but eventually I had to go if I was to make it home for a quick shower and back to meet Red Forrest. The lunchtime rush had become the afternoon rush with no lull in the volume of customers. Not even the blistering heat outside could dissuade them. I gave my apologies to Carla, the other counter staff member, rushed out the back, dumped my apron, and then out to my car where I spent a frustrating few minutes trying to get it out of the very tight car parking space because somebody had moved the trashcans and boxed me in. With the severe lack of parking around Harlot Bay it wasn't a surprise, but it certainly wasn't helpful. By the time I got my car going I was sweating like crazy and practically baking alive. It felt like it was about a thousand degrees in there. The steering wheel was so hot I had to use an old towel that I'd been keeping on the passenger seat to protect my hands.

I slowly made my way out of Harlot Bay, the laughably titled air conditioning in my car doing very little to cool me. I eventually got out of all the traffic and tourists, leaving the vampires and other costumed characters behind and got home in time to walk right into Molly and Luce's ambush.

"You're on the inside so tell us what you know—is Bella Shade here yet?" Luce said the moment I walked in the door.

"You need to tell us because we're your family and family is what matters. And also vampires," Molly said.

"Shouldn't you guys be at *Traveler*? Don't you have like a million customers today?" I said throwing my bag on the floor, narrowly missing Adams who was rolling around and purring.

"We've let the staff handle it—we can't be there every single day or it will kill us," Molly said.

"But you didn't answer the question, so confess. When is Bella Shade getting here?" Luce said.

"I don't actually know, I don't have her itinerary. I'm working for a different author entirely. But if I find out anything, I'll let you know," I said.

Molly turned to Luce. "She says she'll let us know. If only she knew true love the way *we* know it," she said.

"Perhaps if her heart had been opened, she would realize how important this is," Luce replied.

"My heart is open. I know what true love is. And yes, I'm going to read those books once I've gotten through writing mine," I said, a little irritable.

I left my cousins behind as they started talking about *Bitten* and rushed in for a quick shower. I had a few moments of indecision in front of my wardrobe wondering what it was an author's personal assistant was meant to wear, but in the end I had to bow in deference to the weather and so I chose a skirt and a light top. There was no way anyone could wear anything heavier in Harlot Bay and expect to survive. I had frankly no idea how those vampires weren't being taken off to the hospital with dehydration.

I came back out to the lounge as the front door opened

and Aunt Cass marched in. She was wearing a sundress with flowers on it, which was quite cute. However the effect was ruined by the kneepads, elbow pads and bike helmet.

"Chop, chop you two, we've got to get going right now," she said, pointing at Molly and Luce.

"What are you wearing?" I blurted out.

"Safety gear," Aunt Cass said.

"No, we're only here for a quick break, we're going back to work now," Luce said, coming up with what I thought was a fairly good lie on the spot.

"No you're not. Your staff members are at work like mine are so you're coming with me into the depths of the house," Aunt Cass said.

"But my elbow still hurts from last time," Molly complained, grabbing at her elbow as though she'd shattered it and had forgotten temporarily.

Aunt Cass crossed her arms and gave both of them a look. "You're coming right now or I'm going to tell you what happens to Rikael," she said.

Molly and Luce both gasped.

"You wouldn't!" Luce stammered.

"Did you think Amis was going to let him play happy families? Especially after what happened with Julius?"

I looked down at Adams, who was watching this back and forth attentively.

"Okay, fine we'll come. Did you bring any safety gear for us?" Molly said.

"Expedition members are responsible for their own safety gear," Aunt Cass said.

Molly and Luce went off grumbling into the spare room to try to find some protective gear that they could wear, leaving me with Aunt Cass and Adams.

"I hear you're going to be working for Red Forrest," Aunt

Cass said, unbuckling her bike helmet. I knew she'd been wearing it for effect.

"Yeah, I have to meet her soon actually, so I need to go," I said, checking the time.

"Do you think …" Aunt Cass looked shy, which was, if you know Aunt Cass, a very unusual expression on her face. "Do you think she would sign my book?" Aunt Cass asked in a small voice.

"I can ask her. I mean, we're going to be working together for the next two weeks so maybe I can go one better and invite her up for a dinner or something," I said.

"A dinner?" Aunt Cass looked alarmed.

"I didn't know you liked her books," I said.

"What's not to like? A red-haired, feisty woman who solves murder mysteries. It is my jam," Aunt Cass said.

"Okay, well I have to go now," I said, heading for the door.

"Come on you two, the darkness of the mansion awaits. Mwahaha," Aunt Cass called out and gave an evil cackling witch laugh.

As I was walking out the door Aunt Cass called out, "I'll see you tomorrow for training."

I made some noncommittal noise, rushed out to my car which had returned to its hot oven temperature, and then drove back to town.

A recent development, Aunt Cass had decided that we should explore the mansion to see if we could find any clues as to who the unknown Torrent witch was or anything about our family tree. I'd only been along on one such expedition, going up into the roof space which, thanks to the extreme temperatures, was now a no-go zone. We'd spent a very hot and dusty hour in one of the upper rooms going through ruined boxes of books, hoping to find anything written on them that might indicate who they belonged to or where they might fit in the family tree.

After that, I'd managed to avoid going on any more expeditions but Molly and Luce hadn't been so lucky. Aunt Cass seemed to have a sixth sense as to when they were taking any time off from *Traveler* and would force them to come with her into the under-mansion to explore. It was the type of thing where you'd want to wear a helmet and any kind of protection you could. A while ago, Luce had fallen through the floor when Molly and I were down there snooping around. It was only pure luck that she hadn't fallen down to the next story below.

I headed down the hill into town, the windows wide open, the rush of air providing some cooling, although not much.

Given that I was now Red Forrest's personal assistant I'd probably be able to get out of training with Aunt Cass tomorrow, which was simultaneously a good thing and a bad thing. It was bad because yes, honestly I did need training and so did Molly and Luce. Being a Slip witch and not wanting to be, I'd avoided learning spells for years. Molly and Luce had only learned the bare basics, I think all three of us somewhat preferring to leave our witchy natures behind. The moms' and Aunt Cass's philosophy was: we'll teach you, you just have to ask. We hadn't asked and so they hadn't taught us.

That approach all changed once we'd had our encounter with the Shadow Witch. Subsequent events, such as the magical salamander that had brought both love and war to Harlot Bay, had further cemented the idea that we needed to be prepared for whatever supernatural things were happening in our town.

I checked Meredith's address on the back of the itinerary. It wasn't too far away from Jack's house that he was renovating. As I parked I realized I didn't have any idea what Aunt Cass had done with the magical salamander that she'd captured. The last I'd seen of it was in a magical cage when she'd given it to Molly and Luce to take back to the mansion. I could only hope that Aunt Cass had taken it somewhere where it couldn't escape and cause trouble again.

I parked in front of Meredith's and looked up and down the street, seeing a beautiful blue sports car parked across from me. Was that the rental?

The area was on the halfway tipping point between quite wealthy and quite poor. There were a few touristy holiday homes and ones that had been upgraded by retirees moving for the nice weather and the beach lifestyle. Then right next door would be some ancient wreck of a house that needed a severe renovation in the form of a bulldozer. Meredith's house was an old one, but it was clear it had been well loved and cared for. It had a beautiful white picket fence and a squeaky gate that led to an amazing front garden that unfortunately was wilting in the hot sun.

I ducked under the shade of the porch and knocked on the door. I heard someone call out "there in a minute!", and then it was almost a full two minutes before Meredith opened the door.

She was wearing a cast on her leg that went from ankle to knee and was moving on a pair of crutches.

As soon as I saw her I remembered who she was, having seen her at one of the orientation meetings for Writer-palooza.

"Are you Harlow? I'm Meredith," she said and held out her hand. Before I could shake it though she turned and yelled angrily back into the house. "Rex! Get the car keys!" Then she turned back to me and gave me a smile.

"Hi, sorry you injured your leg," I said.

"These things happen... of course, they wouldn't have happened if a certain someone could have done a lift properly!" Meredith shouted back into the house.

Rex appeared, holding a set of car keys. She snatched them and gave him a glare. His arm in a sling, obviously a casualty of the accident that had taken Meredith down.

Rex went skulking back into their house, leaving Meredith and me at the front door.

"Here you go. It's the blue one right there," Meredith said, pointing across the road.

I turned around to look again at the beautiful blue sports car on the other side of the road, the sun glinting off its polished exterior.

"It's a sports car," I said.

"Zero to sixty in... hey Rex, how fast does the sports car go?" Meredith yelled.

I heard Rex yell something back. I didn't quite get it, but it *possibly* sounded like zero to sixty in a few seconds? Meredith gave me the car keys and then sighed in disappointment.

"I love Red's books so much, I'm incredibly jealous that you're doing this job now," she said.

"I'm sorry you hurt yourself," I said.

I checked the time and saw I was going to be late if I stayed any longer. I said goodbye to Meredith and went on my way. As I was rushing out the front gate I heard her shouting from inside the house at Rex again.

I don't know cars, but I know luxury and this car was *pure* luxury. Inside were soft leather seats and it had that new car smell. It was also blazing hot because it had been parked in the sun, but only a moment after I started the engine and turned the air conditioner on, an icy breeze was blowing out, quickly dropping the temperature. It was so cold I swear you could have frozen a glass of water into ice cubes by holding it in front of the vent.

I took a few minutes to adjust the seat and then grinned at myself in the rear-view mirror. Then I saw my ancient car parked a little way down the street and cringed. That car had been with me through thick and thin, and now here I was abandoning it!

That slight pang of sorrow disappeared a moment later when I turned music on and the thudding sound system vibrated my very bones.

I realized I'd have to come back to get my car at some point, maybe later tomorrow, and perhaps take it around to Jack's.

I carefully pressed the accelerator and then squealed as the car lurched forward. It was powerful but quiet.

I drove into town, grinning the whole way until I reached *The Hardy Arms* where Red would be staying for the duration of Writerpalooza. I wasn't expecting there to be a parking space but then one opened right in front of me with perfect timing.

I was sitting in the car with the engine running when my phone rang from an unknown number.

"Harlow Torrent," I answered.

"Good afternoon, Harlow, it's Red—Angela sent me your number. We're driving up to the hotel now and wondering where we could meet you?" she said.

"I've parked out the front so I can meet you at the visitor car park," I said.

"Sure thing sweetness," Red said. "We're the ones driving the yellow military truck. See you in a few minutes."

Her voice had a kind of throaty raspiness to it with a slight southern twang. As soon as she hung up I breathed an intense sigh of relief. I know it was a little much to judge from a few seconds of phone call but I could already tell that she wasn't some horrible person or a megalomaniac.

It wasn't long before a bright yellow military truck turned the corner and went around to the rear of the Hardy Arms. I only caught a brief glimpse of the driver. She had vivid red hair that practically looked like it was aflame in the hot sun.

I turned the car off and stepped out into the heat that hit me like a thousand bricks in the face. I swear I nearly burst into flames on the spot. I hit the button to lock the car and rushed over to the safety of the shade, although it wasn't much cooler.

By the time I got around to the rear of the Hardy Arms I was drenched in sweat, which is exactly what you want to look like when you're about to meet the person you're going to be working for. I turned the corner and saw four people gathered around the yellow truck, hauling luggage out of the back of it as fast as they could, to avoid staying in the sun. There was Red, who I presumed was the woman with the vivid red hair, and then beside her was a mountain of a man, his arms and legs roped with muscle and covered with tattoos. He had an enormous black beard and spiky hair and was wearing a pair of mirror sunglasses. Next to him was a small Asian woman who seriously looked like she only came up to his waist in height. She was struggling to pull a bag from the back of the truck. Beside her there was a man with curly brown hair and glasses who looked like he'd stepped straight out of an office somewhere, wearing a pair of slacks and a buttoned blue shirt that was, unfortunately, looking quite sweaty at the armpits.

"Hi everyone," I called out and rushed over to help them.

"Don't you look as sweet as a piece of pie. I'm Red," the woman with the red hair said and then gave me a quick hug, which in my surprise I forgot to return entirely.

"Let's get out of this sun and then we'll do introductions," she said. I helped them unload their luggage and then the five of us rushed inside the Hardy Arms as fast as we could. We clattered into the foyer with a mass of suitcases on wheels and other bags.

"Last time I was that hot was in Iraq," the giant said.

I looked over at the counter and saw Aveline Hardy, the owner of the Hardy Arms, was watching us with a welcoming smile.

Red turned to me and then whacked me on the shoulder with her hand.

"You have strong muscles, excellent for hauling luggage. Thanks for helping us," she said and gave a throaty chuckle.

"Not a problem, that's what I'm here for," I said.

"Introductions," Red said.

"This is Jenna Cheng, she writes cozy mysteries solved by cats," she said, pointing to the shorter lady. "This is TJ McKenna. He writes Grandma Gough, who's always making pies and cakes and also solving murders. Finally, this is Jay Savage who writes the most amazing bloodthirsty murder mysteries that are so *wonderfully* gruesome," Red said. I greeted them each in turn, shaking their hands one by one. TJ was a giant; my hand practically disappeared in his.

"You have the hire car, right?" Red asked me.

"Blue sports car out the front," I said.

"A blue sports car Red? Geez you're making us look bad here," Jay said with a smile.

"I didn't pick it, darling… well, actually I did, that's just something I say," she said.

Red handed a set of keys over to TJ and then they all went to the counter to check in, talking as they went. I realized they were all close friends and that TJ, although he looked like he was a barbarian, was quite soft-spoken. Aveline checked everybody in, gave them the room keys, and then I followed them into the elevator.

It was only when we were walking down the corridor to Red's room that I realized the last time I was in the Hardy Arms I'd been breaking in. It felt like it was ten lifetimes ago. I'd put myself under a concealment spell to break into someone's room who I thought was connected to some old murders. It turned out I'd been wrong and had in fact pointed the finger of blame at someone who'd ultimately been innocent. He'd actually been in town searching for his lost friend. He'd forgiven me somewhat for that but as we walked down the corridor I felt a small twinge of guilt that Red must have seen.

"You okay darling?" she asked me.

"Uh, yeah, just recovering from the heat," I said. I followed Red into her room and helped her move her luggage over to the bed. The air conditioning had been running in here and so it was lovely and cool, but somewhat dark because the curtains were closed to keep the sunlight out. Red opened them and looked out into the street.

"Harlot Bay, the small mysterious town with a mysterious past," she said, as though she was narrating a movie trailer. She moved over to the bed and started unzipping her suitcase.

"You're the one who used to write that online newspaper aren't you?" she said.

"Oh, you read that? I sort of shut it down, although I left it still online," I said, stammering a little.

"I always research the places where I'm doing readings or going to visit. It's excellent grist for the mill and makes my books better," she said. "You have a good writing style. Have you written any fiction?" she asked.

As she was saying this, she was pulling book after book out of one of her suitcases. They all had her name emblazoned on the side. She piled them on the desk that was against the far wall. All the front covers featured a woman with fiery red hair wearing a trenchcoat.

"Um… I've been working on a story recently. It's about halfway done I think," I said, feeling quite put on the spot.

Red looked at me and then narrowed her eyes and

pointed her finger. "What kind of story is it? Cozy? You trying to come on to my turf?" she said in mock outrage and then laughed.

"It's about a ghost. I think it's a ghost romance, I guess."

"Good choice, very popular, heartbreaking. When you're ready you should send some to me to read," Red said.

I stammered some reply. I wasn't quite sure whether it was a yes or no and then Red came over and patted me on the arm.

"No pressure at all, Harlow. I never talk about my books until they're done anyway. But if you do want to send it to me I'm serious about that," she said and then she gave me a grin.

"Now let's get in that sports car and find out what there is to do in this town," she said.

She grabbed me by the hand and pulled me out of the hotel room laughing as she went. I could barely keep my feet but soon I was laughing too.

CHAPTER FOUR

"*I*t is a truth universally acknowledged, that a single man in possession of a fortune must be in want of a wife," I said.

The assorted writers around me cringed and Jay shook his head and pointed his finger at the shot of vodka that sat in front of me.

"Sorry, Torrent. The correct line is 'It is a truth universally acknowledged, that a single man in possession of a *good* fortune must be in want of a wife.' Drink," he said.

The surrounding writers cheered as I groaned and then drank the shot of vodka, the fiery liquid burning its way down my throat. I slammed the shot glass down on the table and sat down, my head starting to spin.

Beside me, TJ shot up out of his chair like a furious giant and waved his arms in the air.

"However, little-known the feelings or views of such a man may be on his first entering a neighborhood, this truth is so well fixed in the minds of the surrounding families, that he is considered as the rightful property of some one or other of their daughters," he recited.

"Perfect!" Jenna Cheng shouted out. TJ high-fived her so hard she almost fell over and everyone cheered in drunken celebration.

Since leaving the Hardy Arms with Red... things had gotten a little bit out of control.

Firstly, the woman drove like a madman. Or madwoman. Whatever it was, she was mad.

She couldn't drive fast in Harlot Bay, of course, given the streets were clogged up with tourists, vampires and other assorted fans who had gathered in Harlot Bay for Writer-palooza.

We'd even seen a couple of girls dressed up as Red Herringbone, the main character from Red's book series. Red had beeped the horn and opened the window and given them all high-fives as we'd driven by, much to their delight and amazement. She wanted the tour of Harlot Bay, but as soon as we got bogged down by traffic she wanted to know the quickest road out, and so we went in the direction of the lighthouse. It was still closed to the public. Whoever had been renovating it had apparently stopped and so there were no more tours up to the top to look out over the bay. That was quite fine by me. The lighthouse and I didn't have such a great history. The last time I'd been there I had only barely managed to stop a man from leaping to his death. I'd saved his life, but he'd ended up with a broken leg and other injuries instead. The time before that, there had been a gigantic fire and me, Molly, Luce and Adams had been up the top. We'd used a cleaning broom and a bunch of spells to fly off and land in the icy ocean. So I was happy to pass on by and as soon as we hit the coastal roads, Red hit the gas and I swear we were zipping along so fast that I felt like I was going to blink and next minute we were going to end up in Florida. It was slightly scary but also it was a sports car so it felt very comfortable to be speeding along in such a beautiful machine.

As we drove, we talked non-stop. She'd had a husband, Eoin. He'd died eight years ago in a workplace accident that she didn't go into. He'd been a carpenter, working on building houses, much like Jack. They had a single daughter Rionach, Ri for short. She was due to go to college next year and with that line Red had looked at me and said, "And, yes, if you do the math you can work out exactly how young I was when I first had her."

She told me that her husband had only seen the beginning of her writing career before he'd passed away. She hadn't remarried, although she had, in her words, a few flings here and there, giving me a devilish smile. She'd spent all the years since writing books and traveling around the country going to readings and meeting her fans. She'd even been over to the UK twice and had included a tour through Germany where her books had taken off unexpectedly after they had been translated. Sitting beside her in the sports car as we zoomed along it sounded like an absolutely divine kind of life. I told her about Jack, my former policeman now carpenter boyfriend, and then talked about my family, leaving out of course any witchy business. I wasn't entirely intending to lure her to the Torrent mansion, but I guess I did talk up its mysterious past. As soon as I mentioned it, she knew exactly what I was talking about, given that as you drove in Harlot Bay, it was practically impossible to miss. I then let slip that Aunt Cass was one of her fans and Red had then clapped her hands and said, "That settles it then. We must have dinner out there; let's arrange it."

Time had flowed by easily. At one point we'd stopped and went out onto the beach, Red wading out to her knees while I stayed in the shade under a tree. When she returned I was surprised to see that she was wiping away tears. She'd told me it had always been her husband's dream to retire to the seaside, but they'd never got to achieve it, and he'd never got to see the success that her books had brought her.

She told me that her character Red Herringbone was dating a man in the book series and really it was Red's husband in different form, immortalized in prose.

I even wiped away a tear at that point, feeling the sudden loss of someone I'd never met. We returned to the sports car and continued down the coast before Red checked the time and turned us around and we raced all the way back to Harlot Bay. When we arrived at the Hardy Arms, I discovered that she and the other writers had arranged to take the conference room and a party was underway. There were more varieties of alcohol than you can imagine: bottles of champagne and wine and spirits; and soon I had a drink in my hand and was eating fish and chips that one of the writers had ordered. Varieties of take-out kept coming— Indian and then some pies, more fish and chips, Chinese and Thai. There were at least thirty writers and their names went by in a blur. Some of them I thought I recognized but I couldn't be sure.

Soon there was a flood of food and wine, and then shots that were tied to a literary quiz that I knew those sneaky writers had the advantage in.

"Once upon a time there were four little rabbits, and their names were Flopsy, Mopsy, Cottontail and Peter," Jenna yelled out.

"And then the murders began..." Jay quipped. I laughed along with everyone else as the drinking game descended into chaos, everyone reciting first lines of famous novels and then saying "And then the murders began."

The night spun on in a blur. I found myself talking to TJ at one point. He was telling me about his books featuring Grandma Gough, a lovely old lady in her seventies who baked pies and cakes and also solved gruesome murders. It seemed almost every writer I spoke to was able to tell within a minute that I too was working on something and they were always encouraging, telling me to keep working, keep going and I could get it done.

Near midnight, the party began to wind down. I'd had too much to drink and so when Red suggested we all head out for a midnight stroll down to the beach I shouted out *yes!* along with everyone else. The party burst out into the streets and then exploded, going in different directions. I soon found myself with the original four: Red, TJ, Jenna, and Jay. I'd confirmed during the afternoon drive that they were close friends and had been for many years always helping each other and frequently meeting up on tour.

I'd also learned that TJ had been a former Navy Seal who'd spent quite a lot of time in hot countries. When he left the military, he'd turned to writing and now was an incredible success with his little old lady who solved mysteries.

Even at midnight, it was still hot, the road under our feet warm from the sun during the day. The five of us went roaming down the street. I think we'd somewhat forgotten that we'd intended to go to the beach because we were all still babbling along in that way that people who have had too much to drink do. We'd turned away from the beach, heading into town again for who knows what reason when somewhere close by there came a bone-chilling howl that ripped the night. We stopped and then Jenna blurted out "Are there wolves in Harlot Bay?"

The howl had echoed away, but it didn't sound like any wolf I'd ever heard before. There was pain in that howl and anguish, and I think, also fury.

"No wolves here," I said, shaking my head, I think trying to convince myself as much as them.

Although I'd had far too much to drink, and it was

certainly helping numb the senses, it couldn't stop the sudden feeling of wrongness that I had. The surrounding magic that ebbed and flowed in its own rhythm was stirred up like a muddy glass of water with chunks of grit throughout it. I took a breath and tried to calm my thudding heart. Of course, that failed a moment later when a man came staggering out of an alleyway toward us.

He was a tourist, that much was evident from his ridiculous Hawaiian shirt and shorts and the sunburn. His clothes were shredded, torn as though he'd been attacked. His arms and legs and face were bloody with deep scratches from something with sharp claws.

"Help me, help," he slurred and fell into us. None of us were quick enough to grab him so he sort of bounced off TJ's leg, leaving a streak of blood before he crashed to the road.

"Call an ambulance," TJ said kneeling down to roll the man onto his side.

I reached for my phone, but I didn't have it. I must've left it back at the hotel. Jenna had hers though.

"What happened to you?" Red said.

The man looked up at her, and I realized behind the blood and his wounds he'd been crying too.

"A monster attacked me," he said before he passed out.

The anxiety began to win its battle against the alcohol in my blood. The magic all around me was still wrong, and I had a sudden vision of a vicious creature leaping out of the dark to kill us all, me trying to perform magic to save us, and failing badly.

Red and TJ didn't seem to be taking it as seriously as I was though. TJ was inspecting his wounds, touching his fingers to the blood and then sniffing it.

Jay had knelt down beside him as well and was checking the wounds.

"Is this real?" Red asked them.

"What do you mean is it real? Hasn't he been attacked by something?" I said.

"Yeah, I think I recognize this guy. I'm pretty sure he's that one from Chicago," TJ said.

"Still, that's real blood and these are real wounds. Either this guy is the most intense method actor ever, or he was attacked by someone," Jay said.

"Method actor? What's going on?" I asked. My anxiety and confusion was making my stomach turn. Who knows, *maybe* that was all the alcohol and take-out.

"There is an author who likes to promote his books by putting on crazy stunts. Last time it was some a sea monster that apparently attacked somebody. The *somebody* in that case I'm sure being this man. But I don't know, this does look like he was attacked," Red explained.

I knelt down and examined at the man. The wounds on his body were very real indeed. From somewhere behind us came another howl.

I turned around with everyone else but all I saw was a dark shape up on the roof, a glint of glowing eyes, and then it was gone.

"If this is a hoax, it's the best one I've ever seen," Jay said.

The unconscious man stirred and started mumbling. "Something attacked me, something came out of the dark," he said before lapsing back into unconsciousness.

I couldn't help but think that he'd chosen his words precisely, despite his wounds. Not *someone* had attacked him.

But some *thing*.

CHAPTER FIVE

J awoke in the morning hung over and boiling hot with a thudding head, alone in Jack's bed.

The bedroom door was open and I could hear him down in the kitchen, whistling softly to himself. He was cooking bacon and eggs, but this morning the sound wasn't friendly at all. The thought of eating made me want to throw up.

I groaned as I remembered why I felt like this, bits of the night coming together and whacking me in the brain. The ambulance and police had eventually arrived. Sheriff Hardy wasn't with them, which I was happy about. I didn't want my brand-new uncle to see me out on the street with blood on my hands having severely over-imbibed.

That's right, I'd had *blood on my hands* because when you let a girl who's had too much to drink examine someone injured she doesn't realize what she's touching with her hands.

I'd had a brief interview with one of the officers and then called Jack to bring me home. Turns out I did actually have my phone with me, but inebriated Harlow didn't realize that.

The writers had gone their own way, heading back to the Hardy Arms. Jack had come to pick me up and I remembered being in his truck and then waking up sometime in the night to stand over the bathroom sink trying to convince myself not to throw up, splashing water on my face and then gulping down a glass of it. Now it was morning, and I was certainly paying for last night.

I rolled out of bed and found I was just in a T-shirt and my underwear that had little cats wearing bowties on it. I looked around for the rest of my clothes but couldn't see them. I dragged my sorry self down to the kitchen, trying to breathe shallowly, the smell of bacon was making my stomach turn.

"Ah, there she is, aspirin's on the counter," Jack said, pointing a spatula at a glass of chilled water with two white tablets sitting next to it

I gulped the tablets down and swallowed the water, feeling my stomach gurgling in protest.

"What time is it?" I croaked.

"Just past seven which means you had about five and a half hours sleep," Jack said. "Do you want any of this?"

"I never want to see food again," I said and closed my eyes. "Wait, I was out until two in the morning?"

"It must have been some party. You'd better watch those writers, they're trouble," Jack said and gave me a smile.

I gave him a weak one in return and tried to cudgel my brain into thinking up a solution for my current predicament of feeling terrible. Unfortunately, my brain was feeling terrible too and so didn't have anything apart from drink water, try to eat some food at some point, and then stay in bed until you either felt better or died. Your choice.

My stomach growled again and a wave of nausea washed across me.

"I'm going to go sit in the lounge room," I mumbled. I

started staggering in that general direction when there was a loud knock on the front door right as I was about to pass by it. For some reason (well, we know the reason, I was tired and hung over) I decided that while in my T-shirt and underwear and holding half a glass of cold water to open the front door.

I pulled the door open to find an older version of Jack looking at me with a grin on his face. The woman beside him had deep red hair and was wearing a cheerful smile, far too cheerful for this time of the morning.

"You must be Harlow, we're Jack's parents," the man said.

Two things happened at that point. One, I gasped. Two, I dropped my glass of water which exploded at my feet.

"Urk," I said and then I bolted away from his parents, away from the broken glass and water, around the corner and down the corridor into the bedroom.

I don't know exactly what I was doing. Perhaps trying to get away. The moment I ran into the bedroom I tripped straight over Adams who must have stepped out of the darkness to speak to me, cracked my leg against the side of the bed and then toppled over it, bouncing off and landing on the floor on my back. As I lay there gasping, Adams moseyed up beside me and nuzzled at my head, tickling my face with his whiskers.

"Jack's parents are here," he said to me.

"I know," I gasped, trying to calm down.

"Do you think that seeing as I warned you that perhaps you could get me a little more–"

"I already met them so your warning's too late, no food for you," I said, not intending to be harsh but perhaps still a little shocked at what had happened.

Adams nuzzled against me, then walked off under the bed, vanishing into the dark.

I heard the bedroom door open and then Jack popped his head in and saw me on the floor.

"You okay? Did you cut yourself on the glass?" he said.

"I wish I was dead. That was so embarrassing," I groaned.

Jack came into the bedroom and closed the door behind him. He came over beside me, gently stroked my face and then helped me up off the ground. The room swirled around for a moment before he sat me on the bed. He handed me a cold bottle of water he'd been carrying in his other hand.

"It's fine. My parents have seen far worse," he said.

Despite my shock and my hangover and my stomach I could hear the slight joke in his voice.

"Oh yeah? How many girls exactly is it that they have met in underwear at your front door?" I said, trying to make a joke.

"Twenty-six," Jack said, matter-of-factly.

It's a good thing I hadn't had any water yet because I would have splurted it.

"What do you *mean* twenty-six?"

"Adele, Bianca, Charlize, Devon, Emma, Fiona, Georgina, Harlow, Indigo…" It took me a second to realize he was simply going through the alphabet and making up girl's names. I punched him in the arm as he laughed and then I groaned again, tipping forward, pushing my head into his chest as he wrapped his arms around me.

"Why did I drink so much?" I moaned.

"You'll be fine, I'll take them away for breakfast. You can recover and then we'll meet up, okay?"

"No it's fine, I should meet them," I said protesting weakly.

Jack made some noncommittal noise and then left me alone. I went to the shower, which did help somewhat, got dressed into some clothes that were living at Jack's house, and then made my way back to the kitchen where Jack and his parents were chatting and drinking coffee.

"She appears!" Jack's father said and gave me a grin.

"Don't throw any water glasses at us this time," his mother joked and gave me a smile too.

"I am *so* sorry. You've met me at probably the *worst* time of the last year. I'm working as a PA for an author and we had a big party last night and I lost too many drinking games and I promise the next time you see me I'll be witty and charming and *not* hungover," I said.

"It's not a problem. We thought we'd scared you with the old *we'll be there in two days* trick," Jack's dad said.

"It's the best trick of all," Jack said, rolling his eyes but smiling.

"I'm Harlow, by the way," I said.

Jack's dad stood up from the stool. He was about the same height as Jack and his eyes were roughly the same color, hovering on that point between blue and green. He had crinkles around his eyes from smiling. He shook my hand and then hugged me. You could see where Jack and Jonas had gotten their looks from.

"I'm Jonathan but you can call me Jon," he said.

"Jonathan, Jon, Jack, and Jonas, so you must be Julie or Jello?" I joked, smiling at Jack's mother.

"Almost. I'm Jasmine, you can call me Jas," she said and gave me a hug and a quick kiss.

Before we could get to talking, Jack abandoned his bacon and eggs, bustled his parents out of there, gave me a kiss, and said he'd talk to me later. I was soon left alone in his house. I opened the cupboard, took a two-second glance at a variety of cereals that my stomach decided it wanted nothing to do with, and then remembered that it was Jack who had driven me to his house in his truck last night. The rental car was still at the Hardy Arms, which was in the center of town. I groaned, grabbed another bottle of cold water from the fridge, and then stepped outside and locked the door behind me. Although it was early, the heat was rising, so I took off as fast as my hangover would allow me, heading for the center of town. It wasn't long before I was sweating and feeling very much worse for wear.

I was about halfway in when I saw the giant figure of TJ jogging his way up the road towards me. He was wearing a bright yellow fluorescent tank top and a matching pair of shorts, plus his mirrored sunglasses. As he approached, I could see his face was red, and he was sweating so much it looked like he'd fallen into a swimming pool. He came to a stop near me and pulled off his sunglasses, looking me up and down.

"I've gotta say this, but you look like you've been dragged through a hedge backward," he said and gave me a wink.

"I feel like that's what happened," I said. "What are you doing jogging, are you crazy?"

"It feels bad, but believe me, if you have a hangover, drink some water, exercise and you'll get rid of it faster than doing nothing. I guarantee it. You should eat some fried junk food, too," he said.

Now that he said it, I guess I was starting to feel a little better, perhaps from walking and the water. The thought of something fried and salty was actually starting to sound good.

"Have you seen anyone else this morning?" I asked.

"I think Red and Jenna went down the beach. I'm sharing a room with Jay and he's still asleep after spending quite a bit of time in the bathroom last night," TJ said. I groaned at the thought of it, took a sip of my water, and then I suddenly remembered TJ and Red claiming the man attacked was an actor.

"What did you say about that man last night? That he's an actor?" I blurted out.

"Yeah, I checked it out last night online. Carl Stern. He's the same paid guy who was in Chicago who was 'attacked' by a sea monster. Of course, it was all promotion for a book. I don't know what happened last night though. Maybe he fell off the roof or something, or perhaps he did get attacked. The wounds looked real to me."

"Who's the author who does the stunts?" I asked.

"His name is Markus Hornby. Writes monster stories. They're pretty good but for some reason he's into doing these crazy promotional stunts as well. I guarantee with the howling last night and if that guy was attacked, that Markus's next book is probably going to be about werewolves," TJ said.

The watch on his arm beeped at him in what I thought was quite an angry manner.

"Okay, heart rate is coming down, I've gotta get going. I'll see you later though," he said. He put his sunglasses on and jogged away.

I continued into Harlot Bay. The sun was well and truly up now. I could feel it beating down upon me, the temperature rising as I scurried from shadow to shadow trying to avoid being burnt to a crisp.

Publicity stunt or not there was something strange happening with the magic last night.

The lonely howling may have come from some hidden sound source, but in my heart I knew that wasn't true.

As I walked into town, heading for the Hardy Arms, I saw a young vampire heading down the street with a loaf of bread under his arm. I was fairly sure there was no such thing as *real* vampires of course. I mean, yes, there were entities that would drink blood but vampires weren't real. But what had TJ said? He'd bet that Markus Hornby's next book would be about werewolves. They weren't real... were they?

I needed to talk to Aunt Cass or the moms.

I finally made it to the car, started the engine and then relaxed in the chilled air conditioning.

The first event of today was at two in the afternoon, the grand opening of Writerpalooza at the Town Hall, so I didn't have anything to do until then except get home, maybe talk to Aunt Cass, have some food, and try to sleep. I drove home slowly, being careful on the bumpy road so I didn't damage the car.

I parked at our end of the mansion, stepped out of the car, and then my stomach growled. I was suddenly starving. I sniffed the air and caught the scent of delicious food coming from the other end of the mansion. It was still early, and I knew the dining room would likely be crowded with guests, but I couldn't resist. I had to get some of that food right now! I made my way as fast as I could down to the other end of the mansion and went inside to find the large dining table already filled with guests enjoying a delicious breakfast. I gave them a smile and wave and then went through into the kitchen where I found Mom frantically cooking and, surprisingly, Aunt Cass helping ferry out dishes to the guests.

"Oh Harlow, you look terrible, did Jack see like that?" Mom said.

"Yes, he did," I said with absolutely no tone in my voice. Despite the heavy early morning judgment, Mom was already putting together a plate for me, which she passed across and then also a cup of coffee which I sipped from gratefully. She'd handed me a plate of bacon and eggs and fried tomato. There were also some slices of watermelon on the side. The coffee had a vanilla flavor through it, courtesy of the beans that the moms had been experimenting with. It was yet another side-effect from Peta taking over The *Traveler Café* and rebranding it to *The Cozy Cat*. Molly and Luce had been right about trying to make each ingredient unique. Breads baked from special flours, free range eggs, goat's milk and things like that. Peta had dived headfirst into it and every time she got access to some great produce she shared her supply with the moms who were now incorporating it into the breakfasts out of the Torrent mansion. They were also making different breads at the bakery using the unique flours that they'd discovered.

As I thought of Peta I realized I hadn't seen her for at least a week. Between all of us being busy and her at *The Cozy Cat Café* we'd only managed to catch up in brief moments. I decided on the spot that I would find some time to hang out with my girl. Maybe a dinner?

I ate my breakfast, my stomach slowly starting to feel better as Mom cooked frantically and Aunt Cass moved dishes in and out. Eventually, the flow of food slowed as the table reached capacity and all the guests had come down to eat. That was when Aunt Cass sat down across from me with a hot cup of coffee and fixed me with a look.

"Was that you last night who did that to the magic?" she asked.

"You mean when it went all gritty and sort of muddy?"

"So it *was* you," Aunt Cass said.

"No, it *wasn't*. I was out at a party and then we went out into the streets, and suddenly there was a man with his clothes all ripped to pieces and wounds all up and down his arms," I said. I told Aunt Cass and Mom the story. Mom had been cleaning dishes at the beginning of it, but by the end was standing across from me with a worried look on her face.

"Do you think it could be… this feels ridiculous to say… could it be a werewolf?" I said.

"No, not possible," Aunt Cass said.

"Not possible because werewolves don't exist or not possible for some other reason?"

"I don't know if they exist, Harlow. That's not important. Something happened last night to make the magic all muddy like that and I felt it before, out on Truer Island before I had to fight that monster and there was an explosion," Aunt Cass snapped back at me.

"If you'd felt it before, why did you ask if it was me?"

"I hoped it was you," Aunt Cass said.

The details around exactly what Aunt Cass had fought were quite vague, not because she was being her usual secretive self but because it was difficult to explain exactly what it was. That it was magical was undeniable. Aunt Cass had said it *looked wrong in our reality* and she'd fought against it, casting one desperate last spell which had resulted in an explosion that excavated a hole about half a mile across and flattened the trees out on Truer Island. Aunt Cass had had to freeze herself to protect herself from it and it had taken us some time to find her stuck out there in the mud.

"So you fought a monster back then and you think this is *another* monster?" I asked.

"It could be. That's why it's good you're here so we can go training," Aunt Cass said.

I groaned and hung my head, but both Mom and Aunt Cass weren't having any of it.

"You're going to go, Harlow, because you have the morning off and you need to do it," Mom said, quite sharply. She went back to washing some dishes, clanging the spoons and knives around.

"I'll give you something for that headache first," Aunt Cass said. "Come with me."

As I was about to leave the kitchen, thinking that the day couldn't get much worse, Mom called out, "Oh we're going to be having a dinner now that Jack's parents are in town so make sure you invite them and please don't turn up hungover."

I spun around in disbelief.

"How do you even know they're here? I only met them this morning," I said.

"Adams told me," Mom said.

"That little snitch," I muttered and followed Aunt Cass out through the dining room of chatting guests.

As I followed Aunt Cass down to my end of the mansion I was trying to think up reasons I could use to get out of doing any kind of magical training, apart from me having a hangover.

"I'm working for Red Forrest. I can't do this right now, I need to prepare," I said, saying the first thing that came to my mind.

Aunt Cass passed me a small bottle and told me to drink it, which I did. It had an odd taste. Imagine if you took the scent of a sea breeze and compressed it into liquid. After I swallowed it I felt a momentary twinge of sadness that I couldn't be out on the ocean sailing.

"What is that?" I asked.

"I call it Sailor's Help. It'll get rid of that hangover," Aunt Cass said.

We kept walking on as though she hadn't heard me say a single thing about Red. It was only when we reached our end of the mansion that she finally spoke again.

"Give me two hours, Harlow, and then you can sleep and rest. I think it's better if you give me these two hours," she said.

Her tone was serious and for a moment I caught a flicker of worry on her face.

"Okay, I'll get changed," I said.

"You know where to meet me," Aunt Cass said and headed in the direction of the forest behind the mansion.

I went inside to find Adams sitting on the sofa watching the morning news.

"You're a little snitch," I said and pointed my finger at him.

The little black cat had the gall to look offended.

"What did I do?" he protested.

raining with Aunt Cass was a disaster. I was meant to be picking up pebbles and floating them about the place like Aunt Cass demonstrated. She picked up stones and leaves and other small things and then made them dance in a beautiful ballet. But when I tried it I ripped giant clods of earth out of the ground. At one point I managed to pick up three pebbles at once but then I sneezed and one of them shot sideways, ricocheted off a tree trunk and broke a window in one of the abandoned slumped over cottages nearby. Magic sometimes is precise words and chanting and ingredients and things like that, but at other times it's like a song—you have to listen and try to play along. Of course if songs go bad, they don't often *kill* you. So after two hours of unsuccessfully trying to move around small pebbles I ripped up my final clod of dirt and then I'd had enough. I left Aunt Cass up in the forest sitting on a tree stump saying she had to think about some things, went back to our end of the mansion and immediately crashed into bed where, thanks to the concoction Aunt Cass had given to me and the delicious breakfast, I managed to sleep off the hangover.

By the time I woke a little after lunch I was feeling like a million dollars. I had a shower, ate some food, and then of course now that I was able to think clearly, I had a lot more time to think about what had happened last night.

The man had clearly been attacked, and the magic had felt muddy and gritty but was there a connection? The writers certainly thought it had been part of some hoax. Maybe we were all getting ahead of ourselves immediately leaping to it being some sort of supernatural monster. Perhaps it was a publicity stunt gone terribly wrong.

I looked through the itinerary as I ate a late lunch. Today was the grand opening of Writerpalooza and so all I had to do was collect Red and take her to the Town Hall, and then probably deliver her home again after that.

I had a little time before I had to go, so I hit the Internet searching for Markus Hornby, the author of the monster books who was apparently behind the publicity stunts.

I found the incident the writers had referred to. There had been a writing festival in Chicago where Markus was launching his novel *The Sea Monster Lives!*

Right around the same time a man had staggered into one of the local hospitals, his clothes slashed up, bits of seaweed all over him claiming that he been attacked by some horrible sea monster. It had gathered a burst of media attention until it had been revealed that the man was a paid actor by the name of Carl Stern and it was nothing more than a stunt. I found a page that had a photo of him on it. Yup, it was the same guy from last night.

I sat back in my chair and stared for a while as I thought things over.

It did seem that I had jumped the gun telling Aunt Cass and Mom of my suspicions. Yes, the magic had felt odd, gritty and muddy, but it was possible that was due to something else.

I decided I would talk to Red about it to see what she and the other writers knew, and then after that I would talk to Sheriff Hardy to let him know that there was possibly a hoax going on in town. Who knows, maybe even the ex-military man TJ McKenna had been fooled by wounds that would turn out to be fake.

Soon it was time for me to go, so I rushed out to the sports car, waited the ten seconds until the brilliant air conditioning had cooled it down, and then drove into town. The traffic was worse than I'd ever seen it. I hit pretty much what you'd consider the outer edge of Harlot Bay and immediately the traffic came to a dead grinding halt. I sat there for what seemed like ages before we finally slowly started moving again, only to stop a few seconds later to wait some more. I was glad I left a little early because it took a good half hour to inch my way into town to get to *The Hardy Arms*. Once I was in town I could see the reason why. The streets were filled with people as though there was a festival going on. They were constantly crossing the road, blocking the traffic, and cars were having a hard time moving.

Maybe Aunt Cass's potion had had something in it that made me feel extra good, but whatever it was I was quite enjoying myself even though I was stuck in traffic. The air conditioning was on, the music was playing, and I was watching vampires and other people in costumes crossing the street all around me. I even saw a few people dressed up as Harry Sparkle.

As I sat there waiting for the traffic to move, I thought about Jack's parents and opening the door to them, only to drop my glass and bolt. This time instead of cringing in embarrassment I smiled to myself and shook my head. They were his parents and they seemed lovely! And yes, there was a dinner coming up but given that the *Torrent Mansion Bed and Breakfast* was full to the brim, it was unlikely we would have some private crazy dinner. That meant we'd have to go somewhere public and like Jack hinted, I suspected that the witches would be on their best behavior if we were out in the world. Well, *most* of the witches. Who knew what Aunt Cass would do?

Eventually I reached The Hardy Arms and then ran inside before the heat could get to me. When I knocked on Red's door she called out "It's open!" I went in to find her tapping away at high speed on a laptop.

"Give me a minute, Harlow," she said, focused on the screen. I sat on the edge of the bed and waited as she typed away, her fingers moving at a blur. Then she hit a button, closed the laptop and smiled at me.

"Done! The latest chapter in *Red Menace*. My heroine, Red Herringbone is currently trapped in a bookshop that's on fire. All the windows are barred and someone has bolted shut the front door," Red said.

"How are you going to get her out of that?" I asked.

Red shrugged. "*I'm* not going to get her out. I hope she *does* get out because only half the book is done and I would hate to have to explain to all the readers why she was killed in a bookshop fire, but it's not up to *me* what happens."

Red's phone next to the laptop chimed away. She picked it up and read the message, and then chuckled before typing one in return.

"It seems your small town is full of secrets," Red said.

"I guess it is. It has a long history," I said, a little unsure what she was referring to.

"Jenna thinks she has a line on where some old documents are stored, possibly connected to some of the bizarre stuff that's gone on in the past. She says we should check it out some night. Do you think you'll be in?" she asked.

For a moment I was so stunned I didn't quite understand

what it was she was saying to me. Was she suggesting that we break into somewhere together?

Close on the heels of that confusion came the realization that there were actually plenty of strange things going on in Harlot Bay and a lot of them were connected to my family. Were Red and the authors investigating like private detectives?

"I don't know if I'm up for breaking into places, is that what you mean? Are you guys being detectives?" I said.

"We got to talking last night and it seems there's a lot of strange stuff going on in the town... starting with that guy who'd been attacked last night," she said.

"I looked him up this morning. He's a paid actor like you said. So maybe we all got it wrong because we'd had too much to drink? Could it be possible that his wounds weren't real?" I said.

"That's an excellent question, and after we do the opening ceremony we need to go to the hospital to see him," Red said.

That happy-go-lucky, cheerful feeling that had carried me all the way into town was starting to ebb away. If the man being attacked was a publicity stunt gone terribly wrong and the writers investigated that, well, that was fine. But what if there was something? Particularly something *magical*? It could go very bad very fast.

I had the very unwelcome feeling that I should try to sidetrack Red to dissuade her from investigating anything that might turn out badly. If not for her safety, at least for ours as well.

"I guess we can go to the hospital then and see what happens," I said weakly, frantically trying to think of something better.

Red got ready and then we raced out to the car to avoid the heat. Red was chatting away, commenting on all the costumes and the vampires lurking through the streets, but I was only half-listening, my mind running through various plans of things I could use to distract the writers. I was wondering if there was a spell that I could use. Maybe I could get the man at the hospital to say it was all a joke, a stunt that had gone wrong. If he told Red that then perhaps they would stop investigating.

On the other hand, maybe I shouldn't do anything. After all, what's the worst that could happen? They were just a bunch of authors and they weren't here for long.

We were sitting at a crosswalk, waiting for what seemed to be a never-ending flood of people to pause so we could move on when two figures on the sidewalk resolved themselves into the two strange people who had stayed at the Torrent Mansion some months back. Later on, I'd caught them filming outside the theater where we were putting on *The Taming of the Shrew*. The woman was still wearing her ridiculous beehive of hair and the man had on his absurd clothes, including a pair of fake yellow buck teeth. The last time I'd seen them they'd been filming outside *The Taming of the Shrew* and I, perhaps under the influence of a magical salamander that made you either fall in love or get quite angry, had given chase, bolting after them. They had escaped in a car and I hadn't seen them since. The moment I saw them on the sidewalk, I gasped.

"What is it?" Red asked in alarm. I pointed at the couple who were standing in the shade of a building talking.

"Do you see those two over there, the woman with the big beehive and the man with the fake teeth? They're wearing costumes. There's something weird about them. I caught them filming a theater production I was in a while ago, and before that they'd come to stay at the Torrent Mansion. I'm sure they were under fake names and now here they are again. There's something suspicious about them," I said in one long rush.

"Let's confront them," Red said immediately, looking very eager.

"What?" I said.

"I'll get out and go over this way, you drive up ahead and park, and then come down the sidewalk towards us. If they try to run this way I'll herd them back towards you and we'll see if we can catch them and find out what they're doing," Red said.

"No, that's crazy. I mean, yes, they're weird but I..." I stammered.

"Come on Harlow, you said they're up to something. Let's find out what it is," Red said. Without waiting for my agreement she leaped out of the car and slammed the door shut.

With no choice now but to take part I drove through the next available gap in traffic and up the road. It was still terribly slow going though and it was only by pure chance that a parking spot opened up right in front of me. I parked the car and stepped out of the deliciously chilled interior into the maddening heat. I scurried across the road with the rest of the tourists thinking to myself that what I was doing was crazy. At the same time though I was excited. It felt like some kind of mad adventure. My phone buzzed in my pocket. It was a message from Red. *They're on the move coming your way.*

I walked down the sidewalk, keeping an eye out for the strange couple. In the far distance I could see a head of flaming red hair, which I thought was Red. I realized I could be wrong a moment later when I saw one or two other women in the distance with the same hairdo.

It wasn't long before I spotted the couple and about five seconds after that they saw me. They both pirouetted on the spot and hurried away.

"Hey, you two, stop!" I called out, breaking into a run.

The two of them bolted down the street but then there

was Red, her arms outstretched and yelling at them. In a perfect moment of synchronicity the paid took a left, heading into an alleyway, and Red and I followed. The alleyway was narrow, cool and dark and away from the hustle and bustle of the main street. It was also, as we saw a few seconds later, a dead end. The strange couple were cornered. They turned around to face us and the man started fumbling in the bag he was carrying before eventually pulling out a small handheld camera.

"Leave us alone. We have a permit to film here!" the woman said, her hands out in front of her as though she was about to karate chop Red and me.

"Who are you?" Red demanded.

"None of your business," the woman said.

"You were at the Torrent Mansion and you were wearing disguises, and then I saw you filming outside *The Taming of the Shrew*," I said.

"Show whatch, thrreee country," the man said, spitting as he spoke through the fake teeth.

The adrenaline running must've caught up with me because I'd had enough. I lunged forward and pulled the woman's ridiculous beehive hairdo wig right off her head.

"Hey, give that back," she said and then we struggled for a moment before she pulled it back off me. The man was trying to turn on the small handheld camera but Red snatched it from him.

"Take out those ridiculous false teeth and tell us what you were doing," she demanded.

The couple looked at each other and after the woman nodded, the man pulled out his pair of fake yellow teeth and then took off his thick glasses before removing the heavy overcoat that he was wearing. The woman removed a thick pair of glasses and then undid the pins in her hair.

"Wait, I know you two. You're from that show online, the *Mysterious Mysteries*," Red said.

I had no idea what she was talking about, but I was feeling very nervous about what it was exactly we were doing. It was one thing to chase people to ask them a question, but then snatching wigs off heads and stealing their camera? All the while boxing them into a dead end alleyway? I was starting to feel less heroic investigator and more crazed vigilante.

"Our show is called *The Mysterious Mysteries*," the man said, his voice smooth, even pleasant sounding now that he had the fake teeth removed. "May we have our camera back?" he asked.

Red handed it back to him. He held it in his hand but didn't turn it on.

"My name is Dawn and this is Rufus. We're here in Harlot Bay to investigate the many strange things that go on here," the woman said.

I'd never heard of them or their show but I had a very bad feeling. They'd stayed at the Torrent Mansion for at least a night that I knew of. Had they been there secretly filming? Oh Goddess, what if they'd seen something magical or witchy?

"Why were you staying at our bed-and-breakfast in disguise?" I asked.

Dawn shrugged and waved her hand. "Our show is getting quite popular and we don't want to be known, so we travel in disguises while we're doing our investigations."

"We came to the Torrent Mansion because it is one of the oldest buildings in Harlot Bay and according to our research many strange things have happened there and on the land surrounding it," Rufus said.

I saw Red looking at me with a raised eyebrow.

I had to handle this carefully.

"Plenty of strange things have happened in Harlot Bay but we're only running a bed-and-breakfast, that's all," I said.

"That's what we found too. There wasn't enough there to make a show about," Rufus said.

I breathed an internal sigh of relief. Still, I would have to track down the show and see if they'd said anything about my family or our home.

"What strange things are you talking about?" Red asked.

"You might have heard that last night a man was attacked, and he claimed it was by a monster. More than a hundred years ago the stories say that people living out on Truer Island were attacked by a monster also and on one bloody night half the people out there were killed. We're here investigating that," Dawn said.

"But why were you filming outside *The Taming of the Shrew?*" I blurted out.

"It was another dead end," Rufus said. "We thought we could tie in something about all the various murders that have been around Harlot Bay, but then it all came to nothing. Can you explain why you chased us?" he asked.

I was put on the spot, but thankfully I had well-honed lying skills from years of dealing with the moms.

"Someone had been sabotaging *The Taming of the Shrew*, as you know, and so when I saw the two of you filming outside, I thought you might have something to do with it. That's why chased you," I said smoothly.

"I know you, you're that author Red Forrest, aren't you," Dawn said.

"That's me," Red said. I heard in her voice that she was thinking the same thing that I was. We'd *chased* two people and cornered them in an alleyway.

"Now the introductions are done would you please move out of our way and let us go about our business?" Rufus asked.

He turned away from me to pick up the bag he'd dropped and then took in a sharp breath.

"Look at this," he said to Dawn.

He turned on the camera and Dawn began narrating as he filmed.

"We've come into this alleyway off the main street in Harlot Bay. We've been led here by some of the locals who have heard that we're here investigating the strange rumors of a monster that is stalking the town. Look what we found," she said dramatically. She pointed at the brick wall. Both Red and I stepped forward to take a closer look and saw there were long scratch marks running the entire way up the wall. They looked like they'd been carved out of the stone by enormous claws.

"Something has scratched its way up the wall, higher than any man could jump. Perhaps it was the monster fleeing from people, or perhaps giving chase," Dawn said in an ominous tone, looking back at the camera.

"We need to take a plaster cast of it," Rufus said from behind the camera.

We watched as Dawn stepped closer to the camera and then looked directly into the lens. "One thing is certain, there is something strange in Harlot Bay," she said. Then Rufus stopped filming and they both turned back towards us.

"So this is what we do if that's okay," Dawn said, rather sarcastically to us.

"Of course it is," Red mumbled. She turned away and I followed her, making our way out of the dark alleyway. It wasn't until we were back out on the street that we finally spoke.

"Do you think that was a setup? Maybe *they* made the scratches and they were filming it, and *that's* why they ran there?" Red asked me.

"That never crossed my mind. Have they been caught faking things before?" I said.

Although I was confused and, yes, somewhat embarrassed that we'd chased two people who apparently were just trying to make a documentary, Red's question had made me feel quite relieved. The moment I'd seen those marks I had imagined a huge beast clambering its way up the wall. But perhaps once again I was leaping ahead of myself and there was a much simpler explanation, such as an odd couple possibly faking things so they could make their show.

"We need to get to the opening, but I think there's something to investigate here," Red said. I followed along beside her thinking yes, there was something to investigate but also that I would have to do my best to sidetrack her and the writers to ensure they didn't get into any trouble. It was looking like it was going to be a very busy two weeks.

CHAPTER SEVEN

J was standing backstage at the Town Hall quietly hyperventilating when Molly's message arrived.

"Be there five minutes. Traffic!"

I checked the time. She, Luce and Peta would be cutting it close. I took a sip of my cold water and went back to quietly panicking.

After confronting Dawn and Rufus of the *Mysterious Mysteries* so-called fame, Red and I had rushed to the Writer-palooza grand opening at the Town Hall. Inside the building was pure chaos as fans came streaming in to fill up all the seating in the main area, as authors ran around like chickens with their heads cut off, and the organizers tried to keep everyone, well, organized. Thankfully, I didn't have much to do except follow behind Red. I hadn't been feeling great about confronting the *Mysterious Mysteries* in the alleyway and that feeling had only gotten worse when I'd gone to the kitchen to fetch some cold water and returned to find the writers having a conspiratorial conversation. All I caught was Jenna Cheng saying, "I've scouted the place out. I think we can go at night," before they all shut up when I arrived. I handed over the water bottle to Red and pretended I hadn't heard anything.

But it was clear the writers were investigating the strange things that were happening in Harlot Bay. Now, not only did I have to worry about Red possibly running into some kind of supernatural monster, but the rest of the writers as well. Sure, TJ McKenna could probably handle himself, being a former Navy Seal, but as for Jay and Jenna? I suspected they'd be eaten alive.

I found myself hoping that Rufus and Dawn of the *Mysterious Mysteries* were the ones behind carving claw marks into a wall for their show. That would wrap up everything neatly. Yes, there was still the matter of Carl Stern, but perhaps he was involved in doing a publicity stunt and then the *Mysterious Mysteries* had attacked him to whip up publicity for their show?

It was far better than the alternative: there was a monster in Harlot Bay attacking people.

I was standing sipping water when Red appeared out of nowhere and came rushing over.

"Hey, that guy who got attacked can have visitors now. Let's go see him after this, figure out what's going on!"

"You want to go to the hospital?" I said, my heart sinking. Witches and hospitals don't get along. We can sense the emotions there and most of them aren't good.

"We can find out if he was faking it or not. I've been thinking that maybe the *Mysterious Mysteries* could have been the ones who attacked him for their show," Red said.

"I was thinking the same," I said.

"So you're in?"

"Definitely," I said. Red said goodbye and rushed off to get ready for the opening ceremony. My phone buzzed again. It was Molly and they were waiting outside.

As staff members we'd been given guest tickets to

various events throughout the week. I'd used mine on Molly, Luce and Peta. Because of their businesses they couldn't afford to wait in queues so we'd arranged to meet at a side entrance. As soon as I let the three of them in Luce grabbed me by the arms and looked deeply into my eyes.

"Harlow, what's wrong?" she asked.

I had all of about a minute to explain that I suspected the writers were investigating and it would surely lead to something terrible.

"Better them than us," Molly said, seemingly unconcerned.

"What do you mean better them? They're not witches! Someone could get killed!" I said.

"Or maybe they find out the truth and we don't have to get involved and we have a nice lovely calm Writerpalooza," Molly said.

"Doesn't sound our style," Luce commented.

"You said they're already investigating–have they found anything out?" Peta asked.

"They've found some location apparently that they've scouted out. I think they're going to break into somewhere," I said.

We all shared a look. The look was generally *we disapprove of breaking into places* mixed with *we say that having had broken into many places in our time*. It was complicated being a witch.

"Sounds like you need to get on the inside. Find out where they're going and go there first," Luce said.

I groaned. "I was afraid someone would say that. They want to go to the hospital next to talk to the guy who was attacked last night supposedly by a monster."

"Yeah, there's not much you're gonna be able to do there. Even if you can see him first they're still going to turn up," Luce said.

"I need a plan and quick. Is there something we can fake to distract them?" I asked.

"Sounds like that would make them *more* curious, not less," Molly said.

Our conversation was cut off by the lights in the adjoining hall lowering. The opening ceremony was about to begin. We hustled our way in and stood on the sides, finding a somewhat clear spot.

In the dim light I looked around the Town Hall. It seemed like it was about ninety percent vampire. Bella Shade coming to the Writerpalooza had pulled in thousands of fans, many of whom were still waiting outside as the Town Hall was filled to capacity.

The house lights went from romantic evening to pitch dark and then a spotlight lit up and the crowd went wild. It was Harry Sparkle dressed in his bright clothing wearing his crazy hat, holding a ukulele covered in glitter. Despite my worry about what messes the writers would get themselves into I found myself cheering and clapping along with everyone.

Another spotlight lit up on the far side of the stage to reveal yet another crazy character - the Mayor of Harlot Bay. He was dressed in a glittering sequined coat and today his mohawk was bright blue.

"Welcome to Writerpalooza!" the Mayor shouted like he was introducing a wrestling special. The crowd went wild again, the spotlight on the Mayor dropped away and then Harry Sparkle began to play his ukulele.

The opening sped by. We laughed and sang along with Harry Sparkle, an entire Town Hall full of adults turned into children. He told us how excited he was that we were all there, and then went off the stage to a cheering that wouldn't have seemed out of place at a rock concert.

Next up a brunette woman with pale skin wearing a fabulous red dress came up to the microphone. At this, the vampires in the crowd lost their minds.

"It's Bella Shade!" Luce said.

"She looks so normal for a genius," Molly whispered.

Bella tried to give an opening introduction to Writerpalooza, but the cheering was crazy, people standing up and clapping and yelling. It probably went on for about five minutes before it calmed down. In that time Bella's pale cheeks had flushed pink and she was blushing and smiling at everyone. Once the room had gone somewhat quiet, Bella gave the opening speech to Writerpalooza. After that it was a quick succession of authors, including Red, saying their small parts before the Mayor came on and welcomed all of them and all of the crowd to Writerpalooza. And then it was done! I let Molly, Luce and Peta back out the side door so they could return to *Traveler* and *The Cozy Cat Café*. Then I went backstage to find Red was searching for me.

"You're here, excellent, let's go!" she said.

I tried to keep the smile on my face as we left Writerpalooza, got into the rental car and drove across to the Harlot Bay hospital. Outside I knew I was looking calm but inside my stomach was churning. It was probably a good thing it took us almost an hour to get out of the traffic jam caused by the opening ceremony. It gave me some time to calm down and also to talk to Red.

"So... you guys have decided to investigate the apparent monster attack?" I said.

"We'll look into it," Red said and started tapping away on her phone.

I know that she hadn't told me to be quiet or that she wasn't going to answer my questions and, yes, she was still as friendly and fun as ever, but I got the distinct impression that she wasn't telling me the truth. I decided to try another route and so we chatted about inconsequential things until we reached the Harlot Bay hospital. This sounds like it may have calmed me down but it further cemented the idea that Red was keeping from me her plans for snooping and investigating, given that she would talk to me about trivial things but not about what she and the other writers were doing.

I followed along behind Red who rushed into the hospital like she owned it, bracing myself for the pools of sadness I would be forced to walk through. There were even some in the lobby, but thankfully we didn't have to stay long.

"What do you mean he's gone?" Red asked the receptionist.

"Mr. Stern checked himself out about thirty minutes ago," he said.

"Was he with anyone?" Red asked.

The man glanced around to make sure no one was listening and then lowered his voice.

"I know I'm not meant to say this but you're one of my favorite authors so I'm going to tell you. A man dressed in all black with blue tattoos down his arms and the backs of his hands took him away. I swear the guy looked like he was straight out of a horror movie."

Red thanked the receptionist and then we went back outside and got into the car. I started the engine immediately to get the cooling working.

"If he checked himself out he might still be in town somewhere. Maybe we could see if he's at any of the hotels?" I said.

Red shook her head and narrowed her eyes as she tapped away on her phone. It brought up an image which she showed to me. It was of a pale man, his skin as white as alabaster, wearing all black. I couldn't see his arms, but his hands were etched in vivid blue tattoos. Underneath the image was a name: Hannibal Blood.

"I'm going to bet that this is the man who came to collect him," Red told me.

"It says there that he's an author. Was he possibly the one behind the publicity stunt of Carl being attacked?" I asked.

"That's what we're going to find out," Red said.

CHAPTER EIGHT

"*I* hate you Hannibal blood," I muttered as my car chugged up the hill in the blazing heat.

I'd been caught up in Red's excitement about the big clue we'd received about Hannibal Blood checking out Carl Stern but then that excitement had come crashing down when we discovered that Hannibal didn't have any sessions for Writer-palooza on until Thursday. I'd called Angela, the organizer, and discovered that no one knew where Hannibal was staying either. Suddenly, the trail had turned cold. Red was slightly disappointed but seemed to take it all in stride. I was pretty much feeling the same until a fresh new disappoint-ment hit me when I learned I'd have to give up the sports car for the day. Red decided she was going to go for another drive down the coast by herself and so she asked me where she could drop me off. I asked her to take me back to my car, which is still parked across the road from Meredith's. At least Red had the grace to wait to see whether my car would start. The moment the engine turned over she roared off down the street, the luxurious icy air conditioning blasting, leaving me sitting inside my portable oven. So now I was creeping up the hill heading towards Torrent Mansion cursing Hannibal Blood, the sun, monsters, and anything else I could think of.

I eventually reached the mansion and rushed inside to the blessed coolness. The place was empty, of course. Molly and Luce were at work. The moms were at the bakery and only one of them would be down at the other end of the mansion, and Aunt Cass was probably down at the Chili Challenge. Not even Adams was around. I spent a minute drinking some deliciously icy water from the refrigerator before turning on my ancient laptop and going hunting for the *Mysterious Mysteries*.

It turned out the *Mysterious Mysteries* was an online show. Dawn and Rufus investigated supernatural events across North America. As I watched, skipping between different episodes of the show, I started to relax. The entire thing was ridiculous. I watched the two of them creeping through a mansion at night, Rufus carrying something that was apparently meant to detect whether there were ghosts in the house. When the needle moved, he and Dawn looked shocked.

I flicked through a few more episodes until I came to one titled *The Monster of New Orleans*. I sat sipping my cold water as I watched Rufus and Dawn explain how a strange monster had been stalking the streets of New Orleans. It was when they reached an alleyway, and "discovered" the claw marks that I paused it and shook my head at myself. What had I been thinking? I'd been so worried about these two, but they were a couple of charlatans! The claw marks in the New Orleans alleyway were identical to the ones in Harlot Bay. I played the video for a little longer and then shut it off before looking through the rest of the videos to make sure there weren't any about Torrent Mansion. The fact was that even if these guys found anything supernatural in Harlot Bay I doubted anyone would believe them.

After that and feeling somewhat more relieved, I looked up Hannibal Blood and saw that he was an author, publishing over the last decade. He'd apparently appeared out of nowhere and it was evident that his whole get-up was a costume. He wore all black and had tattoos down his hands, never gave interviews, and wrote grisly horror books. The Internet was full of strange rumors about him: that he was actually a vampire or involved with necromancy; that he hadn't aged; that he was a crazy man. Given that the legend seemed to feed into his book sales it appeared to me that he'd discovered that pretending to love the darkness was actually quite a lucrative act.

I was browsing around some of his book titles aimlessly when my phone rang. It was Sheriff Hardy.

"Harlow, my men received a complaint today that you and the author Red Forrest chased two people into an alley-way," he said without bothering to say hello.

Oh no.

"Hi Sheriff," I said.

I took a hasty gulp of my cold water, accidentally choked myself and then started spluttering. It was only when I caught my breath that I realized that Sheriff Hardy had been talking the whole while.

"... and you don't want to be following these people around and so you need to leave them alone, okay?" he finished.

"Sure, yes, absolutely," I croaked. Sheriff Hardy said goodbye and then the phone went silent.

They'd gone to the police!

...although that wasn't too hard to believe. After all two strange people *did* chase them into an alleyway, one of them ripped off a wig, and the other one took their camera.

It took me a little while to recover from the Sheriff's phone call. Although I hadn't heard what he'd said I could guess the gist of it. Leave the people from the *Mysterious Mysteries* alone. It was only after I had calmed myself that I realized I should have told him my suspicions that they were faking that there was a monster around Harlot Bay and they'd probably done it before. Yes, I admit now there was a *slight* bit of spite to it. The idea that they had gone to report *us* when in fact it was *them* who were possibly doing something illegal. I certainly wouldn't put it past them to have attacked Carl either directly or using someone they hired perhaps to get more attention for their show, which as far as I could tell wasn't doing *that* well.

I decided I would think on it for a while and then *maybe* I'd tell Sheriff Hardy. If I called him back right now it would seem like a child who had stolen someone's toy shouting out "No, but they stole *mine* first!"

I returned to the Internet, remembering something that Dawn and Rufus had said. There had been deaths out on Truer Island over a hundred years ago. It didn't take long to find information on it and it came from none other than Harlot Bay's resident historian superstar librarian Ollie. He'd written an article about the mysterious deaths out on Truer Island. As I read through it I knew that I had to show it to Aunt Cass because Ollie had stumbled upon something quite extraordinary.

More than a century ago in Harlot Bay, a woman had been attacked in the street at night. She'd been going to the local bar to find her husband and along the way had apparently been attacked by a large monster with sharpened claws and gleaming eyes. She'd staggered into the drinking hall with her dress shredded and with deep cuts down her arms. It seemed that first attack had been blamed on local vagrants who were promptly charged, convicted, and then sent away to prison all in the space of a few weeks. It was only when another man was attacked that the townsfolk began to wonder if it was something else. Harlot Bay and the fledgling colony out on Truer Island had been gripped by fear over the course of a year as it became unsafe to walk the streets at night. Men and women had been attacked and some killed.

These attacks, of course, had caused the people to turn on their fellow citizens. Women were accused of witchcraft and men too, and local beggars and widowers were often targeted by angry and fearful townsfolk. There were images interspersed through Ollie's article of book pages taken from old records. A strange looping symbol appeared through them. It had been carved on doors throughout town and on other buildings. Many had said it had been the symbol of the devil that was plaguing Harlot Bay and Truer Island. The terrific fear over what was stalking them had reached a peak and then came that single bloody night out on Truer Island where half of the residents were murdered in their beds. After that, there was nothing. It was as though whatever was behind the attacks had simply vanished.

I immediately emailed the article to Aunt Cass. So far only one man had been attacked and it was entirely possible it was a hoax, but after all the time I'd lived in Harlot Bay I was suspecting there was a good chance there was a monster stalking the town.

I spent the rest of the afternoon scouring the Internet and not coming up with much. I eventually found myself looking up the other authors and even reading part of TJ McKenna's Grandma Gough book, which featured the diminutive Grandma Gough, a wisecracking crazy old lady who used her wit and charm to solve murder mysteries.

I was sitting on the sofa, reading Grandma Gough's first adventure, when Molly and Luce arrived home and I was shocked to see it was the end of the day. After the research and reading everything had gone so quickly.

The two of them staggered inside, Molly flopping down

on the sofa and Luce dragging herself over to the refrigerator, where she pulled out a tall bottle of chilled water and drank half of it in one go.

"Water, now," Molly muttered, waving her arm in the direction of the kitchen.

Luce came over with another bottle of water and gave it to Molly before flopping down beside me on the sofa.

"I don't want to be rude, but both of you smell like coffee and sweat," I said, wrinkling my nose.

"Air conditioning broke down, brain is cooked," Luce said and took another huge gulp of water.

"Only cooling was from café next door and it wasn't enough," Molly said. It took a few minutes for both of them drinking cool water to finally recover.

"What are you reading there?" Luce asked me, nodding towards my laptop.

"Grandma Gough in *The Case of the Deadly Muffin*," I said.

"Why are you reading *that* when you could be reading *Bitten*?" Luce said.

"There are other books in the world, you know," I said.

Molly and Luce both gave me a pitying look.

"She says there are other books in the world," Molly said.

"It's like seeing one of those eyeless fish bobbing around in the depths of the ocean and it has no idea of all the color and light that it's missing," Luce said.

"Hey! This is a good book and I'm still going to read *Bitten* one day," I said.

We talked a bit about *Traveler*, which had been packed to the gills even with the non-functioning air-conditioning, and then eventually got on to what the writers were doing.

"Better them than us," Molly declared, going to the kitchen to get another cold drink of water.

"I think I've seen that *Mysterious Mysteries* show. They're the ones who always set up a temperature detector and then say that's when a ghost has come by. You should send them up to your office and see if John Smith is there," Luce said.

"I don't think he's ever affected the weather. I mean, not that much," I said.

I hadn't thought about John in some time. It wasn't as though we'd officially stopped his sessions at my office, but rather I'd stopped going there because of my crazy need to work and have money and eat food. I hadn't seen him around in a while either. Normally, I would see him in town, often up on buildings planning to throw himself off, but sometimes floating down the street looking around in amazement. I guess it's the upside to a serious memory problem: the familiar is new and interesting even though you see it every day.

"I don't know if John has been visiting my office. I haven't been there in ages actually," I said.

"You should be glad that the writers are investigating and even the *Mysterious Mysteries*. Do you know what happened to us when we went under the house?" Molly said, much more animated.

"Did you find something?" I asked.

"No, but I did get *set on fire*," Molly said.

"It was only for a minute, and you were *hardly* on fire," Luce corrected.

Molly turned to Luce with a shocked look on her face.

"Only for a minute? Perhaps you'd like to be set on fire and you see how long you can put up with it," she said. Molly and Luce started bickering, but I eventually got them to calm down and tell me what actually happened. It turned out that somewhere in the depths under the house in a random corridor Molly had stepped into the leftover remnants of an old spell. Thankfully, she'd been wearing long pants at the time and only the hem had caught fire. It had burned for a moment before Aunt Cass put it out and then Molly declared she was never going on an expedition under the house again.

"This place is a death trap," Molly muttered.

Because it was Summer, it was still broad daylight as we made ourselves dinner - reheated pizza from the refrigerator - and talked about random things until night came. Adams eventually arrived, demanding food and refusing to tell me where he'd been and so I fed him and then finally spent the last part of the night messaging back and forth with Jack who was babysitting his parents.

Of all the things I had discovered today that had caused me some shock, from the fact that there possibly could be a monster stalking Harlot Bay, to Molly being set on fire underneath the mansion, and everything else, Jack sent me the piece of news that was simply the worst: there was a big family dinner arranged for Tuesday evening. The moms had already been in contact and his parents had already accepted the invitation. I'd been expecting a dinner but I thought it would be *out* where there would be *witnesses*.

"Make sure there is plenty of wine!" Jack had written.

I had a shower and went to bed, promising Jack by message that there would be. As I lay in my cool room and Adams walked in circles at the end of the bed before settling down, I found myself thinking about Rufus and Dawn in the alleyway and the deep scratches on the wall. How crazy was it that I was more concerned about a big family dinner than the idea of some clawed monster stalking Harlot Bay?

CHAPTER NINE

*M*e, Molly and Luce were bustling around getting ready for the day when Mom came barreling through the front door and headed straight for the spare room.

"Girls, clean this out, quick, quick," she commanded.

"Um, why?" I asked, putting my piece of toast down.

Mom opened the door of the spare room to reveal the chaotic destruction within.

"Kira is coming to stay. Now, help me. I'm making breakfast for the guests and I need this done straight away," she said, quite frazzled.

The three of us went to help, moving boxes and piles of clothes and other bits of junk.

"Why is she coming to stay with us?" Luce asked.

"Hattie is going away," Mom said, pulling another random box of junk off the bed. We heard a car door slam out the front of the mansion. Me and my cousins walked out to the lounge to see Kira appear in the front door lugging a huge heavy suitcase. She dropped it to the ground and grinned at us.

"What's up bitc–" she stopped halfway and coughed when she saw Mom. "I mean… what's up witches?"

I saw through the open door behind her that Hattie was parked out the front and there at her window stood Aunt Cass. She was saying something to Hattie and then passed her a small package wrapped in brown paper. Hattie took it and then, I swear, wiped a tear away. What was going on?

I was headed for the front door when Mom appeared in front of me.

"I need you to finish clearing that room," she said.

"I will, give me a moment," I said, dodging around her. By the time I got to the front door, Hattie had driven away and Aunt Cass was nowhere to be seen.

"I have to go now. Ask these three if you need anything," Mom said to Kira. She gave her a kiss on the cheek, and then rushed out, heading back to the main part of the mansion to continue serving breakfast to the guests.

"She seems stressed," Kira said. Adams appeared out of nowhere and came running up to Kira, leaping up into her arms. She caught the little black cat who then snuggled into her and immediately asked her for something to eat because *he hadn't eaten in days.*

Kira laughed and started scratching him behind the ears before she sat down on the sofa.

"So, why are you staying with us?" Luce asked.

Kira ran her fingers through Adams' fur, the little black cat purring loudly. "It's all very *mysterious* why my Grandma is going away. I don't know why, she wouldn't tell me. She said she'd be back in about ten days to two weeks. So that's how long you get to enjoy my lovely company," she said.

"She really didn't say where she was going?" I asked.

"Nope," Kira said. Adams jumped off her lap and then started giving himself a bath, wiping a paw over his ear.

"Okay, well, I guess you'll be coming with me then," I said, going back to pick up my piece of toast.

As I munched away on it I came up with a plan for the day. Today was quite busy with Red doing a number of sessions but interspersed with breaks at odd times. Sometimes there was less than an hour between them, so although I would have *some* time to get away I suspected most of the day I'd be waiting around for her to finish a session so I could drive her to the next one.

I resolved to get away to see Aunt Cass at the Chili Challenge to find out exactly what she'd given Hattie in that small parcel. Although I gave myself about a one in a hundred chance of finding out the actual truth, I could also talk to Aunt Cass about the *Mysterious Mysteries* and the things I'd discovered thanks to Ollie's article. Although I was sure Dawn and Rufus were charlatans, there was possibly some connection behind the attacks all that time ago and what had happened to Carl Stern.

I was brushing my teeth when I heard the front door open and then a familiar voice. I came out into the lounge to find Red crouched down, scratching Adams on the back of his neck as he rolled around at her feet. Molly and Luce were standing nearby, looking somewhat starstruck. Kira was tapping away on her phone.

"Red, what are you doing here?" I asked.

Red gave me a smile and stood up. "I saw that car of yours yesterday and I'm not sure it'll even make it to the end of the driveway let alone back into town and home in this heat, so I thought I should pick you up," she said. "Plus I wanted to see the mansion up close... and it is *spectacular.*"

"Oh, thanks for coming to pick me up then," I said trying to find my bearings somewhat. "These are my cousins Molly and Luce, by the way."

Red gave each of them a big smile. "You are the ones who

run *Traveler*. I've heard so many good things about it. It's right next to that delightful *Cozy Cat Café*, isn't it?"

"Yup, that's us," Molly said in a somewhat dazed voice.

It was Luce who came to the rescue. "Best coffee in all of North Carolina," she said. "Bring your friends some time."

"That sounds delightful," Red said and then looked at Kira.

"That's Kira. She's coming to stay with us for a little while. She's one of the Writerpalooza volunteers, so we need to take her too," I said.

Kira looked up from tapping on her phone and smiled at Red. "Hi," she said and looked straight back at her phone.

Red chuckled to herself. "Nice to meet you. You remind me a lot of my daughter." She then jingled the car keys in her hand towards Kira. "Do you want to drive the sports car today?" she said.

Kira glanced outside, her face going pale when she saw the expensive sports car.

"I think that car's too expensive for me to drive," she said hastily.

"I'll do it," I said.

We all left at once, Molly and Luce going to Molly's car. The three of us piled into the sports car and once again I was struck at the pure luxury of it. The contrast from my car driving home yesterday was stark. There is no way I'd ever be able to afford a car like this, but an idea was beginning to weigh on my mind that I would finally have to get rid of my car and upgrade. But for that, of course, I would need money, and although I was being paid fairly well for these two weeks, after that I was looking at a nice lovely stretch of unemployment again.

Molly and Luce went roaring away, heading down the hill at high speed. I followed at a somewhat slower pace, wary of the potholes.

"I discovered something interesting about the *Mysterious Mysteries* yesterday," Red began.

She told me that they'd been taken in for questioning in Florida two years ago on vandalism charges.

"But what were they vandalizing?" I asked.

"They were never charged and I think it all went away, but from the information I could get I suspect they were possibly carving scratches into walls or something like that, and they got caught," she said.

I told Red I'd watched some of the episodes too and mentioned the *Monster of New Orleans* in particular. Red nodded and flicked through her phone, turning it to me so I could glance at it and see she'd brought up an image of the scratch marks from that episode.

"I saw those yesterday, and today when I've got some time I want to go back to the alleyway to compare them because I'm sure that they're faking them," Red said.

"But what about Carl Stern? He was attacked and I'm sure they were real wounds," I said.

Red shrugged. "I've been thinking that's one of those coincidences where something happens and it looks like it's connected, but it's not," she said.

We soon reached the edge of Harlot Bay and the seemingly permanent Summer traffic jam. We slowed down to a crawl. Even early in the day the streets were full of tourists and vampires stalking the place. We were creeping down the street when Kira called out "Hey there's Sophira, let me out," before saying goodbye and jumping out of the car.

"Now that we're alone, did you get a visit from Sheriff Hardy yesterday?" Red asked me.

"A phone call about chasing Rufus and Dawn down that alleyway," I said.

"He came to visit me at my hotel room. Apparently they'd made a complaint and so the Sheriff very politely told me to not chase them down any more alleyways and to leave them alone if possible. I told him that I suspected they were responsible for the scratches in that alleyway and possibly could be connected to the man who was attacked," Red said.

"Oh, that's good, saves me some time from telling him then," I said, watching the stream of tourists cross the road ahead of me, wishing once again that Harlot Bay would put in a decent traffic light system so at least cars could move through the middle of the town slightly faster than walking pace.

"He's a quite an interesting man that Sheriff isn't he? I believe he's married to your aunt?"

I was somewhat taken aback. How did she know that?

"They got married a few months ago up in the forest behind our house," I confirmed.

"Oh, that's where we're going to be having dinner tomorrow night?"

Now I was thoroughly confused.

"Sorry, dinner?"

"Yes, after the Sheriff left, your mother rang me and invited me to dinner tomorrow. I'm going to be bringing along a signed book for your aunt," Red said and gave me a smile.

"Oh, of course, yeah," I said. My mind was spinning. How many people were going to be at this dinner now? Jack's parents, my whole family, boyfriends, and Red as well? The poor woman didn't know what she was in for, although I suspected with her quick wit she would be able to hold her own. I silently cursed my mother for once again going behind my back to invite people in my life along to family dinners. The meddling was quite infuriating sometimes. We started chatting away again and in our conversation Red revealed that Sheriff Hardy had come past her hotel not long after she'd left me. I realized that she'd told me she was going for a drive down the coast, but it appeared she'd gone straight back to her hotel. Without thinking, I blurted it out. "I thought you went for a drive down the coast yesterday?" I said.

"I went back to my room to pick up something when I met Sheriff Hardy," Red said, a little too quickly. As someone with a finely honed ability to lie thanks to living with three witchy meddling mothers, I had the very strong impression that Red wasn't telling me the truth. But why? Was she off doing something that she didn't want me to know about?

We moved through the center of town at an incredibly slow pace, Red now tapping away at her phone like Kira did, and me musing over what it was *exactly* this group of writers were doing.

I couldn't blame Red for being a little secretive, after all that was practically a witch's middle name. But if she and the other authors were going to go investigating, I needed to be on the *inside* of that and not the *outside*, especially if they got themselves involved in something dangerous. Unfortunately, at the moment I had no idea how I could do that.

Eventually, we reached the center of town and it wasn't long after that that we were parking at the location of the first session. Red was almost late due to how long it had taken us to get through the hordes of vampires crossing the roads. We locked up the sports car and went rushing inside, Red handing me a huge sheaf of notes and other materials that I was to hand out to the participants in my role as personal assistant. I slipped into the flow of helping her but in the back of my mind I was thinking of the first break I would have and whether I should go straight to see Aunt Cass or track down Ollie.

CHAPTER TEN

inally, after lunch, I was able to get away. Red was doing a two-hour in-depth cozy mystery writing session. I decided to walk to Aunt Cass's to avoid the ridiculously slow traffic. The moment I stepped outside I realized this was a colossal mistake but for some reason I kept scurrying down the street, moving to any spot of shade I could find, and by the time I came to my senses I was already too far gone to go back.

Despite the blistering sun overhead the streets were crowded, packed with tourists, most of whom were eating ice creams and drinking bottles of cold water. I kept rushing down the street, dodging tourists as I went. I passed *Traveler*, which was packed with tourists. Molly and Luce didn't see me. They were standing red-faced behind the counter and the door was wide open. It looked like the air conditioning wasn't working again. I looked through the front window of the *Cozy Cat Café* next door and saw Peta, who was serving customers. She waved me in and then gave me an ice-cold can of lemonade from the refrigerator. I took it gratefully and continued on my way, gulping down the sweet chilled liquid as I went. By the time I reached Aunt Cass's it looked like I had swum there. I was dripping with sweat and I wasn't quite sure what I was going to do to clean up given I had no spare clothes. Oh well, that was a future problem.

Inside the Chili Challenge offices it felt like a meat locker compared to the temperature outside. I swear the sweat on my skin almost froze instantly as I walked into a blast of cold air. Aunt Cass's three staff members were working hard, packing boxes to send chili sauces cowboy hats, nappy wipes and stopwatches all over the country.

I waved hello to them and went into the small office where Aunt Cass was sitting with her feet up on the desk, a laptop perched on her lap and a pair of headphones on. She waved me into the seat across the desk but didn't say anything else. I sat there in the cool of her office for a few minutes recovering until finally Aunt Cass closed the laptop and took the headphones off.

"So the *Mysterious Mysteries* are faking scratches around the town are they? Very interesting," she said, a sort of mad gleam in her eye.

"Why is it interesting? What are you planning?" I asked.

"I'm not planning anything. I think it's very interesting, that's all," Aunt Cass said, clearly lying.

"The writers seem to think that the man who was attacked was a publicity stunt. Is it possible there's something magical going on in town *and* someone could be coincidentally attacked as part of a publicity stunt?"

Aunt Cass opened up her laptop, tapped away for a moment and then turned it around to face me. She showed me the symbol that I had discovered on Ollie's website. The one that had been around the town back when the attacks had happened a century ago.

"Do you think the *Mysterious Mysteries* know about this?" Aunt Cass asked me.

"They seem like they've done their research on a few things."

"Very interesting," Aunt Cass murmured.

Oh Goddess, she was doing it again, being mysterious and refusing to answer questions. I didn't have the time for it. I needed to know whether there was something truly dangerous in the town otherwise Red and the other writers could get seriously hurt. But instead of saying this to Aunt Cass, something else entirely came out of my mouth. "What was in that package you gave Hattie this morning?"

"It was a protective charm. Half of it's an amulet, the other half is a potion that you drink to protect you."

"But why would you need to give Hattie that? Where is she going? What is she doing that's so dangerous?"

"She didn't tell me. She said she needed it and it was important, and so I gave it to her."

I shook my head. For as long as I've known, Aunt Cass and Hattie have been pretty much mortal enemies. I don't know why Aunt Cass would be helping Hattie Stern do *anything*.

"She didn't tell you what she was doing?" I said.

"Nope," Aunt Cass said, a challenging note in her voice.

"Okay, fine, you don't have to tell me if you don't want to. But seriously, what are we meant to do? I don't want Red or the other authors to get hurt if there is something magical in town. I did feel the magic turn gritty—what do you think that was?"

"My guess is that whatever monster it was I fought out on Truer Island has a relative or something similar. Perhaps it escaped, attacked one man, and now maybe it has returned to the island."

"Is there any way we can find out what happened, though? Should we go to the island?"

"As it turns out, I have a plan," Aunt Cass said templing her fingers like a supervillain.

I groaned. "This isn't going to be one of those plans where I end up having to travel all over town setting up beacons is it? I don't want to go down into the sewerage system to collect water samples again."

"Even better, we're going to go monster hunting," Aunt Cass said.

"Gah?"

"You, me, Kira, your cousins. We'll head out at night and track it down."

I couldn't believe what she was saying. Had she completely lost her mind?

"But there are tourists everywhere! Even late at night."

"It already attacked one man, what if it strikes again?"

I shook my head not believing what I was hearing and then I saw the cheeky twinkle in Aunt Cass's eye.

"You're not serious are you? You're toying with me because you're bored," I said.

"A little," she admitted.

"Okay, but do you have a plan?"

"We'll go out and see what happens. We'll start in the alleyway with the claw marks and then walk around to see if we can sense anywhere the magic has gone gritty. That's the best I have right now. Given that it's going to be all of us together it's not like we're going to be in any danger."

"Great, more wandering around the town in the middle of the night. I do have a job, you know."

Aunt Cass waved her arm around, indicating the office and warehouse. "What do you think this is? We all have jobs. I'll let you know when I've decided on what night we'll start," she said. Then she dismissed me with a wave of her hand, returning to her laptop.

I left her office slightly disgruntled at being dismissed so abruptly, unhappy about the idea of trekking all over town in the middle of the night. However, part of me was thinking that *maybe* it wasn't the worst idea in the world. Aunt Cass was right: with me, Molly, Luce, Kira and her together, what could go wrong?

I came walking out of the Chili Challenge building and got punched in the face by the heat. After the meat locker temperature inside, I wasn't prepared for it and felt myself sway on my feet. I had a quick look around, seeing that the streets were still clogged with cars and tourists and knew that calling a taxi would be out of the question. Besides, I didn't have the money. I bolted away from the Chili Challenge, heading down the street, darting from shadow to shadow and dodging tourists. I think in my heat-fuelled daze I was heading to my office thinking that perhaps I had some spare clothes there. I was rushing down the street in that direction when I felt a hand grab me by the elbow. It was Carter Wilkins and his face was bright red from the heat.

"Didn't you hear me calling you? I need to talk," he said.

"What?"

"I've been following you for a whole street now. Can we go to your office and talk?"

I mumbled something that Carter took as a yes, and then he followed me down the street to my office building. The front door was unlocked and as I passed by Jonas's office, I could hear him inside talking with another man. Carter followed me up the stairs. With each step we ascended the temperature jumped. I found the keys to my office, fumbled them into the door and unlocked it. I opened the door to the oven that was now my office to find John Smith sitting on the sofa watching the television.

I walked in, trying not to look at the dust that was covering every surface. My poor neglected office was well on its way to being *abandoned*.

"Why is the TV on if there's no one here?" Carter asked.

Oh yeah, he couldn't see John.

"I think it's faulty. Turns itself on and off sometimes. Maybe it's the heat," I said. I headed for the television looking at John and trying to convey with my eyes that I was very sorry, but I had to turn the television off now.

But I don't think John saw me, he was so intently focused on the television.

I flicked the switch to turn the television off (it was showing a terrible infomercial about some exercise equipment that wouldn't have looked out of place in a bondage dungeon) and only then did John look up at me.

"Oh, Harlow, you're here, is it time for our appointment?" he asked.

I couldn't answer him, of course, not with Carter there, so I was stuck trying to make faces, winking and nodding my head in his direction. John frowned and then looked over at Carter.

"Oh, it's the one who writes that trashy newspaper. He was a little snot when he was a teenager and he's a little snot now."

"You know, you need to use your office if you want to stay in the free rent program. If someone came up here they would see that this place is clearly abandoned," Carter said.

"I know that. But I also need money and if it comes down to it I'll choose having money and no office over having an office and no money," I said, snapping a little.

"Why did you leave those twenty dollar bills on the desk?"

I had no good explanation for them. John had left them, of course, as payment for his sessions with me that I had abandoned but he still kept turning up and bringing money even when the office was empty. The last time I'd seen him I had told him to stop bringing money but due to John's memory problem he'd clearly forgotten this.

"I must've left it there," I lied.

Carter swiped his finger across the desk and lifted it up. It was covered in settled dust.

"It's weird that everything is covered in dust except the note on the top is clean, like it's new and only recently been placed there," he said.

"Did you come up here to do some Sherlock Holmes-style investigation about why there's a clean twenty dollar bill sitting on my desk?" I said.

I could feel my anger rising along with the temperature. I turned away from Carter and rushed over to the window, opening it up. It spoke to how hot it was up in my small office that the blistering heat outside felt like a relief. I turned around to see Carter take a seat on the sofa. He always carried a satchel bag which he dropped down, raising a cloud of dust. John was still standing there, glaring at him but not saying anything.

"Would you like a drink of cold water?" I asked, heading for the refrigerator.

"Yes, thank you," Carter said, opening his satchel and beginning to pull out papers.

"I don't trust him," John growled in an undertone.

I said nothing as I walked by him. What could I say? I didn't trust Carter either. But he was in my office and it felt somewhat rude to throw him out so abruptly. I opened the refrigerator and found that past Harlow had left two large glass bottles of water in there. I had no idea how old they were but they were chilled and that was enough. I cleaned two dusty glasses and then filled them with the water, handing one to Carter. I sipped mine, which tasted a little stale, but the chill of it more than made up for the flavor. As soon as the cold water plumed down into my stomach I felt my senses returning. What had I come up here for again? Ah, that was it, to see if I had some spare clothes.

I went to my desk, opened a drawer, and found some clothes inside. But they weren't mine. One was a miniskirt that would only fit me if I went on in intense dieting regime, and the other piece of clothing was a small top, the type of thing a teenage girl might wear. I turned the clothes over in my hands going through the very short list of suspects as to who these might belong to. The first name on the list was Kira. The second was Sophira, her friend. Oh no, had the local teenagers been using my abandoned office for their romantic dalliances?

"Whose clothes are those?" Carter asked.

I stuffed them back into the drawer and closed it before turning around. John was still standing there, glaring at Carter.

"You should ask if those are his real eyebrows," John said.

I stifled a laugh but couldn't escape a smirk making its way onto my face.

"Something funny?" Carter said, those eyebrows of his moving up and down, almost causing me to burst out in laughter.

"No, it's nothing. What did you want to talk to me about that was so urgent?" I finished my glass of cold water and went to the refrigerator and refilled it again. It felt like I could drink all of the water in the world at the moment.

"I think those scratches in the alleyway were faked by the *Mysterious Mysteries*. I wanted your help to investigate them," Carter said.

I gulped down some cold water and then opened the refrigerator door again to luxuriate in the cool air streaming out from it.

"Are you offering me a job?" I asked.

Carter shuffled through his papers for a moment before giving a half nod. "I can't keep writing the paper all by myself. I need help and I can pay you," he said, not looking me in the eye.

Perhaps with the crazy heat I was feeling a little crazy, but it didn't sound like the worst idea. Carter and I had clashed many times in the past. He'd in fact written a few lies about my family and me in his paper. *The Harlot Bay Times* had started off as a credible source of news and then slipped in the direction of tabloid garbage. I had understood why Carter had done it–after all, my own online newspaper was dead and buried. There was only so much attention you could get writing about foreshore restoration and council matters and whether the potholes in the main street were going to be filled.

As a result, Carter had turned to scandal and making up things to keep his newspaper going.

Was I considering working for him? How financially desperate would I have to be that I would call him my boss? In an instant I decided that there was no way he was going to be my boss... but perhaps I *did* need the money. Once Writerpalooza was over I was looking at a nice stretch of unemployment again, perhaps broken up with a few shifts at the bakery or working as a waitress at the *Cozy Cat Café*. Although I was sure there would be a lot of work for the Summer at the café, eventually the seasons would turn again, the entire town would shut down and I would be back to unemployment and writing my ghost story up in my lair behind the mansion.

"I need to think about it. But I would never be your employee, it would have to be a partnership," I said.

Carter nodded and then picked up one of the pieces of paper. He stood up to pass it to me and walked straight into John who bounced off him like he was made of rubber. John went shooting straight through the wall, letting out a surprised yelp that made me jump.

"You okay? You're not dehydrated or something are you?" Carter said, handing me the paper.

"Just a cold chill from the water," I said. John walked back through the door looking positively furious.

"Push me around, will you," he thundered and took a swing at Carter. I flinched again as John's fist connected and then he went shooting off, flying off in the other direction through the front window and down into the street below.

"Maybe you should see someone if you keep having shakes like that," Carter murmured.

To hide my shock I looked down at the paper he'd given me. It was a police record from a little town called Walkerville down in the Mississippi. I had to read through it a few times before I understood what it was saying. It seemed to be a report of Rufus and Dawn of *Mysterious Mysteries* fame being questioned for trespassing after being caught on private land. The interesting part of the report indicated that they'd been setting up a trap of some kind, described as a "modified bear trap".

Carter tapped his finger on the paper.

"I think they'd planned to trap someone. They were going to fake a monster and then have *that* person get terribly injured which they would claim was the *real* monster attacking," Carter said. I passed him back the piece of paper and closed the refrigerator door and went back to my desk with my cool glass of water. I took a seat in my dusty chair and Carter returned to the sofa.

"So do you think Carl Stern being attacked was these two?" I said.

I was feeling that familiar journalistic tingle. Honestly, I had missed it. I loved being a journalist and going around collecting stories, trying to hunt down the truth, and it had been a great pain in my heart to abandon that career.

"I think that's exactly what happened. It's possible they're working with one of the authors too. I found one of them who sets up stunts in all the towns on his book tours. Maybe they're in cahoots or perhaps Rufus and Dawn were taking advantage of that, of him setting up some publicity and trying to make it real. I'm thinking one of them attacked Carl Stern," Carter said.

I sat back in my chair and took another gulp of cold water. Somewhere down in the street behind the sound of the tourists and slow-moving traffic jam, I heard John Smith shout out something.

Although I'd come from Aunt Cass's where she'd concocted a plan for us to go monster hunting in the middle of the night, I considered it still possible that there could be *both* a monster and also someone faking that there was a monster and an attack. Now that I'd seen the police report, which seemed to suggest that Rufus and Dawn had been setting up a trap, it gave greater weight to the hypothesis that they may have been connected to the attack in some way.

"I did discover that Rufus and Dawn had been involved in some vandalism in the past," I told Carter. I briefly took him through what Red had told me, leaving out the source of information and making it seem as though I'd discovered it myself. Carter grew more animated as we spoke and started writing down notes. By the time I was finished, he was grinning.

"This is amazing, both of us can investigate and I think we can nail them! So what do you say, do you want to work together?" he asked.

I was kind of getting excited myself but I managed to stop from blurting out *yes*.

"How about this? I'll pass you any information that I find and you do the same. Once we have a bit more, then we can talk about what to do," I said.

I think Carter must've expected I would bluntly say no

because he looked quite joyous at my noncommittal answer. He held out his hand and I shook it without thinking. "It's a deal," he said.

I suddenly remembered that I only had a two hours break. When I checked the time, I saw I only had fifteen minutes before I was due back to meet Red.

"Okay, I have to go back to work now," I said, hurriedly. I rushed Carter out of my office and locked it behind me after grabbing the bunch of twenties off the desk, and then followed him down the stairs. We'd hit the bottom when the door to Jonas's office opened and Sylvester Coldwell, real estate developer and general all-around sleazy bad guy, came striding out. Jonas was behind him, his face flat and displaying no emotion. Coldwell turned and looked at me and Carter, his eyes traveling up and down.

"The two of you wrestling in the dirt up there, were you?" he said. I looked down at my clothes and saw they were covered in dust from my office. Carter was the same. It was all over his clothes and his bag, and his hands too. Given how sweaty and disheveled we both looked it did in fact appear as though we'd been wrestling up in my office. I knew however that Coldwell hadn't said this as an accurate guess, but rather as an insult to both of us.

"I found that council member who's renting off you for a fifty percent discount. That's not going to slide," Carter said coldly.

Coldwell ignored him and looked at me. "You need to use your office three days out of five or you lose it. I think I need to talk to the council about what you've been doing." With that he turned on his heel, said goodbye to Jonas, and marched out the door. The three of us watched him go, Carter and I wearing identical scowls.

"Goddess, I hate him," I said, gritting my teeth. Jonas

looked at me and then Carter, appeared as though he was about to speak but then merely nodded and closed his door.

"Are they working together?" Carter asked.

"I have no idea," I said, rushing out the door away from Carter and his questions and down the busy street.

CHAPTER ELEVEN

"*B*ut I don't want to go monster hunting at Goddess knows what hour," Molly complained, waving her arms around dramatically.

"I didn't say you were going monster hunting. I said we were looking for where the magic *might* be a bit gritty that *might* coincidentally be a monster," I said.

It was the night of the ridiculously big family dinner and all three of us were slightly on edge. The two boyfriends and now one fiancé were late and the heat hadn't done anything to improve anyone's mood. Yesterday after I'd left my office and Carter behind and gone back to meet Red, the rest of the day had been a blur of exhausting work. Although at first it seemed that being an assistant wasn't that difficult, there was quite a lot of organization to do. I was taking names of students and people that she was talking to, arranging materials to be sent out to them, collecting lists of email addresses, and other things. Red had dropped me off back at the mansion last night and after a quick dinner and a shower, I'd gone to bed early. I hadn't heard Molly and Luce come home and in the morning they'd left before I'd gotten up, a note on the kitchen bench saying they had to meet an air conditioning repair man early at *Traveler*. Today had been another blur of work helping Red out and in the flood of it all I think I'd honestly forgotten that a man had been attacked or that there was some magical mystery going on. I'd forgotten all about the *Mysterious Mysteries* people and had to focus on my job.

Today, Red had had a full day with only two breaks of one hour each in which we both hastily ate and talked through what materials she needed for the next few days. I hadn't mentioned to her what she or the other writers were doing and neither had she. I think maybe there was even some part of my mind that was hoping that after a few days of investigation, they'd all let it go and were too busy to follow up on anything.

The day ended at about five in the afternoon and Red had dropped me off before promising she would return soon. Molly and Luce were already home, having shut *Traveler* early, and after fighting for who got to go in the shower first we'd finally gathered in the lounge. It was the first chance I'd had to talk to them in two days. Kira was currently in the shower, having lost out on that particular argument and having to go last.

"I don't like to be tired but I don't know, it could be fun," Luce said.

"You think walking around the streets of Harlot Bay at night with Aunt Cass looking for a monster is *fun?*" Molly said.

"It could be," she said. She was fiddling with her engagement ring again, a habit she'd picked up now that she had one to play with.

"I'm going to tell Aunt Cass I'm not doing it. I think if you get set on fire going under the house that you should be given a pass on any future adventures," Molly said. Kira emerged from the bathroom with wet hair and rosy cheeks. She was wearing a somewhat skimpy sundress with two small stitched pockets on the front, and as soon as I saw her I remembered the clothing that I'd discovered in my office.

"Have you been going up into my office? Did you leave a miniskirt and a top there?" I blurted out.

Kira frowned, looking puzzled. "I don't know what you're talking about," she said. She reached to pull out her phone.

"No, no, no, no, no, that's not gonna work," Luce tutted.

"What?" Kira said.

"The correct answer is 'No, I haven't been to your office'. Then ask follow-up questions about what clothing, like a normal person would," Luce said.

"Rookie mistake," Molly said, crossing her arms and shaking her head.

"What do you mean rookie mistake? That was the perfect lie," Kira said.

"Aha! So it was you who left the miniskirt and the top in my office," I said, pointing my finger at her.

Kira looked at the three of us and then poked her tongue out at us. "Okay, you got me you bunch of sneaky witches," she said.

"Going there for romance?" Molly teased.

"We were using it as a place to get changed. Someone must've left their clothes behind or gone back later," Kira said.

"Great, so my office *has* become a teenage changing room." I said.

"Better than what we used to have to do. I hated that old water pipe," Luce said.

When we were teenagers intent on sneaking out and getting up to no good, we had an old unused storm water pipe outlet that we would go to. It was a short detour on the way from school so what we would usually do was sneak our clothes out in a bag, hide it in the drain, and then that night when we went out we would go there to get changed. Then, usually we'd head out to one of the parties out on Truer Island or at someone's house around town. Before we would return home we would have to go to the storm water drain again and get changed back into our old clothes. I had to admit it that Kira had come up with a better solution than we had. Even back when we were teenagers, there were plenty of abandoned shops and empty houses around the town. Given that sometimes teenagers would hold parties in abandoned houses I couldn't quite understand why we'd never thought to use one as our changing room.

"Try not to get caught," I said. "I think the council is going to be having a close look at that office building soon and you don't want to get caught there." I briefly explained about bumping into Coldwell and his threat.

After that, the conversation went off in a few directions as we waited for the boyfriends and everyone else to arrive. We were chatting about whether I would take a job with Carter once Writerpalooza was over (I was thinking *not* but perhaps there would be some way I could work with him without having to murder the man), when finally some headlights splashed across the front of the mansion. A whole lot of cars pulled up in quick succession and before we could walk out there Mom came bursting through the front door. She was moving so fast it was like she was a film that was running at high speed.

"Okay everyone take a guest, go up into the forest, there's a chair for everyone. We're going to be bringing some bottles of wine so you need to carry those and we might need some help with some of the food as well," she said all in one breath.

"How many guests are there?" Luce muttered. We wandered outside to find that this dinner was going to break a record. Jack and Jonas were there with their parents, Jon and Jas, as well as Peta. There was also Will and Ollie, Mom's boyfriend Varrius, the banker, Freya's boyfriend Boris Dubois of the Dubois Cheese Company, and Aunt Cass's boyfriend Artemis who ran Fogg's Island Tour Company.

There was also Aunt Cass, our moms, the three of us, Kira, and then a moment later two more cars pulled up. One was Sheriff Hardy and the other one was Red.

"My this is going to be a big dinner," Red called out as she stepped out of the luxurious sports car.

"Everyone up into the forest and then we'll do the introductions," Mom said, sounding somewhat manic.

I grabbed Jack by the hand, kissed him on the cheek and then said hello to his parents.

"No hangover or throwing a glass of water at us this time," Jon said with a chuckle.

"Not tonight," I quipped. I saw Mom shoot me a look. She'd overheard what he'd said and I knew she would ask me about it later. I waved Red over and despite Mom's instructions gave her an introduction to Jack and his parents, and also Jonas and Peta. Molly and Luce had already grabbed Will and Ollie and had led them away along the path, going up into the forest. It had only been a few months ago that Aunt Ro and Sheriff Hardy were married up here. We'd set up tables in the forest for the wedding, which we then had left in place.

There were glimmering fairy lights in the trees, and although our non-magical guests wouldn't know it, there were spells on the area to keep out any bugs and other insects that might disrupt the meal. Aunt Freya and Aunt Ro followed behind with Sheriff Hardy, each of them carrying a cooler that I'm sure was filled with wine. The large group soon reached the clearing and everyone found their seats.

Normally when we were eating inside Aunt Cass sat at the head of the table, but out here the tables were so long the head was somewhere off in the distance. Aunt Cass sat in the middle and looked over each of the guests in turn. As she did, Aunt Freya and Aunt Ro opened up the coolers and began pulling out bottles of tequila and other ingredients.

"Tequila? This is going to be good," Jack whispered to me.

As the alcohol came out onto the table I got the impression this was going to be a Mexican themed night. It looked like the moms had grabbed all the ingredients for margaritas, including two large buckets of crushed ice that Sheriff Hardy pulled out of a cooler and put onto the table.

"Introductions and drinks," Aunt Cass commanded and then pointed her finger directly at Jon.

"I'm Jon. I am Jack and Jonas's dad, and this is my wife Jas. She used to be a schoolteacher and also a musician," he said. As we went around the table Aunt Ro expertly began mixing up margaritas at high speed and passing them around. Mom had gone back to the mansion, disappearing into the dark. With so many guests it took a while to go around to meet everyone. Red, who was sitting directly across from Aunt Cass, introduced herself and I saw that shy look on Aunt Cass's face again.

"I love your books," Jas said and smiled at Red.

"Thank you so much, and I brought something for you," Red said, talking to Aunt Cass. She reached under the table into her bag and brought out a copy of one of her books which she passed across the table to Aunt Cass.

Aunt Cass opened the cover where it had been inscribed "To Cassandra Torrent" and then signed by Red Forrest.

"Thank you, I will treasure it," Aunt Cass said in a somewhat small voice.

It must've been something quite extraordinary to see Aunt Cass momentarily silenced because practically everyone around the table who knew her well took a big gulp of their margaritas. We all started chatting away as the moms vanished and then all three of them returned, bringing with them covered platters of food. My earlier guess had been right: the evening was Mexican themed. Soon there were a variety of nachos on the table, some with bacon and cheese, others with beef and chorizo. There were cheesy chicken enchiladas, and black bean and sweet potato chimichangas. Me, Molly and Luce were forced to leave the table momentarily to go to the kitchen, passing through the main dining room of chattering guests. In the kitchen there were two women there that I didn't recognize. Mom explained to us in an undertone that they had hired them for the night to help out with the guests so we could have our family dinner in the forest.

We grabbed more platters of food and carried them out to the dark. It was still stifling hot up near the mansion, but we were all feeling good, our stomachs full of food—and the margaritas were certainly helping too. We returned to the tables, setting out the platters which turned out to be a variety of tacos. I took one and bit into it. It was a prawn taco with black bean salad and creamy avocado dressing. I groaned in pleasure and then took another bite before washing it all down with a mouthful of delicious lemon and lime margarita.

I'd been hoping to get the chance to talk to Jack's parents tonight but without a proper seating plan they were over the other side and too far away to have a conversation. I didn't mind though. Jack had arranged for me, Jack, Peta and Jonas to go out with his parents to Valhalla Viking. Jack had even booked a booth, so although the place would be busy we would be able to have a conversation at least.

In all the talking and eating I overheard that Jon had been a builder in his life, mostly houses and then moving to smaller renovations that he did every now and then. Jas had been a teacher, first in secondary schools and then moving to primary schools, and she'd even been a musician working in piano bars for a time.

We were all eating and laughing, the conversation flowing all over the place, when I felt the magic push against me like a gentle wave. It was enough for me to notice it but thanks to my third margarita I ignored the feeling.

"Hey, Jonas what are you doing meeting with Coldwell?" I called out to him across the table.

I hadn't intended to bring it up in front of everyone, perhaps the alcohol in my drink was loosening my tongue, but everyone else continued their conversations and didn't appear to be listening in.

"I'm was making sure everything is okay for the Governor's mansion restoration," Jonas said. He gave me a significant look that I didn't quite catch the meaning of until I looked to Peta next to him. She mouthed *we'll talk later* and I nodded back at her.

"So we've had one proposal and acceptance. When are the other two happening," Aunt Cass called out.

Suddenly, all the conversations came to a grinding halt.

"They'll happen when they happen," Molly said.

"There's no rush," I said and waved my margarita happily.

"Marriage is wonderful," Aunt Ro said and put her arm around Sheriff Hardy before kissing him on the cheek.

I was about to say something else when the magic surged again and this time every witch at the table felt it. It pushed harder this time and then felt gritty, as though it was muddy water.

"Eat up everyone, you know there are wild animals out here so we don't want to stay for too long," Aunt Cass said, coming up with a lie on the spot.

"Wild animals? What do they have here?" Jon said.

I'm sure Aunt Cass was about to come up with another lie, but in that perfect moment of silence somewhere in the forest there was a cracking sound and then we all heard a tree snap and topple, crashing to the ground.

"What the hell was that?" Art said, peering into the darkness.

"Some of the old trees have been rotting and they fall over from time to time," Aunt Cass replied.

"Maybe we should finish this dinner down your end of the mansion, inside" Mom said, looking at me, Molly and Luce.

There was another crash in the darkness. This time it sounded as though something large had hit a tree. A moment later, there was a snapping sound as the tree fell and crashed down.

"It sounds like there's an animal out there. Are there wild pigs here?" Jon said. Jack looked at me and I nodded. I understood his question well: *Is this something magical?*

Before any more lies could be told, there came a piercing howl from the darkness that sounded like a animal in great pain. Aunt Cass shot up from her chair so fast she knocked over her drink.

"That sounds like a wolf to me," Red said. By now everyone was on their feet, peering into the dark.

"Harlow, come with me," Aunt Cass commanded. She took off, not caring what it looked like, and I followed behind. I heard Jack call out to me, and Mom say something about everyone heading back, the protests from Jon that it wasn't safe, and also from Varrius, Art and Boris. I'd had three margaritas and I could feel the alcohol sloshing around in my blood. It was probably the only thing keeping me from feeling completely terrified. The moment we were far enough away from the forest dinner table Aunt Cass threw up a small globe of light ahead of us.

"Is this safe?" I gasped as I followed along behind.

"Not at all," she said. The magic around us was gritty, full of mud, and the further we went through the dark, the worse it felt. It began to feel rough, like sandpaper.

Aunt Cass stopped so abruptly I crashed into the back of her. There in front of us was a clearing. Kneeling on the ground, hunched over, was a man wearing ragged clothing. He had black hair and his face was in shadow.

Aunt Cass walked slowly forward into the clearing, her arms stretched wide as though she was trying to calm a wild animal.

"You're safe," she said to the man. At the sound of her voice he turned towards us. He looked past Aunt Cass and then at me, his blue eyes glinting in the moonlight.

"Marguerite? Is that you?" he said. I took a step towards him and from the way his expression changed he must've understood that I was not whoever this Marguerite was. He groaned in pain and then leaped to his feet.

"Stay away Torrents," he said through gritted teeth. Then he bolted faster than any man should be able to run, disappearing into the darkness. We heard another tree crash to the ground, felled by his passage.

It wasn't long before it was only me and Aunt Cass standing in the clearing, the quiet sounds of the night around us.

"Is *he* the monster? Who's Marguerite?" I asked.

Aunt Cass looked at me. "I think *you* are," she said.

CHAPTER TWELVE

$\mathcal{J}$ was unloading boxes of books from the trunk of Red's sports car when I Slipped. Sometimes a slip is unnoticeable except for the effects. This was *not* one of those times. It was yet another blistering day but I was hit with a deep chill as though someone had thrown a bucket of ice cubes at me. It went through my body in a shock and then I stood there, gasping, clutching a box waiting to see what would happen next. I didn't have to wait long–lines of frost crept up the sides of the box where I was touching it. I dropped it back into the trunk in alarm.

"No, no, no, no, *no*," I moaned. If I was going to turn into some Ice Princess, that would ruin everything, including my job. I'd likely have to quit and stay stuck at home, or worse head out to Truer Island to hide in that cave again.

As I stood there, gulping air and feeling my heart thudding in my chest, I realized I could no longer feel the heat beating down upon me. A moment ago I'd been sweating like crazy. Now I felt as though it was simply a pleasant day.

I took a few more deep breaths to calm myself and then reached out to touch the box again. It took only a few

seconds for thin white lines of frost to creep out from the tip
of my finger and down the side of the box. I held my finger
there for a moment until the icy line stopped moving. Well
that was a relief of sorts. It seemed there was some limit to
how far it would go, at least at the moment. I pulled my hand
away from the box and watched as the stripes of frost
vanished in the sun glaring down.

Another experiment was in order. I touched the box with
my elbow. No frost. I put the box on the ground and rested
my toe against it. All clear. It looked like it was contained to
my hands, at least for now.

Maybe it would be okay. Hey, who knows, *maybe* for once
one of these slip powers would come in handy. Like carrying
around my own air conditioning. I only had a few more
boxes to take inside for Red's session and then I'd be free. I
wasn't due to see her again until after lunch. It would give
me time to figure out something.

I reached out and grabbed one of the boxes with both
hands but then put it down when it frosted over. I had to
come up with a plan and quick if I was to drop off these
boxes without anyone seeing that they were covered in frost.
I certainly didn't need to add another fiasco to the list of
recent fiascos. Such as last night, for example. After Aunt
Cass and I had returned from the forest there had been a
blister of lies. Aunt Cass had said she thought she'd seen a
wild pig in the forest a few days earlier that had had an
injured leg and *that* was why she'd rushed out into the darkness. Our guests understandably weren't quite sure what to
make of this excuse. I knew the moms' boyfriends, Boris and
Varrius, simply thought that Aunt Cass was eccentric, or
perhaps crazy. Everyone else who knew she was a witch tried
to take it in their stride. The meal had finished soon after
that. Mom appeared afraid that something else would occur
and so she'd served dessert and then the night had fizzled

out. As we were walking back to the cars, I had told the lie to Red that Aunt Cass was eccentric and cared deeply about injured wildlife. I overheard Jack saying the same thing to his parents. Whether they'd believed us was another thing entirely.

Me, Jack, Jonas and Peta were due to go to dinner with Jack's parents at Valhalla Viking on Thursday night and I hoped it would give us a chance to talk properly. I was hoping that they would see that although *perhaps* certain members of my family were a little kooky, *I* was perfectly normal. It was starting to look like this might not be possible though, not if every time I picked up my glass of water it would freeze solid in my hand.

At that thought I wondered how powerful it was. Could I pick up a glass of water and have it freeze in my hand?

My thoughts were interrupted by Red calling out to me from the exhibition hall doorway.

"Harlow, can you bring the boxes in, we're about to begin," she said before rushing back inside.

It didn't look like I had any other choices - I was going to have to make a run for it. There were no gloves in the sports car, and nothing else I could use to put a barrier between my hands on the boxes. So I grabbed one and rushed inside as fast as I could, dumping it hurriedly with the others. Red was sitting at a table going over her notes for the morning session and didn't look up to see the spiraling frost on the side of the box. I went back and forth two more times before I finally delivered all the boxes. Thankfully, as soon as I put them down, the frost disappeared due to the hot weather.

"Thanks for that, Harlow, so I'll see you after lunch?" Red asked me.

"I'll see you then," I said and then got out of there as soon as I could. I needed to find somebody I knew, somebody who knew I was a witch and see if when they came close to me if I felt cold. It might certainly be possible to hide this slip witch power but not if people who walked by me started freezing.

I'd planned to see Ollie this morning to talk to him about the name Marguerite so perhaps this could be two birds with one stone. As I walked away from the exhibition center heading in the direction of the library, it did feel as though this new slip power wasn't *so* bad. The sun was glaring down and all around me tourists were red-faced and sweaty but I felt fine. I made my way through them, careful to keep my hands close to my sides to avoid any accidental bumps. As I walked through the streets my mind drifted back to last night. The man in the clearing who had bolted after speaking to us had looked at me and called me Marguerite. I was convinced it was no coincidence. Some time ago, after defeating the Shadow Witch, I'd seen a glimpse of the past. Juliet Stern, young and wild, riding on a horse galloping past the Torrent Mansion being chased by her friend, the unnamed Torrent witch. The second girl on horseback had looked like me. I was convinced that thanks to the man last night we now had a name for her: Marguerite Torrent. She'd had a daughter Rosetta. Neither the moms nor Aunt Cass knew who Marguerite might be.

I hadn't had a chance yet to discuss this properly with the family. After everyone had left last night, Aunt Cass had vanished, presumably heading to her lair, and the moms had returned to their end of the mansion to look after all the guests up there. Molly and Luce had gone with their respective boyfriends, and Jack had given me a kiss before taking his parents with him. I'd been left at home with only a sleeping Adams to keep me company.

As I headed towards the library, my mind kept drifting all over the place. I wondered if I should read Juliet Stern's journal again. It was sitting in my lair up in one of the abandoned cottages behind the mansion. Now that I knew the name Marguerite, would it appear in her journal?

I even briefly wondered whether Hattie Stern would recognize the name before I remembered she was gone, off on some mysterious expedition that required a protective charm from Aunt Cass. As for the man himself–who was he? There was no doubt the magic around him had turned muddy but he had simply been a man, not a monster. Could he transform? How could a man be destroying trees in the forest? He hadn't looked *that* strong.

I was pondering these things when I turned a corner onto the road where the library was and then stopped dead in my tracks. There, across the road, was an abandoned hardware store. The large weathered door had seen better days. In the middle of it, about two foot high, carved into the wood, was the strange symbol that I'd seen on Ollie's website. The one that had been drawn on doors and carved into trees around Harlot Bay more than a hundred years ago. I crossed the road, moving between the tourists who were seemingly ignoring the symbol. As I came closer to it I saw there were chips of wood on the ground left over from the symbol carving. I approached it cautiously, expecting to feel some magical influence but there was none. It was merely a symbol carved into a door. I touched it with my fingers. Where the symbol had been carved the wood appeared new, light pine in color, a contrast to the aged wood around it. I ran my finger down it. It was smooth as though it had been done by a machine.

Was this the work of the *Mysterious Mysteries*? Had Rufus and Dawn been out here last night carving a symbol into a door so they could later "discover" it?

Given they had a history of vandalism it seemed entirely possible that they could be to blame. After all, what better way to hype their show than to claim to have discovered some monster from the deep past and then replicate the symbols that had appeared the last time it had been roaming the streets.

I stepped back from the symbol and used my phone to take a photo. I'd have to talk to Ollie and the family, and also possibly Sheriff Hardy.

It was already bad enough that the writers were investigating in town. If the *Mysterious Mysteries* brought attention to Harlot Bay who knows how many wannabe monster hunters would turn up?

I left the symbol behind, shoving my phone back into my pocket after it started to ice over. That was certainly a problem I hadn't expected.

I passed by Sheriff Hardy's car as I went into the library and briefly wondered why he'd be here. I didn't have to wonder for long. As soon as I went inside I saw Ollie and Sheriff Hardy standing over in a small alcove talking in low tones. I walked over and after have a quick look around to make sure no one was listening said, "This might be a strange question, but do you feel freezing cold when you're around me?"

Both men looked at me, not quite sure what to say. Sheriff Hardy had many years on the police force to bring out his police face, a sort of impassive wall that gave away nothing. Ollie didn't have this experience, though, and so he was merely puzzled.

"Is this a... you know, thing?" Ollie said, almost in a whisper.

"I think I've accidentally turned into an Ice Princess. Here I'll show you," I said. I grabbed a book from a nearby shelf and it only took a moment of holding it for frost to coat the cover. I handed it to Ollie, and his eyes widened as he looked at it.

"It happened this morning. So what I need to know is that

if you're near me do I feel freezing cold? Because that's going to be a big problem," I said.

"No, I don't think but let's try this," Sheriff Hardy said. He reached out and before I could stop him, grabbed my wrist. He only held it for a moment before he let go with a start. When he turned his hand towards me. I saw that there were thin streaks of frost across his palm. Oh Goddess, had it started to spread already?

"Okay, well, it's not as bad as I thought, but it's still pretty bad," I sighed. "Anyway, what were you guys talking about before I interrupted?" I asked.

"You were walking through the town. Didn't you see all of those symbols? We have at least ten carved into doors and walls, and twenty more spray painted everywhere," Sheriff Hardy said.

What? I had only seen one. But then again I hadn't been concentrating on my surroundings, my mind full of other things.

"I saw the one across the street but there's more?" I asked.

"A lot more. It looks like they all happened last night," Sheriff Hardy said.

"I can check my website, but I'm not sure it's possible to know who read the article to be honest," Ollie said, picking up the conversation they'd been having.

"My guess is that it's the *Mysterious Mysteries*. This would fit perfectly into their story that there's a monster in Harlot Bay," I said.

I may have spoken a little louder than I intended, because Sheriff Hardy took a quick look around before responding.

"But didn't you see some man out in the forest last night, someone possibly supernatural who'd been knocking down trees. Could it have been him?" he said.

For a moment I felt sorry for Sheriff Hardy. I think he'd always known there was something very strange about our family and he ignored this when he would turn to us for unofficial help with mysterious police cases. Then he'd gotten together with Aunt Ro and discovered that she was a witch and so were the rest of us. Now he was trying to be the Sheriff of a small town where he never knew if the crimes that occurred were ordinary ones or had some supernatural origin.

"I have no idea if it was that man in the forest. But doesn't spray paint sound like a modern thing? That symbol that's down the road looks like it's been carved with modern tools. I don't know why but I don't feel that the man last night would know anything about spray paint," I said. Even as I spoke I realized I was suddenly understanding something about the man we'd seen last night. Sure, he'd been dressed in ragged clothing but now I realized it had been very *old* ragged clothing, not a modern style. The last time I'd seen people dressed like that was when I'd had the problem of seeing into the past. I filed this piece of information away. It was something to tell Aunt Cass and the moms later on.

"Do you know of anyone else who has come to talk to you about the symbols, or anyone who seemed too interested?" Sheriff Hardy asked Ollie.

"There are a lot of people. I get emails from all over the world. This morning there was a couple here asking me about it."

"What did they look like?" I blurted out before Sheriff Hardy could say anything.

"Tall guy, muscly, quite scary looking. Looked like a Navy Seal," Ollie said.

"Was the woman with him much *much* shorter?" I asked.

"Yeah, that was right," Ollie said.

"It sounds like you know them," Sheriff Hardy said.

"The tall one is TJ McKenna, he's an author, and the

woman would be Jenna Cheng, another author here for Writerpalooza," I said.

"Why would they be here asking about the symbol?" Sheriff Hardy said.

Although Sheriff Hardy was married to Aunt Ro and now technically my uncle, and therefore on the inside, I still hesitated as I thought about what to tell him. Should I tell him that the writers were investigating on their own? That they thought something strange was happening in Harlot Bay, but I didn't know *exactly* what they were doing?

I took too long thinking though and I must've had some look on my face because Sheriff Hardy growled, "Harlow, tell me the truth."

"Fine. I don't know for sure but I think some of the authors in town who were with me that night Carl Stern was attacked have been running their own investigation," I said.

Sheriff Hardy pinched the bridge of his nose and let out a sigh.

"Bad enough that I've had the Torrents tangled up in investigations, but now I have a bunch of authors too? That one from last night, Red, is she involved as well?" he asked.

"Um, I think she might be," I said, feeling like the biggest snitch in the world.

"Should I have *not* told those two about the symbol?" Ollie asked.

"It's fine, it's historical information. It's free for anyone. But now I'm going to have to question them to see if they were involved," Sheriff Hardy said.

"Do you think some of the authors might have put all those symbols around the town?" I asked.

"I'm not quite sure, but I've also become aware that perhaps the man who was attacked a few nights ago, Carl, was involved in a publicity stunt and that it may have gone terribly wrong. So they could be involved, although I don't know why they would be," Sheriff Hardy said. He said goodbye to us after that, leaving Ollie and me alone, standing in the alcove looking at each other. Ollie ran his hands through his hair and let out a sigh.

"I know this is all about... you know... *magic*, but it still feels so crazy sometimes," Ollie said in an undertone.

I was once again reminded that although both Ollie and Will knew that our family were witches, it was a recent discovery for them. I didn't want to start talking about magic and possibly upset him any further, so I changed the topic.

"I have a name I need you to research for me," I told him. "I think she's one of our family members. Her name is Marguerite Torrent and she would have had a daughter, Rosetta. We only know as far back as my grandmother's grandmother and I have a suspicion that she is somewhere in our family tree before that. Could you look into it for us?" I asked.

Ollie's mood brightened noticeably. He loved research and so constructing a family tree was perfect for him.

"I'll get right on it, Harlow," he said and then touched me on the hand. He pulled his hand back an instant later though, obviously at the cold that was emanating from my skin.

I hastily said goodbye and left. I didn't want the poor guy to freak out more over the magical slip power that was currently afflicting me. When I walked outside, although I knew intellectually it was blisteringly hot, it felt like a pleasant day, so it wasn't *all* bad.

I checked the time and saw that I still had a few hours before I had to return to Red. Now I had a clue to follow up on–TJ McKenna and Jenna Cheng researching the mysterious symbols. With a renewed fire in my belly I headed back into town to find a copy of the Writerpalooza itinerary so I could track the two of them down.

CHAPTER THIRTEEN

*D*amn, he was good.

By the time I found TJ and Jenna, Sheriff Hardy was already there interviewing them. They were doing back-to-back sessions with a small fifteen-minute break in between them. I waited around the corner, trying to look like I was in line for the next session to start. I kept peeking around at TJ and Jenna talking to Sheriff Hardy. Eventually the Sheriff nodded at them and left. The moment he was gone I went walking over.

"So the Sheriff's questioned you as well?" I said by way of greeting.

"Hey, Harlow," TJ said and put his hand up for a high-five. Without thinking, I slapped his palm. He immediately pulled his hand away.

"Why are your hands so cold?" he said.

"Amazing air-conditioning in the car," I said.

"You'd better be careful with that, you'll get frostbite," TJ said, shaking his head.

"What did you mean by we got questioned *too*?" Jenna said, looking at me with a slightly suspicious expression.

Okay, time for *another* lie.

"Ollie the librarian is my cousin's boyfriend. I work with him casually at the library sometimes. I was over there talking with him when the Sheriff arrived to question him about all those weird symbols that have appeared all over the town. I happened to be there when he mentioned that you two had been at the library asking about it as well," I said.

"Oh right, well I guess a giant like this guy would be pretty obvious to spot wouldn't he," Jenna said, looking at TJ.

"You think he tracked us down because of me? You're the suspicious one," he said back and poked her in the side. Jenna laughed and swatted his hand away.

I got the sudden feeling this was a *little* more than innocent flirting.

"What did the Sheriff say anyway?" I said, trying not to sound too concerned about it.

"Not much. I think he was trying to find out if we were running our own investigation. He didn't seriously believe that we had anything to do with the symbols around town," TJ said.

"If you *were* running your own investigation who do you think was behind the symbols?"

"My guess is it's the *Mysterious Mysteries*. Red told us they've already been in trouble for vandalism and now they're here, and all these symbols appear in a single night? I bet they're doing it to promote their show," Jenna said.

"I still think it has something to do with that guy who was attacked, Carl what's-his-name. I think Markus Hornby is somehow involved... or maybe there's just a lot of weird things that go on in this town," TJ said.

I suddenly saw an opportunity to put the writers on to a false trail.

"I think you're right, Jenna. I bet you that it's the *Mysterious Mysteries*. Last night, one of my cousins saw them skulking around down a side street. We didn't see if they were doing any of the graffiti but I bet you they were involved. Someone should find out where they're staying. I bet ten bucks that they'd find spray paint there. Or maybe even some kind of monster costume," I said.

For a moment I thought I'd overdone it, trying too hard to lead them in a false direction but then both the authors nodded and Jenna grinned at TJ.

"Yeah, let's find where they're staying and sneak in," she said.

Before they could say anything else, one of the Writer-palooza organizers came out and told them their next session was due to begin. I said goodbye to TJ and Jenna and rushed out of there, feeling quite pleased with myself. If I could keep the writers away from investigating mysterious supernatural things, then perhaps they'd be safe.

I still had a little time before I had to return to Red so I had to solve the problem of everything I touched being frozen. I'd have to talk to Aunt Cass for a more permanent solution but in the meantime I'd have to buy a pair of driving gloves and find an excuse to wear them.

I dodged my way through all the hot and sweaty tourists until I found a small clothing store that I knew sold leather driving gloves. Wincing a little at the price, I paid for them and then slipped them on before walking out of the store.

The rest of the day was a blur again of helping Red. She didn't ask about the gloves until much later. I told her I had an allergic reaction to something and needed to keep my hands covered for the next couple of days. She seemed to accept this lie without question. I got a message from Kira saying she was skipping the ride home with us; she'd find her own way back.

It wasn't long after that that Red was driving me back up the hill to the mansion.

Now it was time to put her off the trail as well.

"I talked with TJ and Jenna today. They think Rufus and Dawn are behind all the symbols around the town," I said.

"Oh, they already told me. Jenna is putting together a plan to find out where they're staying so we can break in."

I had a sudden moment of doubt. Yes, I *wanted* to put them off the trail but what if they broke in and then something bad happened?

"Maybe they should find where they're staying and then tell the Sheriff?" I said.

"It's strange you say that… because they pretty much said it was *your* idea," Red said, looking sideways at me.

Uh-oh. I'd been successfully telling lies all day but it looked like I might have accidentally tripped myself up. Never mind, I always had another fresh lie ready to go.

"Yes… I kinda did. But then I thought about it a bit more. If these people have been spray painting around town and with all that stuff you told me about them setting up a trap, maybe they *did* attack that guy that we found. I wouldn't want anyone to get injured," I said.

"No, me neither," Red agreed. We arrived at the mansion and Red said goodbye, telling me she'd see me in the morning.

I walked inside to find Aunt Cass sitting on the sofa stroking Adams behind the ears like she was a villain in a movie.

"Word on the street is you've slipped," Aunt Cass said, without preamble. I immediately glanced at Adams but he was purring with his eyes closed.

"Did some little snitch tell you that?" I said.

"It doesn't matter where I heard it. Is it true? What's happening?"

Rather than tell her, I took off the leather gloves, stepped forward and picked up a coffee cup that was sitting on the table. Within a few moments it was covered in a thick coat of frost.

"I have a family dinner with Jack's parents coming up. Do you have any ideas?" I asked.

"I'll think of something, don't worry. I'll get you to that dinner," Aunt Cass said.

I told her about the writers and attempting to put them off the trail but as I did Aunt Cass started shaking her head.

"No, no, don't try to put them *off* the trail. We want them *on* the trail as much as possible. We need as many people as possible *on* that trail," she said.

I went to the refrigerator and opened it, searching for something to eat and found I had to remove the food quickly, lest it freeze over in my hands. Was it my imagination or was the frost faster now?

"But it's not safe for nonmagical people to be investigating this kind of thing," I said.

"I think there's something bigger going on and the more people look into it, the better," Aunt Cass said with finality.

"This is gonna be impossible," I complained. I was trying to cut cheese and the knife had frosted over.

"It'll be okay, I'll help you, and by the way, we're going out tomorrow night," Aunt Cass said. She was out the door before I could protest.

It was looking like tomorrow was going to be a big day. Red had a jam-packed schedule and then at night we were going to go to the Hannibal Blood session. Red believed he'd checked Carl Stern out of the hospital, although we didn't know why. Then I was going with my family to stay out till all hours walking the town looking for a monster.

"Can I have some cheese?" Adams said from somewhere near my feet.

I looked down at the block of cheese that had the beginnings of frost creeping up over the packaging.

"Sure," I said and sighed. I gave him some food, put my gloves back on and ate a quick dinner. Then I had a shower, which was an exercise in ridiculousness given I couldn't wear the gloves. The water kept freezing on my hands and then falling to the ground. It wasn't long before I was ankle deep in a kind of slushy snow.

By the time I got out of there and dried myself off I was feeling very unhappy indeed. My unhappiness only grew deeper after I checked my phone and found a message from Jack telling me he would be out entertaining his parents and he hoped to see me sometime soon.

They were lovely people and so were the writers, and I was thankful to have a job, but I also couldn't wait until everyone went home and I could be with Jack again.

CHAPTER FOURTEEN

"*H*ello, earth to Harlow?" Molly said.

"Gah?" I mumbled, waking up to find myself sitting in Molly's car heading down the hill into Harlot Bay.

"I said, what happened with Hannibal Blood?" Molly repeated.

"Oh, yeah," I said and yawned, rubbing my eyes. I was stuffed in the backseat, along with Luce and Kira. Aunt Cass was in the front. It was just past eleven at night and I was having trouble staying awake.

"What's that word for when something doesn't go well? Is it a debacle?" I asked.

"Fiasco? Luce said.

"No, it's a screw-up," Aunt Cass said.

"Disaster, that's the word you're looking for, a disaster," Kira said.

"It could be a blunder," Molly said.

"Okay, yeah, it was all of those: a debacle, fiasco, screw-up, disaster, blunder."

After working with Red we went to Hannibal Blood's reading...

The day had been a crazy blur. Red had packed in so many sessions there was barely enough time to breathe between them. I honestly don't know where she got the energy because I was feeling exhausted trying to keep up and all I was doing was *assisting*. We worked the whole day and then the final session had run late. By the time we'd finally gotten away we were so late we were almost going to miss the end of Hannibal Blood's one and only author appearance.

We'd rushed over there—well 'rushed' is a relative term, given that the traffic was still quite clogged—and arrived as Hannibal's horror audience was getting out. We managed to duck and dodge our way through the horde of people dressed mostly in all black and found our way around to a side exit.

It wasn't long before we found Hannibal Blood but the moment he saw us he headed off in the other direction. Red called out to him and then he'd bolted. We'd given chase, but by the time we'd gotten outside he was gone. We'd then spent the next half hour stuck in traffic trying to drive around the central part of Harlot Bay hoping to spot him again, but there was no use. He'd vanished. Red had finally driven me home, a long silent car trip which wasn't a surprise given how tired we both were.

I'd come inside, eaten some food (take-out from the fridge that didn't require any delicate preparation), fed Adams, had a five-second icy shower, and then crashed into bed.

"And then you guys woke me up and now I'm here and I need some more sleep," I finished.

"That sounds super suspicious that he ran away. Maybe he's behind the attack," Luce said.

As tired as I was, I knew I had to head her off at the pass. She had a way of jumping off the deep end.

"Or maybe he saw two crazy people following him and bolted for it," I said and yawned again.

"Is this him?" Kira asked, showing me a picture on her phone.

"That's the one and man, can he run fast," I said.

Looking at the photo on Kira's phone there was something familiar about him again, but I couldn't put my finger on it. Or who knows, maybe I was imagining it given how tired I was.

"Or *maybe* Hannibal Blood's a shapeshifter! He's the monster *and* also the author writing about monsters and that guy, Carl, was working for him thinking it was some standard publicity stunt and then his boss turned on him and ripped him to shreds!" Luce said dramatically, waving her hands around in the tiny back seat of the car.

I ignored her.

"So now I don't know what we're going to do," I said.

"What we're going to do is get to that alleyway and see what we can find. Do some *real* investigating," Aunt Cass said.

"Or what we *could* do is stay in our beds and have a sleep and go to work because we all have jobs and not worry about authors and monsters," Molly said with a liberal dose of snark. She was clearly not happy about being dragged along on this little escapade.

Aunt Cass pretended that she hadn't heard her. "How is your business going anyway? Did that guitarist work out?" she asked.

Guitarist? How much had I missed when I was asleep?

"His name is Blake and he is amazing," Luce said, her voice turning dreamy.

"What's happening? Who's Blake?" I said thoroughly

confused. I lowered my window to let some air blow in. It was still quite warm but it helped to wake me up.

"I haven't seen him yet but C-Money found a guitarist named Blake and now he's going to be working at the *Cozy Cat Café* and *Traveler*. He's a tourist though, so maybe it'll just be for a few months," Kira said.

"Blake? Even his name sounds scruffy and blue-eyed," I commented.

Molly looked at me in the rear-view mirror.

"No, seriously, you should see him. He's exactly like that. It's ridiculous," she said.

"I'm looking forward to meeting the boy," Kira said.

"Oh, and what about your boyfriend Fox?" Luce said and poked Kira in the ribs.

"I can look, I don't have to touch," Kira quipped with a devilish smile.

The remainder of the trip into town was taken up discussing Blake and his degree of scruffiness and blue eyes. We still hit some traffic although it was nowhere near as bad as it was during the day. This deep into Writerpalooza, it seemed that many of the tourists who had been out wandering the streets at night had been eventually worn down by the heat and so it seemed slightly quieter in the center of town. We parked near the alleyway and then trooped down it. Making sure no one was watching us, Aunt Cass cast a small ball of light to illuminate the deep scratches that ran up the wall. I was now much more awake and as far as I could tell the magic around us felt quite normal. There was no sign of any kind of magical entity, be it a shapeshifting man or not.

"I think these scratch marks are real. Look at the angle on them here," Aunt Cass said, sounding like she was narrating one of the *Mysterious Mysteries* documentaries.

"That's all well and good but what exactly is the plan?" Molly said, still not letting go of the snark.

She had a point. Here we all were standing in the alleyway. There were scratches but what next? Start walking around?

Aunt Cass turned to Kira "You're up K-Fresh," she said and then gave the teenager a high five.

Kira winked at us and then took a deep breath before casting a spell. What kind of spell it was I don't know. I'd never seen it or felt it before. Not only that but wow, Kira was *quiet*. When spells are cast, you can normally feel them, sense how they affect the magic. There was a slight tug in the magic surrounding us, but it was almost a whisper. I had no idea that Kira had gotten so good so fast. She was a slip witch, like Aunt Cass and me, and the thing with slip witches is that we can go from incredibly weak to incredibly powerful in random pattern. Perhaps today Kira was incredibly powerful?

Kira let out a breath and then clapped her hands together at the end of the spell. There was a moment of silence as we waited and then tiny pinpricks of pink light began to sparkle up the wall, like a glittery trail of fireflies. They soon brightened, forming a cloudy pink string that went up the wall and over the rooftops.

"I give you a path," Kira said and then bowed to us all.

"Wow, that's incredible," Luce said.

"How did you learn to do that?" Molly asked.

"Sort of figured it out myself plus I've been training with C-Money a bit," Kira said. She and Aunt Cass high-fived again and I have to admit I felt a *tiny* surge of jealousy. Yes, the moms and Aunt Cass had always had a policy of they would teach us if we'd ask, and of course we hadn't asked very much and so they hadn't taught us. But from my recollection, Aunt Cass had never been like this with *us*.

I had that sudden feeling of what it's like when parents become grandparents. They might not be very good parents but they become amazing grandparents, allowing the kids to have candy before bed and getting involved in all kinds of reckless things.

I pushed the jealousy away. I should be happy for Aunt Cass and also Kira. They got on well together, almost making some kind of crazy superhero witch team.

A sudden image of them both wearing spandex and masks entered my mind and I giggled to myself, earning a strange look from everyone around me.

"No time to wait, let's follow it," Aunt Cass said. Without waiting for response, she found the nearest fire escape ladder and clambered up it as though she were a monkey in the forest rather than an old lady in her eighties. Kira followed and then me. At ground level I heard Molly complaining again to Luce about how they were always getting involved in dangerous situations. Obviously being *slightly* set on fire under the house had made her extra wary.

Up on the rooftops, the glittering pink trail stretched across them off into the distance. We followed it three roofs across until we came to a gap that we couldn't jump. We had to go down the fire escape and this time we went out onto the street to walk the rest of the distance, occasionally Aunt Cass forcing one of us to climb a fire escape to check the direction of the glittering pink path.

As we walked, we talked about all kinds of random things. You would almost think were out for a Sunday afternoon stroll rather than trying to track down a monster. We teased Kira more about her boyfriend, talked about how business was going at *Traveler* and the Chili Challenge.

"Speaking of that, I want Will to help me grow my chili garden," Aunt Cass said to Luce.

"Um…" Luce said, obviously trying to think of some lie as to why Will wouldn't be able to help.

"There's no point making anything up. I know he has the time, so let's get it happening," Aunt Cass said.

"Do you promise it's going to be a standard chili garden though? He knows we're magic, but I don't want him to get, like, *saturated* in it," Luce said, worried.

"Of course they're going to be standard chilies," Aunt Cass said, a little too quickly for my liking. She always played a bit fast and loose with the truth. I think that particular statement hinged on what her version of "standard" was.

"Yeah, and I don't want Ollie getting involved in too much either," Molly said, looking at me.

"Involved in what? I only have him doing some research," I protested.

"No, you don't. You have him looking up witchy things and he's probably going to find papers that all contradict each other again," she said.

"He's a librarian and I think he's okay. He knows we're witches now. If he finds some strange things he'll assume it's magic," I said.

"No, he won't. If he gets too much magic then he might not ask me to marry him!" Molly said, the sentence practically ending in a shriek.

There was a moment of quiet as we continued walking down the sidewalk in the general direction of where the pink path was leading us.

It was a worry the three of us had regarding our men given what had happened to our moms. Our three fathers had had us and then, apparently, within a very short time had all decided to leave our moms and us behind. It was a common problem amongst witches. It was difficult to hold onto a man once he learned the truth about you. But what could you do? Try to keep it secret and not be your full self? There was no good solution.

It was Aunt Cass who broke the silence. "Ollie is madly head over heels in love with you. Don't worry about him doing a bit of research," she said.

Molly gave a double blink. I think she was expecting, as the rest of us were, that Aunt Cass was going to hit her with some snark, to tell her to suck it up princess or something like that.

"We're nearly at the end of the path, I can feel it," Kira said.

We made our way down another alleyway, this one more grimy than the first one. There were trash cans lining one side of it and from the smell of them they hadn't been emptied in a few days. With the blistering sun during the day cooking them it didn't smell good. We found our way to a fire escape and clambered up it until we were on the rooftop. The glittering path went across five more roofs before coiling around itself in a corner. We carefully followed the path until we reached the final rooftop.

"This is where whatever it was that made those marks went to," Kira said.

"But there's nothing here," Luce said, looking around.

She was right—it was a standard rooftop. It was a bit dirty, there was an exhaust outlet not too far away from the building below, and there was nothing particularly special about it at all.

"Let's look around first," Aunt Cass said. We looked around but even after a few minutes of searching the rooftop didn't yield any more clues.

"Maybe the monster or whatever it is came to sleep here?" I ventured.

"No, I don't think that's it," Molly said, staring, looking

down into the street below. She pointed to the building across the road.

"Oh, hey, it's the Chili Challenge," Kira said.

"Maybe the monster wasn't sleeping here. Maybe it was watching the Chili Challenge," Molly said.

"It wouldn't be watching the Chili Challenge, it would be watching *Aunt Cass*," Luce said, diving off the deep end.

We all came to stand against the side of the building and looked down. From our vantage point, there was a perfect view of Aunt Cass's office, where she would sit with her feet up on the desk, tapping away on her laptop.

Aunt Cass turned to Kira. "If we give you a bit of power and you cast the spell again, do you think we could find any more trails?" she asked.

Kira shrugged, looking quite unsure. "Maybe, we could try it, but I don't know," she said.

"It's up to you. Do you want to?" Aunt Cass said.

"Sure," Kira said after a moment.

Sharing magic between witches is easily done. Most the time it's usually holding hands or touching each other, skin to skin contact, like a hand on a shoulder. Sometimes it's standing in specific positions like a ritual.

Tonight we gathered in a circle, me putting my hand on Kira's shoulder and on the other side Aunt Cass doing the same.

This broke down a moment later when Kira had to pull away because of the frost creeping from my palm. I had to leave the circle and stand by, not touching anyone. Kira took a deep breath and pulled on the magic and we lent our power. I tried to give her as much as I could, but without that direct contact it was significantly weaker. I did feel the spell this time though, almost caught a glimpse of how I could cast it myself. The magic flowed through Kira, coiled around her feet and lit up the glowing pink path like it was made of bright neon. A bolt of light shot down it. Gleaming bolts of pink jolted out across the rooftops in different directions.

"Wow," Molly breathed as the night lit up around us, appearing as though there was a pink spider web laid across Harlot Bay. One of the trails headed in the direction of Truer Island, going down to the water and then we could see it faintly in the distance on the beach across the bay. There were others heading across the town, always on the rooftops. I looked up the hill towards Torrent Mansion and there were multiple pink trails heading up into the forest, and one that appeared to be circling the mansion.

"Whatever that thing is, it's been up to the mansion a few times," I said.

"That's all I have," Kira said in a strained voice and let the spell go.

In an instant the pink lines faded away, leaving us standing on the dark rooftop.

I summoned a small ball of light, which didn't work too well. Instead of the normal warm yellow I got a cold white as though I had pulled a ball of ice into existence. Even the light coming from it felt cold, so I snuffed it and let Molly do the honors.

"Any idea what to do next?" Kira said in a tired voice.

"We go home to sleep and then, we need to set a trap," Aunt Cass said.

CHAPTER FIFTEEN

"*A*re you sure this is going to work?" I asked, turning the small perfume bottle over in my hand.

"Guaranteed to work, just don't use too much," Aunt Cass said.

I looked suspiciously at the perfume bottle. It was one Aunt Cass had reused. Printed on the front was *Sunshine by Bella Bing*.

I wondered briefly if Molly knew that her mortal enemy Bella Bing now had a perfume line?

"I guess I should try it out then," I said.

"Dab it on like perfume, don't overdo it," Aunt Cass warned again. I opened the top of the perfume bottle and took a hesitant sniff. I could still smell the original perfume which was vanilla and sickly sweet, something that teenage girls wear and douse too much of it on themselves. Behind that was the scent of the potion. It smelt like a felled tree.

I put my finger over the bottle, tipped it upside down and back again, and then gently dabbed a droplet of it on my neck.

The effect was immediate. From my finger where I'd

touched the potion to my neck there was an immediate burst of heat that spread out over my entire body.

I reached out and grabbed the test glass of water sitting on the kitchen bench.

"It's looking good so far," I said when frost didn't immediately appear. A moment more and I was convinced Aunt Cass's experimental potion appeared to have worked.

"I think we're good to go," I said, feeling happy.

"Make sure you don't use too much though. There's enough in there to get you to midnight and then, like Cinderella, you're gonna turn into a pumpkin," Aunt Cass said.

"I'm pretty sure it's the carriage that turns into the pumpkin not Cinderella," I said.

"I was thought *she* was the one that turned into the pumpkin. Makes more sense to me, messing with magic and all that," Aunt Cass said, now heading for the door.

"What are your plans?" I called out.

"Buildin' mah trap," Aunt Cass said in her best southern accent and then she was gone.

I was wearing a skirt that was light and flimsy, but it had a small pocket where I could fit the perfume bottle.

I slipped it into the pocket and then went to check myself in the mirror. Top was looking nice, slightly demure, not too much, makeup was on point. I had the slightest of bags under my eyes, thanks to staying out late at night and working hard through the day, but in the dim light of Valhalla Viking I'm sure I would look great.

I was wandering around the house, tapping away at my phone when I heard Jack's truck coming up the driveway. For the first time since his parents had arrived, I got to see him alone. The man had barely stepped in the front door when I jumped on him, wrapping my arms around him and kissing him with all my might. It was a good thing the moms were nowhere to be seen because I'm sure they wouldn't have approved of this public display of affection. When we finally pulled apart, he was gasping and his eyes were a little wild.

"Wow, you're warm, did that slip witch power wear off?" Jack asked.

"Nope, I have a potion and that's just as good," I said.

I was thinking that if we finished dinner early enough perhaps I could see Jack alone and take another dose of the potion so I wouldn't be a freezing Ice Princess. The idea of sneaking in through his bedroom window like we were teenagers was *very* appealing.

"You look amazing, and as much as I want to stay here instead, we've gotta go," Jack said.

I smooched him again, harder this time, briefly contemplated dragging him inside into my room, and then reluctantly decided to follow him out to his truck. There were parents to impress. Parents who I'd barely spoken to at the family dinner and who'd seen me then run off into the forest, chasing after Aunt Cass, like a crazy person.

With Aunt Cass's potion helping keep the ice at bay, I was going to be witty, charming and personable. By the end of the night they were going to *love* me.

As we drove down the hill I couldn't stop looking at Jack. It's true that absence makes the heart grow fonder. I kept touching his arm, feeling the strong muscle beneath his shirt and I'm sure I was smiling at him with a dopey expression on my face. We were halfway down the hill before Jack pulled his arm away.

"Ouch, your hands are cold again," he said, startled.

There on the sleeve of his shirt was a frost pattern from where I'd been touching him. It seemed the tiny droplet of potion had already worn off.

"Not to worry, I have the solution right here," I said.

I opened the perfume bottle and touched my finger to its neck, this time rubbing the small droplet of liquid between my fingertips. As before, the wave of heat burst over me and when I touched Jack again, my hand was warm.

"So you need to keep dabbing that stuff on yourself and you'll be okay?" Jack asked.

"That's the plan," I said and gently tugged on his ear.

I had the urge to run my hands through his hair, to grab him and kiss him again. Between all the work I'd been doing with Red, and the fact that his parents were here, I hadn't seen him in ages.

As if reading my thoughts, Jack glanced back at me with a look that sent a shiver down my body, and it definitely wasn't anything to do with being cold.

"I'm quite looking forward to when my parents depart," he said, sounding like a formal eighteenth-century gentleman.

"Me too," I purred, perhaps heading a *little* too far in the sex kitten direction.

Jack grinned as we drove down the hill and into town. As usual, most of the parking spots were taken so we ended up having to park over near the beach. Jonas and Peta were the ones bringing Jack's parents to dinner tonight. Apart from seeing his parents and trying to impress them, I was looking forward to seeing Peta and Jonas too. When I used to work in my office, I would often chat to him as I passed him down the stairs or he would come up sometimes. Occasionally, yes, this was trying to get the inside straight on his brother Jack.

I was excited to talk to Peta about the *Cozy Cat Café*. Molly and Luce had set it up next to *Traveler*, but been overwhelmed until Peta had stepped in and taken it over. She was now in control of it and it was a thriving business. I had a standing offer of a job there. After Writerpalooza was over I was going back to unemployment unless of course I took

Carter Wilkins up on his offer. So it looked like my future would include some waitressing. Working with one of my best friends? It sounded great.

We parked near the beach and then walked hand-in-hand all the way back to Valhalla Viking. This is the place where Jack and I had one of our very first dates. It seemed a lifetime ago. It had been a night of great food and wine and merriment, but then our romantic walk on the beach had been cut short when an arsonist had struck, burning down a building in town. Like tonight, I had been suffering under the burden of a slip witch power. Thankfully, tonight I had a potion that would take the edge off it. As long as I remembered to apply a drop every now and again I was sure I was going to get through the night with no problems.

As we approached Valhalla Viking, we saw Peta, Jonas, Jon, and Jas waiting for us. Jack squeezed my hand and whispered in my ear "By the way my mother has been asking about marriage quite a bit so have fun with that," he said in a rush. I didn't have a chance to reply because we were suddenly at Valhalla Viking.

"There she is, the girl who goes running into the forest to save wild animals!" Jon said with a great smile.

"Here I am!" I said back in a loud voice and then gave him and Jas each a kiss on the cheek. We had a round of hugs, me grabbing Peta and pulling her against me. By the time we walked into Valhalla Viking I was feeling like I was floating off the ground I was so happy. I had my boyfriend, my friend, Jack's brother and parents, and a night of good food ahead of me.

The inside of Valhalla Viking was dimly lit and all around the place were shield maidens dressed in Viking clothes serving great hunks of meat off the bone, pitchers of mead and other alcoholic drinks. We made our way to a semi-private back booth and then slid in. I sat in at the end, only remembering at the last minute that I might have to slip away to apply more of the potion. Jack was beside me and then Jonas, on the other side of the table was Peta, Jon directly across me, and Jas in the middle.

We'd barely sat down when one of the waitresses came up with a notepad that looked incongruous with her braided blonde hair, horned helmet, and enormous breastplate.

"Can I interest you all in some mead?" she asked.

"Mead would be wonderful," I answered, smiling back at her. The shield maiden disappeared and returned in record time before we'd had a chance to start talking. We were given enormous tankards, and then she sat a jug in the middle of the table that looked like it held about a gallon of mead.

"Enjoy. I'll be back soon," she said and vanished.

Jon filled all of our tankards and we held them up to say cheers.

"Here's to saving wild animals and true love," he said.

"Here's to amazing writing studios and what they might *mean*," Jas added.

I felt Jack poke me under the table in the leg. Yes, I had recognized mother meddling as well as he had.

We all took a big gulp of our mead after saying cheers. It tasted of spices, cloves and orange with a honey flavor underneath. After my gulp, I felt it plume in my stomach and seemingly go straight to my head.

"Your Aunt Cass is quite the wildlife warrior. Did you end up finding the wild pig?" Jon asked me.

Oh right, the lie that Jack had told. "No, we didn't find it unfortunately. It seems like it moved on from the area, but it'll probably be back," I said.

"Your Aunt Cass is an interesting woman, isn't she? She's running the chili business and then she's brave enough to go out into the darkness at night to see if there's an injured animal that's strong enough to knock over trees," Jas said.

"It's okay, you can say eccentric, we know she's eccentric. She loves all animals great and small," I said.

"Most of them are hardly wild anyway. They're practically tame they see the Torrents so often," Jack said, stepping in with a quick lie.

"What wild animals are you talking about?" Peta said, blundering in.

It was so unlike Peta, who would usually be able to play along without any notice whatsoever. She'd *been* at the dinner, too. Perhaps the mead had gone to her head too?

"The wild pigs that are up near the cottages in the forest. We thought one of them had been injured a few nights ago, *remember*, and Aunt Cass had gone out there to see and I'd gone with her," I said trying to transmit a lot more information with my gaze. Peta gave a double blink and then smiled at me.

"Oh right, yes, the wild animals," she said.

"So Jack tells me you're writing a book? He showed me the delightful writing studio he's been working on," Jas said.

"Mom..." Jack said under his breath.

"How about we pick what we're going to eat," Jonas said diving in. We'd been given menus, but no one had looked at them yet. I picked mine up but Jas was not to be dissuaded.

"How is your book going?" she asked, smiling at me the way a lion might look at a fresh meal.

"It's about halfway done, I think," I said.

The truth was I'd barely thought about my story since I'd started working for Red at Writerpalooza. Between the packed days and now busy nights I hadn't had the time to work on it–or hadn't *made* the time to work on it. Although the days with Red had been busy there had been something incredibly inspiring about working with her and the other authors.

They were on the other side of an enormous chasm that

at first looked too wide to jump across. I think I must've been absorbing some of Red's session info by osmosis because every day I was feeling more confident in my ability to finish my book and then maybe do something with it.

"That sounds great. I'd love to read it once it's done. Have you seen the writing studio that Jack has been building?" she asked.

"I have and it's lovely," I said, giving Jack a smile and touching his hand under the table.

Two things happened then: one, Jack pulled his hand away in alarm; and two, the waitress returned for our orders.

"How about I order for all of us?" Jonas proposed and then went ahead and did that. While he was ordering I opened the perfume bottle under the table and rubbed a bit more of it between my fingertips. The heat washed out and the chill left my skin. Was it my imagination or had the potion worn off quicker this time?

I slipped the perfume bottle back into my small pocket and then poured everyone more mead. By the time the waitress was gone the conversation had moved on from Jack and his writing studio over to Peta and the *Cozy Cat*.

"A business owner. That's impressive," Jas said, giving a significant look at Jonas.

Jack squeezed my fingers under the table as he tried to keep a straight face.

"It's always great to be in love," Jon said, smiling at us. I said cheers to that, and we clashed our tankards together, some of the mead ending up on the table.

"It's going well and hopefully soon, Harlow might come work with me," Peta said.

"Maybe, but I also have a job offer as a journalist again," I said.

"Oh, really?" Peta said, her face falling slightly.

Oh no, why had I blurted that out? Oh right. Too much mead on an empty stomach. I'd have to take it easy.

"How is your business going Dad?" Jack asked, coming to the rescue.

We all drank mead while Jon talked about his business back in Canada. He had been a house builder but now was doing small jobs and sometimes Jas went along to help him. Jack and Jonas were very effective at keeping their parents off our backs, turning all the questions back around to what they were doing and keeping them away from any topics that could lead to questions of marriage.

"But now that we've been down here I don't know how we're going to go back to that cold," Jon said.

"It's so far away. Too far to travel if there are grandkids," Jas said.

Jack and Jonas almost splurted their mead at that. I came close to doing the same and so did Peta.

Grandkids? Oh boy, Jas would get along *wonderfully* with the moms.

"I think that's a *little* in the future," Jonas said.

"How *far* in the future would you say?" Jas asked.

Thankfully, the food arrived, enormous hunks of meat on the bone, salads that I'm sure weren't ever served to Vikings but were delicious anyway, and another large jug of mead.

We dived into eating, me taking the briefest of moments to apply another dab of potion, this time rubbing it on my leg. As we ate we talked about Jonas's business. It seemed it was going well especially now the redevelopment of the Governor's mansion was underway.

The conversation eventually swung around to the newspaper Jon and Jas had been reading this morning, *The Harlot Bay Times*. Carter had reported on the strange symbols all throughout town and had clearly blamed it on the authors, saying it seemed the work of vandals interested in publicity.

"Is that the guy you're going to be working with? Would he be telling the truth?" Jon asked me.

Perhaps I'd had slightly too much mead by then or maybe the potion was having an effect on me because I simply blurted out the truth.

"Carter writes a lot of exaggerated garbage so he can keep selling papers but I think somewhere deep down he is quite honest and I feel sorry for him sometimes. It's hard running a business in a small town," I said.

"She is so honest Jack, I love her," Jas said, taking another gulp of mead.

"Thanks Mom, I love her too," Jack said.

I was blushing furiously and having a wonderful time thinking the night was going incredibly well when there was some sort of commotion over by the door. Valhalla Viking is quite noisy but in that moment there was a lull in the conversation as a new group staggered in. My breath caught in my throat as I saw Red, TJ, Jay and Jenna roll up to the bar, their faces streaked with black and their clothing covered in dirt and grime.

"Wow, how did they get in looking like that?" Jonas said.

It was then that the writers saw me and TJ called out my name. It seemed like the four of them were slightly tipsy, or possibly drunk. Before they could come over to the table and cause a scene I bolted out of my chair.

"There are some friends of mine, I mean, people I'm working with, I'll be right back," I said and rushed over to the bar.

When I got there, TJ clapped me on the back with an enormous hand that nearly sent me sprawling.

"Harlow Torrent, the woman of the hour," he boomed.

"The mead is here," Jenna said and Jay and Red each gave a cheer. A full tankard was thrust into my hands and I was pulled into saying cheers, although I don't know what it was for.

"You guys need to keep it down... what's going on?" I asked.

"We broke in and we found *something*," Jenna said, grinning at me.

"What do you mean broke in? Are you talking about Rufus and Dawn, the *Mysterious Mysteries*?"

"No, not *that*. Jenna found this other place where they keep all this old historical stuff," Red said and touched the back of my hand. She pulled away an instant later.

"Why are you so cold? Is it the air conditioning?" she said.

Oh no, the potion had worn off again.

"It's strong over there," I said, grabbing for the potion bottle. They were all too excited and, yes, seemed a bit drunk to care what I was doing as I rubbed some between my fingers. The heat burst over my skin instantly. I shoved the potion back into my pocket and took a deep breath, trying to ignore the fact that I could see Jon and Jas and everyone else at our table glancing over to where I was.

"Okay, so to get this straight you broke into *somewhere else* and not Rufus and Dawn's?" I said.

"Jay, show her what we found," Red said.

Jay reached behind him and pulled out something from the band of his shorts. He held it out to me.

"It's a map," he said, eyes gleaming.

It was a cloth map, clearly extremely old, sealed in a plastic bag. Up in one corner of it was the strange symbol that had been carved in doors all over Harlot Bay and spray painted everywhere. There were lines showing a rudimentary map of Harlot bay. Printed across the fabric were random letters and symbols.

"Is that a code of some kind?" I said. As I moved to take a

closer look, I felt the magic tingle. Oh Goddess, it was *magic* and the writers had stolen it!

"That's what we are going to figure out," Red said.

"It was all thanks to you! You gave us the idea to break into Rufus and Dawn's and then we felt brave enough that we should go into the place Jenna found!" TJ said. He slapped me on the back again before pulling his hand away.

"You don't feel cold, you feel hot," he commented. Jenna reached forward and touched me on the shoulder.

"Harlow do you have a fever? You're burning up," she said.

Oh no. I felt for the potion in my small pocket and as soon as I touched my dress I realized it was wet. Somehow the stopper had come off and the entire bottle had leaked out and soaked into my clothing.

"Talk to you tomorrow!" I said.

I felt my temperature jump and I was sure the next person who touched me would burn their hand.

I looked briefly back at the table and saw Jack watching me with a look of concern. I gave him an apologetic wave and then bolted out of Valhalla Viking. Two steps down the road I took off my fantastic high heels and ran with them in my hands, heading down the street towards the ocean. As I sprinted I could feel myself getting hotter. It wasn't like a fever where you feel sick and terrible. I pretty much felt fine... but my skin temperature was increasing fast.

I bolted around tourists who were looking at me with a strange expression to see a girl running down the street. By the time I reached the edge of the beach I could smell smoke. My clothing was starting to crisp up against my body. I dropped my heels on the beach, ran straight into the water and dived. There was an audible sizzle like the first moment when you throw a steak into a hot frying pan.

Sadly, the tide was out. Because it's a bay that meant it

was quite shallow. I ended up landing on my stomach in a few inches of water (*oof*). I jumped up and continued sloshing outwards away from shore until eventually I was up to my waist, then I ducked down until the water touched my earlobes.

"Okay, stay calm, stay calm, stay calm," I chanted to myself. At this time of night there were still people swimming but thankfully it was dark enough that no one could see out where I was. The water around me was simmering which then turned into a full boil over the next hour. I kept moving around, going out as deep as I could. Thankfully the tide had begun to come in and the cool wash of water helped keep the temperature down. It was another two hours before the boiling finally subsided, but then I was in serious trouble because once it wore off I was out a long way. I had to rush back to the beach, swimming as fast as I could as the water turned to ice around my hands. By the time I got back to the beach my feet were encased and chunks of ice were hanging off my hair. The cold had spread!

By then it was past midnight though and the beach was mostly empty. I still had my shoes, but I had no phone, no car and I had bolted away from dinner. I was feeling very sorry for myself as I walked along the beach, thinking I'd have to walk home, when Jack appeared out of the darkness.

"Harlow, are you okay?" he said, grabbing me and grabbing me in an enormous hug. I relaxed into his arms but then a sudden sob hitched in my throat and before I knew it I was crying.

"I was trying to impress your parents and then I spilled the stupid potion on myself and boiled the ocean out there. Now I've run off *again*. They're gonna think I'm crazy. I hate being a Slip witch," I said.

"But I love my little Slip witch," Jack said. He had to let

me go then, the lines of frost climbing up over his clothing and up the insides of his arms.

"Your parents are going to think I'm crazy," I repeated again. My tears were freezing on my cheeks and falling to the ground as tiny beads of ice. This new power was worse than I thought and had spread fast.

"I think the word you're looking for is *eccentric*, like Aunt Cass, and as I said, I love my eccentric slip witch," Jack said. He kissed me on the cheek and squeezed my fingers for as long as he was able, and then together we made our way back up off the beach and to his truck.

Jack advised me on the way that he'd told his parents I'd bolted out because I wasn't feeling well. Not the best of lies but hey, what could you do?

I recovered somewhat in the truck and it wasn't long until he was dropping me off at home. Jack couldn't stay; it wasn't safe for him to sleep next to me. So we said good-night, he kissed me again, and promised we'd see each other again soon.

After he was gone, a very sleepy Kira came out of her room and smiled at me. "How did the date with the parents go Torrent?" she said. Then she saw the state of me.

"Oh," she said. Surprisingly, for a teenager, she came over and hugged me, pulling away before the frost could streak up her arms.

"Being a Slip witch sucks doesn't it," Kira said to me.

"No disagreement there," I said.

CHAPTER SIXTEEN

$\mathcal{I}$ was up at dawn with a mission on my mind. Thankfully, the cold had retreated again, affecting only my hands. After a quick test to confirm that I was still frosting up water glasses (which I was), I put on my gloves and rushed down to the other end of the mansion to see if I could talk to Aunt Cass before she left for the day. At this time in the morning the dining room is empty but soon it would fill up with guests. The Torrent Mansion bed-and-breakfast had been full to the gills and every morning and every night the table was packed with tourists.

As I approached the kitchen I could smell breakfast being prepared and hear the clattering of frying pans and chopping of knives, and the other comforting domestic sounds of cooking.

I rushed inside and found Aunt Freya and Aunt Ro cooking like two madwomen possessed. *Frazzled* was exactly the right word to describe how they looked. They barely glanced up as I entered the kitchen.

"Oh Harlow, good, pass me that onion," Aunt Freya commanded.

I passed her an onion and as I did she got a good look at me.

"Oh my Goddess, what happened to you?" she said.

"What?" I said, attempting to straighten up the bird's nest that was my hair.

Aunt Ro took a look at me and tutted. "Did Jack see you like that?" she asked.

Great, Mom wasn't here to *mom* me but my aunts were more than willing to step in on her behalf.

"Yes, Jack did see me like this and he loves it," I said.

"Don't make a big deal out of it. Do you want some breakfast?" Aunt Freya asked.

I was getting hungry, but I had bigger fish to fry at the moment, a fish by the name of Aunt Cass.

"Is Aunt Cass here? Is she up yet?" I asked.

"She's downstairs, but I don't know if you'll be able to get into her lab," Aunt Freya said.

I went down the stairs into the basement.

As usual, Grandma was standing there, although she was over in the corner with a sheet over her. There was also an ongoing concealment spell on her maintained by the moms in a rotation.

I felt a sudden pang of guilt. I hadn't been down to see Grandma in quite a while. Yes, she is frozen and doesn't respond, but still, all of us like to come down every now and again to have a talk with her. I walked over and lifted the sheet.

"Morning Grandma, good to see you," I said softly.

As usual, there was no response. I put the sheet down and turned around, intending to head into the undermansion see if I could find Aunt Cass, but the woman herself came through the door, wiping pink off her hands with a rag.

"Harlow, the witch I wanted to see," Aunt Cass said. I

walked over to her and caught the sharp smell of turpentine from the rag.

"What's that all over your hands?"

"Some paint but it was worth it," Aunt Cass said. She dropped the rag on the floor, reached into a pocket, and pulled out a small, flat black stone. "Here, hold out your hand," she said.

I obeyed, taking my gloves off, and she dropped the stone into my palm. As soon as she did, I felt that familiar burst of heat that I experienced yesterday with the potion.

Aunt Cass closed my fingers over the stone.

"I realized last night that having a liquid isn't very stable or safe, so I thought I could infuse the potion into a stone. It'll only come out a small amount at a time and as long as you just touch it every now and again, it'll work fine," Aunt Cass said, proud as punch.

I stared at her for a moment, having the feeling that I wanted to strangle her.

"I'm very glad you realized that. It's something that would have come in handy last night at Valhalla Viking when I spilled the whole bottle of the potion on myself and nearly caught fire," I said through gritted teeth.

"You nearly caught fire? Wow, that sounds amazing!" Aunt Cass said.

"Amazing? I had to bolt away from Jack and his family again. They must think I'm a crazy person," I said.

"But if you got hot without burning that's an amazing discovery! Imagine what you could do with that potion. Take a gulp and go out to fight crime. No one would be able to grab you without burning themselves," Aunt Cass said.

"You forget the bit where *my clothing nearly caught fire*. I had to wait in the ocean for hours. So your superhero who's out drinking that potion will be fighting crime naked," I said.

I realized I'd been sidetracked from the point of *why* I

went to see Aunt Cass and despite feeling quite annoyed with her, I realized I was being *slightly* ungrateful.

"But thank you very much for the potion. It worked before I spilled it on myself, and thank you for the stone. I appreciate it," I said, softening my tone.

"So is that why you came down here?" Aunt Cass asked me.

"Nope. Yesterday, the writers broke in somewhere, I don't know exactly where but they stole a very old map that had that weird symbol on it and some coded message. They brought it to Valhalla Viking. I sensed magic but that was right around when I spilled the potion on myself and so I had to get out of there and hang out in the ocean for a while," I explained.

"Which one of them has it now? The big hunk of muscle, the little one, Red, or that guy with the curly hair?"

"Jay Savage had it last night. I think that's the one you mean when you say the curly hair," I said.

"Hmm... interesting," Aunt Cass said with that sort of mad gleam in her eye again.

"What do you mean interesting? What are you planning?"

Aunt Cass ducked down and picked up the rag from the floor, using it to wipe the last few smudges of pink from around the ends of her nails.

"I think given it's a magical object it rightfully belongs to *witches* and not *authors*. You could find out who's holding it and I'll arrange to take it," she said.

I took a breath and turned the black stone over in my hands, worrying at it like it was prayer beads. I honestly didn't have any other better plan. I guess it had been floating somewhere in the back of my mind that I would steal the map back from Jay. Who knew if it had anything to do with the monster that was in town but the fact it was magical meant it wasn't good for him to be holding onto it.

"Okay, I'll see if I can find out who has it. But we need to be discreet. I can't be asking them who has the map and then it gets stolen instantly," I said.

My phone chimed in my pocket then, which was unusual considering we were underground and it hardly ever works. It was a message from Luce telling me to come back to our end of the mansion immediately.

"I've gotta go, but I'll let you know," I said to Aunt Cass.

"Don't lose that stone, it's the only one I have," she told me.

She followed me back up the stairs as I went through the kitchen, stealing a toasted ham, cheese and tomato sandwich that Aunt Freya and Aunt Ro had left out. Aunt Cass stopped there, demanding her nieces make her breakfast, but I continued on my way, heading out through the dining room where a sleepy looking guest was making his way to a seat.

I waved hello and rushed outside, only to see Sheriff Hardy's car parked down our end of the mansion.

Oh no. Was he here about the writers? Considering how they'd all barged into Valhalla Viking surely it would be easy to work out that it was the four of them who had broken into wherever they'd gone.

I gulped down my toasted sandwich as fast as I could. I walked into our end of the mansion to find Molly, Luce and Kira all sitting at the kitchen table. Molly and Luce looked panicked, Kira was tapping away on her phone. Adams was on the sofa asleep.

"Harlow, good to see you this morning. You look tired. Were you up late last night?" Sheriff Hardy said.

There it was again, that stone cop look of his. The one that he had pulled many times when we were teenagers. It was one that said *yes, I am related to you through marriage but if you get involved in crime I'll throw you in the cell and lock the door myself.*

"Yup, went out to dinner last night with Jack and his family. It was great until a potion backfired and I had to run down to the beach and jump in the water before my clothes caught fire. Then Jack came to get me about midnight and brought me home where I met Kira," I said, pointing a finger at the teenager.

"That's what happened," Kira said without looking up.

Sheriff Hardy's expression softened. He must have realized he'd slipped into cop interrogation mode, which was far colder than he needed to be with his family.

"Sorry, I wasn't meant to be accusing you of anything," he said. "There was a break-in last night at one of the city storage facilities and we have more of those symbols around town, carved in doorways and spray painted everywhere. I was coming around to make sure that none of you girls are involved in it," he said.

"We're not involved in it," Molly said.

She had her arms crossed with her hands stuffed under her armpits so tight it was like she was hugging herself to death.

"It wasn't us!" Luce muttered. She was sitting on her hands.

What was going on here? Were they *both* hiding something?

"I suspect it's the *Mysterious Mysteries* duo who are putting those symbols all over town. Have you gone to speak to them?" I said. I kept things light and acted casual as I went around to the refrigerator and pulled out ingredients for a second breakfast.

"They're on my list to visit soon given that Carter's article has everyone riled up," Sheriff Hardy said.

There was an awkward silence then, as though Sheriff Hardy wanted to say something else but finally he nodded to us, said goodbye, went outside and drove away. It wasn't until his car was off into the distance that Molly and Luce shot up from their seats and I could finally see their hands. Molly had pink all around the tips of her fingers, and so did Luce.

"Hey, what is that? Is that spray paint?" I asked.

Molly looked at Luce, an incredibly guilty move that gave both of them away.

"No, no, no, no, no, haven't I taught you guys anything? Deny, deny, deny," Kira chirped up, reciting back the advice that we'd given her.

"We went out last night with Aunt Cass to spray a few of those symbols around town," Luce said.

"Correction, we were *blackmailed* into going out with Aunt Cass last night," Molly said.

"I saw Aunt Cass wiping her hands with a rag and turpentine! Why is she spraying the symbols around town? Do you mean it's *her* doing it?" I asked.

"I think she's done *some* of them and we added a bunch last night. She told us the more attention they get the better it is and the faster we'll sort out this whole monster thing," Molly said.

I didn't get to ask any more questions about what exactly was going on because Red pulled up at the front of the house in her sports car.

"Wash the paint off your hands, and Kira, I need you to go with Molly and Luce because I need to talk to Red alone," I instructed.

Red emerged from her sports car wearing a gigantic pair of black sunglasses and moving like a woman who had had far too much to drink the previous night.

I abandoned my breakfast ingredients and opened the front door to let her in.

"Hey, Harlow good to see you," Red said in a tired voice.

"We'll talk in a moment once my cousins are gone," I said

to her in an undertone. Red took a seat on the sofa. She still had her sunglasses on as she leaned back and started stroking Adams behind the ears. He began purring in his sleep.

I made her a coffee and myself one, as Molly and Luce and Kira rushed around getting ready. In some kind of miracle it was about ten minutes before they departed, heading off into town, although it was still quite early. It was only once they were gone that Red took off her sunglasses. Her eyes were bloodshot and she looked very tired.

"That was some night last night wasn't it," she said with a weak smile.

"I'll say, we just had the Sheriff here, trying to find out who had broken into one of the city storage facilities. I'm guessing that's where you guys went?" I said.

That certainly woke Red up. She sat up looking alarmed. "Did you tell him it was us?" she asked.

"No, but if he talks to anyone from Valhalla Viking from last night he might be able to put it together," I said.

In that moment I had a feeling that this is what it must be like for the moms when me, Molly and Luce got involved in things. From the outside it appeared chaotic and dangerous. It was certainly a very *unwelcome* feeling. The only good thing about the whole situation was that Writerpalooza would be over soon and then the writers would go home.

"When the festival is over, are you all leaving Harlot Bay?" I asked.

Red pinched the bridge of her nose as though she trying to push away an incipient headache. "Me and Jay are. I get the feeling Jenna wants to stay and if she does, TJ might as well. Although it can't be for long. There's another festival about three days later that they're booked in," Red said.

"Maybe it's time to stop investigating… whatever it is you're investigating," I suggested.

"Yesterday we got excited and then unfortunately had some drinks and one thing led to another, and suddenly we were being chased by dogs out of the building we'd broken into. Now Jay has that map with what I think is a code on it, this is too juicy to let go," Red said.

Perfect, she confirmed that Jay still had the map.

"But what is it you think you're going to find? Even if it is a code and you decipher it, isn't it going to be something about the past when they believed in all kinds of crazy supernatural things?" I said. As I spoke I pulled out my phone and tapped a message to Aunt Cass. *Jay Savage has it.*

"At first we were only investigating because that guy got attacked and then we discovered some of the history and how it connected, and I don't know... it seemed so *strange*," Red said.

I had a cold feeling in the pit of my stomach. There are plenty of things strange about Harlot Bay and mysteries buried all over the place. But the biggest, strangest thing was *us*, the witches, and there were more than our family in town. I got the sudden very unwelcome feeling that one of the writers would stay to write a non-fiction book about Harlot Bay.

My phone buzzed in my pocket. A message from Aunt Cass. Two words: *On it.*

"I guess we need to get going before we're late. Maybe we can talk about it later," I said.

Red nodded and then handed me the keys to the sports car.

CHAPTER SEVENTEEN

"*H*ot dog, beer, eat, drink," Jack said, handing me the food and cup.

"Thanks," I said, keeping my eye on the beehive I could see bobbing around through the crowd.

"Have they done anything suspicious yet?" Jack asked.

"Not yet, but the night is young," I said and took a bite of my hot dog.

It was Saturday evening and I was down in Scarness Park with what felt like the rest of Harlot Bay and every tourist in the state waiting for the free concert to begin. I was there with Jack, Molly and Luce with their respective boyfriends as well. Aunt Ro and Mom were manning a table amongst all the food booths. We had no idea where Aunt Cass was. I'd been watching Rufus and Dawn since we'd arrived at the concert and spotted them wandering around. Jack had gone off to get food and so I'd been half keeping an eye on them and half watching the assorted vampires and Harry Sparkle imitators wandering around the place with everyone else who was in costume.

"There's probably not much they're going to be able to do

at an open concert, so maybe we should ignore them?" Jack said.

"Yeah, maybe," I said, taking another bite of my hot dog.

Jack touched me on the arm and stepped in front of me, breaking my line of sight.

"My parents won't be coming until later. Your cousins are wandering around. We're alone together for the first time in ages," Jack said, looking into my eyes.

Like a switch had been flicked I was suddenly in the here and now. I had a cold beer in one hand and a hot dog in the other and Jack standing in front of me. Why should I care about Rufus and Dawn being at the concert?

"You're absolutely right," I said and gave Jack a quick kiss that tasted slightly of mustard.

We took a seat on my picnic rug and ate our hot dogs while we both enjoyed people watching. The sun was setting, the lengthening shadows stretching across Scarness Park and all around it glimmering lights were beginning to shine. I saw a few authors I recognized, including TJ off in the distance walking around with Jenna. Every now and then he had to stop to talk to one of his fans. I wasn't sure entirely but from a distance it looked like Jenna was getting annoyed that their progress towards the hot dog van was being thwarted.

I finished my beer and then Jack handed me another one which thankfully was still somewhat cool. As I drank it I felt relaxation spreading out through my body. Yesterday and today had been crazy as usual. Trying to keep up with Red was a blur of hard work. Thankfully that hadn't left me time to worry, such as about what might happen if Aunt Cass went to get that map back from Jay Savage. Out of habit I checked my phone again. I'd sent Aunt Cass a message asking if she had the map yet, but hadn't received any reply. Sadly, I had no idea if this was because she simply hadn't answered, or if thanks to Harlot Bay's twitchy telecommunications she'd never received the message.

"What's up lovers?" I heard Kira say. I looked up to see her and her boyfriend Fox standing there, both holding hot dogs and also, surprisingly, large cups of beer. Kira saw my eyes glance at the amber liquid in her hand.

"We're practically twenty-one," Kira said.

"Better not let the moms see that. While you're living under our roof it means they're responsible for you," I said.

"Is that Sheriff Hardy over there?" Fox asked, pointing a finger in the distance.

"Okay lovers, we have to go," Kira said before she and Fox bolted off in the opposite direction.

"I wonder how they got those drinks," Jack mused.

"I can tell you *we* never used magic to get things we shouldn't have," I said with a sly wink to Jack.

It felt good to sit there on the picnic blanket with the sounds of the murmuring crowd around us. As the sun set, the temperature had been dropping. Thanks to my slip witch power, of course, I wasn't feeling the heat but still, as it fell, I could feel myself relax and grow more comfortable. Did that mean on some level I was actually feeling it? I wonder if I could get dehydrated because I didn't realize it was hot.

Jack's phone chimed a message.

"Jonas and Peta say they're still eating with Mom and Dad, so it's going to be a while," Jack said.

"Let's hope this time I don't have any reason to run away," I said.

It wasn't long before the stage lit up and the crowd grew quiet as the Mayor appeared. As usual he was in a crazy costume covered in glittering sequins. He was red-faced due to the heat as he came out and introduced the opening act—Harry Sparkle. The crowd went wild, cheering and clapping as though a rock star was about to come on the stage. We joined in, and as I yelled out I felt the weight of the week float away. I wasn't going to worry about the *Mysterious Mysteries* or monsters in Harlot Bay, strange symbols or magic maps. I wasn't going to worry about writers doing things they shouldn't be, or me freezing glasses of water with my hands. I was going to enjoy myself, spend time with Jack, and of course the rest of my delicious beer.

Harry Sparkle was a consummate performer. He sang a few songs, talked to the children and adults alike, throwing in jokes that went over the children's heads but had the adults laughing. He played for around forty minutes before he finally said goodbye, running off the stage and jumping into a crazily painted golf cart with *Harry Sparkle* emblazoned all over it. Then he drove his way out of the park and disappeared over the hill, the entire crowd cheering and clapping as he went. Next up was a local band, Flying Pizza, who had recently returned from a trip to Europe, where they'd been playing in bars and clubs over there.

"Hey kids," a woman behind us said.

We turned around to find Jon and Jas smiling at us.

"Welcome to Scarness Park!" I said with a big smile that was partially fuelled by the two drinks I'd had.

"Are you feeling better?" Jas asked.

Oh yeah, Jack had said I'd fled Valhalla Viking because I was unwell. I didn't get a chance to respond.

An ambulance siren pierced the night, echoing across the park. With its lights flashing, we saw it drive into view at the top of the hill. A breath and I realized the magic around me had turned gritty, that same feeling again as when we were up in the forest and we'd seen the man who'd been destroying trees.

A terrible rush of *something is wrong* hit me and before I knew it, I took off running towards the flashing lights.

I heard Jack following close behind.

I reached the ambulance in record time. I saw Sheriff Hardy look at me and then hold out his hand as though to say *stop*. But it was too late. I'd already seen everything I needed to, and I felt my stomach turn. Harry Sparkle was being loaded into the ambulance. His clothing was shredded. There were cuts all over his face and arms, and blood everywhere. I couldn't see if he was breathing or not. The paramedics slammed the door of the ambulance closed and then it took off, the siren wailing.

I was taking deep breaths, trying not to throw up, when Kira appeared in front of me.

"Something attacked Harry Sparkle!" she said.

I looked past her worried face and saw Rufus standing there with his camera filming the crowd. Dawn was in front of him, narrating something. As I looked across at them I saw him swing the camera in our direction so I grabbed Kira and hustled off down the hill.

CHAPTER EIGHTEEN

*B*y the time I reached Harry Sparkle's hospital room I was shaking with the effort of maintaining the concealment spell. I slipped inside and then let it go with a sigh of relief.

Last night had been yet another disaster of epic proportions. After the ambulance had taken Harry away, I had wandered back with Jack in a sort of numb daze to Scarness Park. The music festival resumed although it felt somewhat more subdued with people whispering that Harry Sparkle had been attacked.

Jack had passed off to his parents my running away as my journalistic instinct. I had vaguely agreed and tried to make small talk with them, but honestly I could barely remember anything that we discussed that night. Eventually, Jack had given me a kiss goodbye and then Molly and Ollie had given me a ride home. I tried to call Aunt Cass a few times and sent messages but hadn't received any response, and so I'd gone to bed for a restless night of sleep, waking up in the morning with half my bed frosted over. It seemed when I slept, the cold spread outside my hands. Could I tape the stone to myself?

It was while I was making breakfast alone and flicking through TV channels that I discovered that Harlot Bay had once again drawn the national spotlight. Carl Stern being attacked wasn't important enough to gain attention, but children's entertainer Harry Sparkle certainly was.

Up to that point I was still somewhat in a daze. It was clear the monster was attacking people... if that's what it was. How long would it be before someone *died*? As soon as I realized the national attention was on Harlot Bay I decided then and there on the spot that I would go to the hospital to talk to Harry Sparkle directly to find out what he'd seen. Was it a monster? Or something else?

I'd had a quick breakfast, drove to the hospital, walking directly through a pool of sadness as I came in that nearly knocked me to my knees. With my head full of fire I managed to discover his hospital room and then had to use a concealment spell to find my way there. Now here I was standing inside the door trying to take large, deep, gulping breaths as quietly as I could.

It was still reasonably early in the morning, before visiting hours, but I wanted to be sure I could talk to Harry without being interrupted by any nurses or doctors, so I found a chair in the room and used it to block the door.

Using what felt to be the last of my energy, I also magically locked the door behind me.

I looked over at Harry lying in his bed. He was covered in a thin white sheet up to his waist. I could see that both his legs had been bandaged as well as one arm and up his neck. He had one pale arm resting on top of the bed sheets with an IV line in it.

I crept over to get a closer look and that's when I saw the blue tattooed lines running down the back of that hand.

They went up to about his wrist where they were then covered by what looked like makeup that must have been wiped away sometime last night. I'd seen that pale hand and blue tattoo before... on Hannibal Blood.

"The tattoo isn't real either," a croaky voice said from next to me.

I jumped and turned to see Harry watching me. He had one blue eye and one brown eye.

"You're Hannibal Blood? And Harry Sparkle?" I blurted out, my heart still hammering my chest.

Harry reached up into his eye and pulled out a blue contact lens.

"You're that girl who was chasing me the other day. The one who was with Red. Is this a scheme to reveal who I am?" Harry asked.

"I'm not crazy," I said and realized a moment later that's *exactly* what someone who was crazy would say.

"They put the nurse call button on the wrong side, so I don't think I can get them in here that quick... so if you're here to murder me go right ahead," Harry said.

"I'm not here to murder you. Why would you think that? I do have some questions," I said.

Harry looked at me as though he was considering whether he should lunge for the nurse call button. Then he smiled. He appeared to be Harry Sparkle again, happy and joyous despite the fact he was wounded and bandaged.

"Sorry, someone attacked me so I'm a little jumpy. Ask away," he murmured.

A lie came to me so fast I felt as though my brain had been preparing it during the night and had only now revealed it to me.

"My name is Harlow Torrent and I'm a journalist, I work for myself and also for another paper in town, *The Harlot Bay Times*. Not so long ago a man named Carl Stern was attacked in the middle of the night. He claimed he had seen a monster, but then he didn't stay in hospital long. He discharged himself and you, or Hannibal Blood I should say, drove him away. Then yesterday you're attacked by something. Can you tell me what you saw?"

"My cousin, you mean," Harry said.

"Carl is your cousin?"

"He sometimes works as my personal assistant, but also he does some acting work on the side. He was meant to be helping Markus Hornby with a publicity stunt. They were gonna pull that same thing they did back in Chicago where he apparently gets attacked by, this time, a wolf monster. It looks like someone decided to make it real," Harry said.

"So Carl thinks it was a *person* who attacked him? Not a monster?"

Harry rolled his eyes and gave a shrug before he winced at the movement. "I don't think he's clear on what he saw. At first he said it was a monster, but then he became convinced it could have been someone in a monster suit. Now I guess that I've been attacked perhaps it's just someone out to get us," he said.

"Is Carl still in town? Can I talk to him?" I asked.

Harry gently shook his head. "He got out of here as soon as he could. He's returned home to New York. I think he wants to put this whole thing behind him," he said.

Damn, there goes someone else I could have collected evidence from. Never mind, I still had Harry here and he was talking.

"So what did you see last night?"

"I finished my set and drove my cart back to my truck up the top of the hill. It was secluded so I was taking a few minutes to have a drink of water and eat when something came out of the gloom and attacked me. All I know for sure is it had teeth and claws. The next thing I remember is crawling along the road and someone talking to me. After that, I think I was in the ambulance and then I was here," Harry said.

"Could it have been a wild animal?"

"Maybe, but I doubt it. My cousin gets attacked and then me too? It is clear that someone doesn't like us. So as soon as the doctor says I can go, I'm outta here."

"Do you suspect someone wants to hurt you?"

Harry looked at me, his smile fading away. It was only a subtle transition but then I swear I had Hannibal Blood in the bed in front of me and not Harry Sparkle.

"Success breeds jealousy, jealousy creates enemies. There are plenty of authors in this town who would like to see me taken down, both *mes*, Harry Sparkle and Hannibal Blood. Why aren't you writing any of this down?"

"Oh, I'll remember it."

"Most journalists usually record interviews or take notes and you're doing neither. So I have to wonder what it is exactly you *are* doing."

Oh crap. He was completely right. I could only play the character of a journalist if I was, you know, doing journalist things. I'd been so caught up in getting here that I hadn't bothered to bring my handheld recorder with me.

"I want to keep it off the record because I think there's a bigger story here," I said. Harry seemed to accept my lie, nodding gently.

"Could you please keep my two identities a secret? Harry Sparkle and Hannibal Blood are very important to me. Both would be ruined if the truth came out."

"I won't tell a soul," I promised him. It occurred to me that Harry Sparkle and Hannibal Blood were both fake names.

"If your cousin is Carl Stern, does that make your real name Harry Stern or is it Hannibal Stern or something else entirely?" I asked. I could feel something tugging at the back of my mind. It felt like a word on the tip of my tongue... ideas struggling to come into my consciousness.

"My real name is Harry Stern. I guess that whoever attacked Carl and me doesn't like the Stern family," he said.

I stopped breathing for a moment as the idea hit me like a cold wave out in the ocean. Carl *Stern* attacked; Harry *Stern* attacked; the man up in the forest had called us *Torrents*. The monster that had left the scratches in the alleyway had been sitting up on that rooftop watching the Chili Challenge warehouse where Aunt Cass *Torrent* worked.

Magic can be fantastically unreliable. It's incredibly easy to screw it up, for it to get out of control. Brew up a love potion the wrong way and it wouldn't be only that boy down the corner who wanted you, but all of the dogs and cats and fish and mice in the neighborhood as well.

Brew up a curse and give it two names, Stern and Torrent, and it wouldn't particularly care whether they were witches or ordinary people with coincidentally the same name.

"Are you okay? You look like you're about to faint," Harry said.

"Leave town as soon as you can," I warned Harry and then I was gone, unlocking the door, pulling a concealment spell over myself, and bolting out of the hospital.

CHAPTER NINETEEN

"So... are people coming or can I go back to my very important business?" Luce asked, tapping away at her phone, bored.

"They'll be here soon," I grumbled, checking my own messages. It seemed my ability to call an emergency family meeting wasn't as powerful as I had assumed. We had been waiting an hour now and so far there was only Luce, Kira sitting on the sofa, and Adams gently snoring. The moms said they were on their way and so was Molly, and I hadn't received any response from Aunt Cass yet.

"What is your important business anyway?" I asked.

"Will is currently gardening at his house and when he does that it's in a pair of shorts only and there's a spot inside his kitchen that looks out over the backyard and it's directly beneath the air conditioning. Do you see what I'm putting together here? Me on a chair under the air conditioning, drinking something cool, Will in a pair of shorts. That's what I *could* be doing rather than sitting here listening to Adams snore," Luce said.

The little black cat woke up at the sound of his name. "I'm not snoring!" he retorted, somewhat blearily.

"Fight the power Adams," Kira murmured and scratched him on the back of the neck with her free hand, tapping away on her phone with the other. Adams rolled over and went straight back to sleep, starting to snore again.

"I'm sorry to keep you from your *very important business*, but this is important *and* an emergency. I don't know why everyone's not taking it seriously," I said, pacing around.

Thankfully, I only had another few minutes to wait. The moms came walking down the drive, faces red from the heat. They stumbled inside looking like they'd been running a marathon. All three of them had enormous bags under their eyes, obviously the result of burning the candle at both ends. The three of them slumped down onto the sofa, Aunt Ro pushing Adams aside, who left grumbling to himself to find somewhere else to sleep.

"What is this about Harlow?" Mom asked in a tired voice.

"We have to wait for everyone to get here so I don't have to explain it over and again," I said.

Outside, Molly parked her car and rushed in with Ollie following close behind.

"Could you get us all cold drinks, darling?" Molly asked him in a sweet voice.

"Sure thing," Ollie said and headed for the kitchen. As soon as he was even slightly out of earshot she turned and pointed her finger at me.

"I don't know what this is about but try to keep the magic to a minimum okay? I don't want too much magic today," she said, making sure the moms heard her.

"He already knows you're a witch," Aunt Ro murmured, her eyes closed.

"Listen to what I said," Molly said.

"Why did you bring him if you didn't want any magic business?" Aunt Ro asked.

"Because leaving him for some secret magic meeting is as bad!" Molly hissed in an undertone.

Ollie returned with cool glasses of water, going back and forth from the kitchen ferrying them for us.

I checked my phone again but there was still no response from Aunt Cass.

"Aunt Cass isn't here, but I think we can get started seeing as I don't know when she's going to show up," I began.

Right on cue, Aunt Cass came through the front door. She was dressed in all black from head to toe with a rolled up balaclava sitting on her head and black around her eyes. Her cheeks were red, which was no surprise given the temperature outside.

"What are you doing dressed like that? What have you been up to?" Mom said.

"I've been sneaking and breaking and entering and *stealing*," Aunt Cass said with a wicked grin. "Give me a minute," she said. She rushed past us all and went into the bathroom. As the moms murmured amongst themselves and Molly looked positively aghast, Aunt Cass got changed, coming back wearing a pair of shorts and a tank top with a grinning sun on it saying "I've been down to Florida" on it. She had attempted to wipe the black away from her eyes but some of it was still there, giving her the look of a somewhat crazed raccoon.

"It's good everyone is here because look what I found," she announced, taking over. She held up the map, the one the writers had found.

All of us could feel the magic emanating from it. Had it grown stronger? It felt old and powerful.

"Is that the magic map those writers found?" Aunt Freya

asked. She yawned into the back of her hand, seemingly unable to stop herself.

"Ten points for the tired witch," Aunt Cass said. "I crept in and took it, and there's a spell on it but I'm not sure how to activate it or what it's going to do," she said.

She passed the map to Mom who started turning it over in her hands, examining it.

"The monster is cursed to attack anyone with the last name Stern! I think it's after Torrents too!" I blurted out, seeing my emergency family meeting being taken away from me.

Everyone turned to face me with puzzled expressions. Except for Molly, of course, who was looking increasingly angry that we weren't keeping the magic to a minimum. I presume it was because she didn't want to scare off Ollie, who seemed fine and taking it all in his stride. He was leaning against the counter drinking a glass of cool water, looking like this was a perfectly normal weekend.

"Didn't it attack Harry Sparkle?" Luce said.

"Sparkle isn't his real name!" I said.

Kira had finally put her phone down and was now paying attention. "His real name is Harry Stern?" she asked.

"Yes, and his cousin was Carl *Stern*. The monster was up here in the forest, keeping watch on *us* and out on those rooftops looking over the Chili Challenge at Aunt Cass *Torrent*. I think the man we saw in the clearing is the one behind it," I said.

"The man is the monster? The one who called you Marguerite?" Mom said finally, passing the map along to Aunt Freya.

"Maybe we could take it a bit easy on all the magic talk," Molly said in a brittle voice. Everyone ignored her.

"Yes, I think it's him. Maybe he transforms or he's connected to it somehow. Doesn't it seem like an enormous coincidence that two people with the surname Stern would be attacked, and then he talked to us and said 'Keep away Torrents'?" I said.

"But he hasn't attacked any Torrents, has he?" Kira said.

"We have wards up around the mansion and grounds. That might explain it," Mom said. She gave an enormous yawn and then both Aunt Ro and Aunt Freya followed her.

I looked at the three of them, and realized exactly what was going on. Ongoing magic spells are a dangerous thing for a witch. If you cast one at lunch today, then tomorrow at lunch it will use the same amount of energy to keep itself going. Cast too many spells and you can die.

"So let me get this straight–you've put wards around the property. Plus you have a concealment spell on Grandma *and* you've been cooking for the bed-and-breakfast guests, *and* running the bakery? Aren't you afraid that number of spells is going to kill all of you?" I said.

"Maybe we should talk about this later," Molly said, her voice becoming shrill. Again, everyone ignored her.

"Yes, that's exactly what we've been doing, keeping our family safe and our businesses going," Aunt Ro said, sounding possibly meaner than she intended due to her tiredness.

Luce stood up and began pacing around. "You're telling us there is a man or possibly a monster out there who *could* have attacked us, but he hasn't because there is a ward around the property? Did you put one around *Traveler* too?" she asked.

Aunt Ro shook her head. "Only around where we sleep, which includes Will's house, Jack's and also Ollie's," she said.

"There's a magic spell around my house?" Ollie asked.

"You betcha librarian," Aunt Cass said, giving him the double finger guns for some reason.

"Mom!" Molly protested.

"Do we have any idea of who that man is? The one who called you Marguerite?" Luce asked.

Ollie cleared his throat and stood up from leaning on the bench which caught everyone's attention because he normally didn't talk that much.

"I have something on that. I'd been researching the Torrent family tree trying to find out who Rosetta's mother was, after Harlow asked me. I've also been looking into Juliet Stern and trying to find where she fits," Ollie said.

For some reason Molly started glaring directly at me. She had known I had asked Ollie to research the family tree but apparently having this revealed *again* was upsetting her today.

"It was the strangest thing… this morning at home I was flicking through a stack of old papers I've been through many times before, and then there it was. I found some old property records where one of the local church members had written details about other townsfolk on the back of them. I found Marguerite Torrent who had a daughter Rosetta. She was married to a man called Johannes Tilson. Rosetta had a daughter who, in your family tree, is your grandmother's grandmother. I also found Juliet Stern married a man called Benjamin Mainer and they had a daughter. There are some odd gaps in the family tree so I haven't been able to connect it to Hattie yet, but that's what I found. If that man saw Harlow and called her Marguerite perhaps, if it's magic, he *was* Johannes or Benjamin, or maybe someone who knew her all that time ago?" Ollie said.

"Oh, you brilliant, brilliant boy," Aunt Cass said and grabbed Ollie, planting a big kiss on his cheek.

"Are we saying that the man in the forest, who could possibly be the monster, is the husband of either Juliet or this Marguerite?" I asked.

"Do you remember out at that explosion site? It felt like

there were pieces of old magic scattered around the place. Aunt Cass said it felt the same. You could be right. Maybe it's a man or *men* cursed into monsters, told to attack Stern and Torrent," Aunt Freya said.

Molly moaned into her hands. "I can't have this much magic happening, it's too much," she said.

"It's fine Molly, he knows we're witches," Aunt Ro snapped. She summoned a tiny horse made of gold light that ran across her palm and then dived off, bursting into a glitter of gold on the floor. Considering how tired she was from maintaining the wards, the concealment spell, and everything else she was doing, I was surprised she had the power to pull it off.

"I said keep the magic to a minimum!" Molly yelled.

Just then, when Molly was on the brink of a major freak out, Kira passed me the map that Aunt Cass had stolen. The moment I touched it the magic around it lurched and every witch in the room felt it. There was a sudden burst of white light as though I was holding fireworks in my hands. Sparkles of white and then blue began to shoot off the map, landing on the floor before dissipating. It was a few seconds before it ceased but it sent Molly into complete overdrive.

"That's it! We're going," she shouted.

"Molly…" Ollie said softly but she was too angry to hear him.

"Don't get so wound up," Aunt Ro said, frowning at her daughter.

"Oh, don't get upset? Where are your husbands right now? Where are our fathers? That's right, they're gone, they left because there was too much magic and they couldn't handle being married to witches and so they left. They left *you* and they left *us*. I don't want the same thing to happen to me!" she finished with a shout and then stood there, panting. We were all somewhat shocked into silence, which was quite a strange thing to see considering Torrent witches usually got straight into it.

It was then that Ollie stepped forward. He grabbed Molly by the hand and spun her around to face him.

"You think I'm going to leave because you're a witch?" he said.

A tear trickled down Molly's cheek. "Our fathers did," she said in a quiet voice.

You could have cut the tension in the room with a knife. Ollie gave us a quick glance and then pulled Molly from the room, taking her out the front door to stand in the driveway.

He started talking to her, never letting go of her hand.

Of course every witch in the room tried to see what was going on without being conspicuous about it.

"What is he saying?" Aunt Ro said.

"I'm trying to read lips... you're my fish? No. You're my witch?" Aunt Cass said, peering out the window.

Ollie was fumbling for something in his pocket and as he did he knelt down on one knee.

I swear the collective intake of air nearly broke every window in the house.

"Is he proposing?" Kira asked wide-eyed. The silence was only broken by Adams' soft snoring as we watched Molly say something to him and then nod. Ollie slipped a ring on her finger and then stood up, his knees covered in gravel dust from the road. They hugged and then that was it. I found myself with the rest of my family rushing out the front door in a mob. We were all going far too fast because instead of hugging Molly and Ollie, we crash tackled them to the ground.

"We're gonna get married," Molly said from somewhere underneath a pile of witches.

It took a few minutes for us to all get up. Everyone was

covered in gravel dust, Ollie's hair was sticking up in spikes on his head, and his face was bright red.

Everyone was talking at a hundred miles an hour, all of us hugging and kissing Molly and Ollie in turn, and admiring the ring that Molly had on her finger.

It was finally Aunt Cass who took charge and commanded all of us go back inside before we got sunburned to death. We ended up back in the lounge room where a very grumpy Adams woke up and glared at all of us.

"Cat can't get any sleep around here you know," he said.

"Harlow look at the map," Aunt Cass said.

In the rush of everything it seemed that we'd all forgotten that the map had burst into light the moment I'd touched it. There on its dark brown surface were the lines showing the rudimentary map of Harlot Bay. There was now a new mark faintly glittering on the corner of two of the streets.

I held the map out as everyone gathered around to view this new development. As we looked at the map there was a twitch in the magic and a word shimmered into existence: *Compass.* A small arrow appeared, pointing at a new dot.

Aunt Cass gently took the map from me and the new glowing dot turned brown.

"I have a feeling we need to find this compass," she said.

"And the compass will surely help us find the monster or the man behind it," Luce said. Normally when she went right off the deep end everyone ignored her but this time it sounded as though her voice had the ring of prophecy in it.

CHAPTER TWENTY

*M*onday morning found me inching my way through the traffic on the main street of Harlot Bay with Red.

She was tapping away on her phone and my mind was a million miles away. Or to be more precise about half a mile away down the street at the Harlot Bay Museum. Yesterday after the magic map, the wedding proposal, and everything else, all of us witches scattered to the four winds. The moms very tiredly went back to their end of the mansion. Aunt Cass hitched a ride with Molly and Ollie, taking the map with her. Kira went with Will and Luce. And as for me? I was left alone with only a sleeping cat for company.

After the revelation of the map it felt very much as though I'd been sprinting at full speed and then come to a dead stop.

Honestly, it also felt like I'd been a little abandoned. Aunt Cass insisted on taking the map by herself. Then I got in contact with Jack, only to find he was somewhere far down the coast with his parents. I know I could have used the time to dig further into the mysteries going on in Harlot Bay. I could have read some of Carter's articles where he was now blaming interlopers from out-of-state for carving symbols and spray painting them around the town. I could have gone up to my lair to read Juliet's journal again to see if I could find any mention of Marguerite. But after the week I had, I was exhausted, and so what I actually did was sit on the sofa next to a sleeping cat, put on a movie and do nothing for the rest of the day.

It was only this morning, just before Red came to pick me up for another day of work, that Aunt Cass had messaged me, telling me that the dot on the map was the museum and she was "looking into it".

Red and I had a lot of work on this morning but after lunch the afternoon was free. Normally Red would drop me off at home but perhaps today I would visit the museum to see if I could spot a compass at all and then hitch a lift with Molly and Luce.

I hadn't been to the Harlot Bay Museum since I was in high school on one of the forced trips they'd made us go on. It was a large imposing building in Harlot Bay, but one that I completely ignored, as did most of the other locals. It was pretty much only the tourists who went there. The latest attraction getting all the buzz was their *Weapons of the World* exhibit. After Luce's catapult had been stolen and then recovered, it had been, against her wishes, given to the museum who had then built an exhibition around it.

"Harlow? Did you hear me?" Red said.

I returned to the here and now to find Red looking at me from the passenger seat.

"Oh, sorry, what was it?" I said.

We inched forward a little further, watching as a man dressed as a vampire and a woman dressed as Red Herringbone crossed in front of us.

"Jay confirmed it, the map is gone. Someone stole it from

his room yesterday," Red said.

Gulp. Okay, now I was feeling like a double agent. It had been Aunt Cass, of course, who had stolen the map. She was the one who had it right now. I had to keep calm.

"Did someone go into his room?" I asked watching another flock of vampires cross the street, slowing down the traffic yet again.

"It was the weirdest thing… he says he was *in* the room at the time and then suddenly it was gone. He searched everywhere but it's not there," Red said.

"That *is* weird," I said.

"It's okay. We took photos of it and we have Henry Martin working on cracking the code," she said.

The name seemed familiar. The answer came to me a moment later.

"Is he that author who writes those books with cryptography and secrets in them? Where they're always finding a clue in an old painting and rushing through Paris?" I asked.

"That's the one. He's working on it right now. We've also discovered where Rufus and Dawn of the *Mysterious Mysteries* are staying."

"Oh?" I said, trying to keep it light as I finally pulled off the street and into a reserved car space. We were nearly late again, thanks to the flood of traffic, which seemed to have gotten worse over the last few days.

"We're thinking of going there given that all of the other leads have disappeared. Harry Sparkle discharged himself and left town. The first guy who was attacked has left town. No one knows where Hannibal Blood is, and Markus Hornby, the author who sets up all those publicity stunts, doesn't have a session until tomorrow," Red said.

When she mentioned Harry Sparkle and Hannibal Blood I felt myself involuntarily tense but then I relaxed. She didn't know they were one and the same, that they were actually

Harry Stern and that he had left town at my urging. Now that Aunt Cass had the map perhaps it would lead somewhere.

Aunt Cass had the map, not the writers, and although their code cracking expert author might find something, I sincerely doubted it. Given the map had been made by witches I was sure the code was a decoy or unbreakable by normal means.

"He'd better work quick because Writerpalooza is almost over," I said. My phone rang. It was Jack.

"You take it honey, I can get this stuff inside myself," Red said. I answered the phone as I popped the trunk, so Red could grab her papers for the session.

"Word on the street is that I have a magical ward around my house," Jack said in a pleasant tone.

"Oh, you've been talking to Ollie?" I said. I had fully intended to tell Jack everything that had happened yesterday as part of my *no more secrets* policy. Given that he was away with his parents I didn't want to disturb that and then by the end of the day it had simply slipped my mind. Clearly he'd spoken to Ollie and heard what had happened.

"It was actually another informant," Jack said.

"Would this informant be small and black and have four paws and a weakness for tuna?"

"I may have obtained this information with tuna," Jack said, laughing.

Red closed the trunk, gave me a wave and rushed inside, leaving me sitting in the sports car.

"I did discover yesterday there's a ward around your house and a few other things," I said. I told Jack about Aunt Cass stealing the map and how it had lit up in my hands, a new dot appearing that we think was at the Harlot Bay Museum, along with an instruction to find a compass.

Jack listened as I spoke, and although he didn't say a thing

I could feel his concern radiating down the phone.

"So there is a man, possibly from the past, possibly the husband of some great-great-grandmother relative, or her friend, and he may also be a monster, and he's after Torrents and Sterns?" Jack said.

"That's the working hypothesis," I said realizing it sounded quite dark when it was said out loud.

I heard Jack blow out air between his teeth. "Is there some reason I shouldn't dump my parents on Jonas and then you and me stay together until this is all solved?" he asked.

"I do want to see you but honestly I think it's going to be okay. The monster has only ever attacked at night and at dusk, and given that it's been up at the mansion and watching over Aunt Cass without attacking, it looks like the wards are working. We've put Kira under a curfew and none of us are going to go out into the dark alone," I said.

I heard Jack sigh again. "That actually didn't make me feel better. When there's someone out there stalking you, you don't just hope it will get better. You need to do counter surveillance. Maybe I can set you guys up with some security cameras," he said.

"I think it'll be okay. I don't –" I stuttered to a stop as the phone died in my hand. It was coated in a layer of frost. I reached for the stone, rubbing it between my fingers and feeling the warmth flood out. The frost crept away from my phone and it eventually came back to life. There was a message waiting from Jack: *Cut off, talk to you later, don't get eaten by a monster!*

I smiled at the message and then got out of the sports car, locking it behind me. Jack was right. We had to take action, and as soon as work was over today I was going to that museum to see what I could find.

Happy to have a plan in a direction, I rushed inside to start my work for the day with Red.

CHAPTER TWENTY-ONE

*R*ed and I were loading her teaching materials into the trunk of the car when Jay Savage appeared, dressed in the costume of... I guess what he thought a tourist would wear? Think impossibly bright floral shirt, gleaming white shorts, an enormous pair of sunglasses, a cowboy hat for some reason, and the rest of his body glistening with sun cream. His face was bright red and he was carrying two large bags of food.

"TJ said Rufus and Dawn have left their rental so I think it's now or never. Are we going?" he said without preamble.

Red glanced at me, no doubt seeing the look of panic on my face.

"We're going to break in to see if there's anything where they're staying. Are you in?" she said with a slight smile.

Oh Goddess no, what was with these authors? Couldn't they end up nowhere with the code on the map and then Writerpalooza would finish and they would leave Harlot Bay? That's what I was hoping was going to happen and now they were proposing breaking and entering!

"You're going to break into Rufus and Dawn's?" I said, stalling to give myself time to think.

"The rest of our leads have gone dead so that's where we're going," Jay said. He pulled a wrapped sandwich out the bag and offered it to me. I took it without thinking.

Okay, so I could say *no* to this, let the writers do whatever it is they were going to do, and go to the museum and see if I could spot a compass, do some reconnaissance. Or I could go with the writers, engage in some crime, and see where *that* led. I made a sudden decision. "Okay, I'm in," I said. Red held up her hand for a high five and I slapped her palm. We all got into the sports car and I started it, the amazing air conditioning chilling the interior. Jay climbed into the back seat and was now munching away on a sandwich while talking at a hundred miles an hour. I unwrapped mine (it was chicken salad) and took a huge bite before pulling out into the traffic jam that was now Harlot Bay. Red typed in an address on her phone and then showed me on the map where it was. It was a few streets back from Barnes Boulevard, one of the richest streets in Harlot Bay. That whole area was essentially tourist rentals which I guess explained Jay's costume.

"I also heard that they once got in trouble for damaging an old house by carving scratches into the door so they could film it," Jay said somewhere between taking enormous bites of his sandwich.

"They have to be the ones doing it around town then," Red said.

I kept chewing and focusing on navigating the congested road ahead of me. I suddenly remembered that in all the confusion of the last few days I still hadn't had an opportunity to talk to Aunt Cass to explain why exactly she'd blackmailed Molly and Luce into joining her in spray painting the strange symbol around town. I knew for a fact that Aunt Cass was behind *some* of the symbols.

"You think Rufus and Dawn are the ones doing the symbols?" I asked. I came to a stop and a huge crowd of vampires crossed the street ahead of us, then we were finally able to go.

"What I think we have here is two separate and distinct mysteries, with possibly a third. The *Mysterious Mysteries* people in town faking things, something *else* is in town attacking people, and mystery number three is that I suspect a publicity stunt had gone wrong and maybe somehow Harry Sparkle got tangled up in it," Red said.

"It's like *Deep Dish Disaster*, isn't it," Jay said.

"*Deep Dish Disaster*?" I asked. Jay nodded, taking another enormous bite of his sandwich and talking through a mouthful of food. "It was a book Jenna wrote years ago. Three separate mysteries all connected, intertwining, and it was sorta like this. They ended up fighting a guy in a monster suit," he said.

"I realized... is it safe to break in during the day?" I said. We were reaching the edge of Harlot Bay now and the traffic was starting to speed up.

"We'll look like other tourists hopefully. Besides they're there at night so we need to go in the day and TJ has had them on surveillance. They almost always leave at this time," Jay said. We drove up the hill, the traffic now moving faster, talking about Jenna's old book the *Deep Dish Disaster*. In it a man had been attacked, apparently by a monster, which in the end had been revealed to be simply a person wearing a monster suit. If only that were the truth here...

I was feeling nervous and on edge from the prospect of engaging in some light breaking and entering but the more I talked with the writers the calmer I began to feel. Although they were interested in what the map might reveal, it seemed their focus had turned to Rufus and Dawn, that perhaps *they* were the suspects behind Carl Stern and Harry Sparkle being attacked. As we drove closer to where Rufus and Dawn were staying I began to hope we'd find something because perhaps then the authors would give up this pursuit and us witches could go about our witchy business in peace.

"Up here on the left," Red murmured, pointing at a tall white house midway down the street. I drove by it and then following her instructions went around the corner into the next block where I parked behind the giant yellow truck that belonged to TJ. He and Jenna were waiting inside and so the three of us clambered into the back for a small criminal conference.

"Harlow, you're joining us today. This should be fun," Jenna said with a wicked grin. She seemed almost manic at the idea that we were about to break into someone's house.

"They're usually gone for at least an hour and a half, and it's been thirty minutes already, so we need to get moving," TJ said.

He pulled a small crowbar out of a bag that sat near his feet. It was the exact same model and style as Aunt Cass's crowbar, except of course this one didn't have *Cassandra Torrent* inscribed on it. I almost started laughing out loud at that moment in the car at the absurdity of this all. Here I was with the writers about to break in somewhere and I was pretty sure that as soon as we located that compass I'd be sneaking in somewhere else to commit a little bit more crime. Witches didn't care much about the law, but the way the Torrent family had been going recently you'd think we were full-time criminals.

"We need to look natural. We're going to walk to the front and then go around the back of the house like we own the place," TJ said.

We piled out of the car and walked around the block. The closer we got to the house the more anxious I began to feel. For starters, there were tourists everywhere, coming and going from their rentals, the streets packed with them. Although Jay was dressed in the same kind of absurd tourist costume, the rest of us weren't.

We went in through a white picket gate and around the side of the house which was planted with rows of blooming flowers in shades of red and blue. Thankfully, the fence dividing the properties was quite high and when we went around the back of the property we saw the fence on the other side was too. Usually, houses up here would back onto another property over the fence but this time there was an old grassy alleyway behind each of the houses.

TJ had his crowbar ready and waiting to go, but then we discovered the back door was unlocked. We crept into the house, feeling the temperature drop. They had left the air conditioning going to keep the house cool. The house was well maintained but impersonal. It was simply a holiday rental, bland and functional. A cup in the sink and some groceries sitting atop the bench was the only sign that Rufus and Dawn were here at all.

"Let's split up and see what we can find," Jay said.

"No, you never split up, that's how people end up getting murdered," Jenna said.

"Grandma Gough always splits up and she hasn't been murdered," TJ said.

"The house is tiny. I sincerely doubt anyone's gonna get murdered," Red said and poked Jenna in the ribs.

We split up–sorta. Me with Red, TJ and Jenna together, and Jay by himself. Our first stop was a bedroom. There was a suitcase in the corner full of men's clothing and then another one next to it that contained parts of what was clearly Rufus's disguise. Red and I went through the suitcases as quick as we could, trying not to disturb anything but checking for anything unusual. We didn't find anything. Red was moving a sock into place when we heard Jay call out from the other end of the house.

"Get down here!" he said, his voice echoing down the corridor. We rushed down to a far room, which looked to be a tiny fourth bedroom. There was a single bed against the wall and sitting laid out for everyone to see was a full monster costume.

"It's actually *them* attacking people. This is crazy," TJ said from somewhere behind me. We filled the room, standing around the bed staring at the costume in disbelief. It was the size of an adult man, covered in brown matted fur that looked somewhat realistic. There were long claws on both the hands made out of metal, and they were smeared with red. There was a separate head resting against the pillow of the bed that had small latches where it connected to the body of the suit. The face of the monster was a snarling visage of a wolf crossed with a man. TJ picked up the clawed hand and touched the red stains on the sharpened steel claws. Then he sniffed at it.

"I think this is paint, not blood," he said.

"Look what I found," Jenna said from the corner.

There was a long black bag sitting against the wall. Jenna pulled the top of it open and inside it was glittering steel. The entire bag was full of carving equipment, chisels, drills and the like.

Some of the equipment still had wood shavings on it. There were also a few spray paint cans stuffed in the end of the bag.

"I guess this shows that *maybe* they are behind it," I said.

I realized that my hope that we would find something was going to backfire seriously. Red and Jenna were already taking photos with their phones. I had no doubt that Sheriff Hardy would be notified and then all the clues seemed to point in one direction. The two men who had been attacked and the vandalism that had been going on around town could be pinned on the *Mysterious Mysteries*.

Except I knew it wasn't true. I'd sensed magic when Carl Stern had been attacked and also when Harry had been attacked too. We witches knew there was something magical in town. There was the man or possibly monster who had called me Marguerite. I would have to tell Sheriff Hardy that although the clues and evidence appeared to implicate Rufus and Dawn, it likely wasn't them. But that would put him in a bad position of having to possibly cover it up so they didn't get arrested for crimes they didn't commit.

"What do you think: anonymous phone call?" Jenna said. I didn't get a chance to answer because all four of us heard the slamming of car doors that sounded awfully close.

"They're back! Why didn't we have a lookout?" TJ said.

As one we bolted out of the room, down the corridor, and out the back door. We heard a man and woman out the front of the house and then the sound of keys. I was last out of the house, closing the door as quietly as I could and then sprinting to follow the authors who headed for the back fence. There was a gate but unfortunately it was locked. That was okay–we had a giant on our side. TJ practically flung Jenna, Jay, and Red over the fence and then I was next. One moment I was near the fence, the next I was over on the far side, landing in the thick grass, Red and Jenna pulling me to my feet. We had to get out of the way as a giant mountain of a man appeared on top of the fence and then landed beside us with a thud that shook the earth. Then we were off again, running down the narrow alleyway, and continuing until we reached the end of the street.

"Stop running, we have to look normal," TJ said.

We slowed down and headed back to the cars. I could feel my heart thudding in my chest and I wanted to look behind us to see if were being pursued. My mind was filled with doubts. Had Jenna closed the bag? Maybe TJ had disturbed the costume? Or possibly Rufus and Dawn had heard us climbing the back fence. We had to get out of here as fast as we could. I could only imagine how bad it would be if a police car came around the corner.

We got back to the vehicles and this time Red took the wheel. We were all in a kind of stunned silence as we followed TJ out of the street, down the hill and back towards town. I don't think I came out of it until he stopped in a random street and we parked behind him. Then I followed Red and Jay to TJ's truck and we all got in.

"That was way too close," Jenna said. Her cheeks were red but she seemed almost giddy with joy at our narrow escape.

"I think we need to anonymously call the Sheriff because if they heard us, they might get rid of that stuff and then what proof will there be?" Jay said.

That panic was back again. The idea that they would call the police and get someone *other* than Sheriff Hardy. Then the case would roll along to its inevitable and unjust conclusion of Rufus and Dawn being arrested for attacking Carl and Harry, and also going down for the vandalism.

I had to take charge immediately.

"I'll do it! The Sheriff is my uncle. I'll talk to him in private, not implicate any of us, and then we'll see what happens. He might have to keep the investigation quiet so they might not be arrested straight away," I said.

"How are you going to explain how you came across the information?" Red asked.

The lie came together with startling clarity and quickness.

"Although I'm currently working for Writerpalooza my actual job is being a journalist for *The Harlot Bay Times*. Carter and I have been working on this since those weird symbols appeared in town. I'll say I had a tip off and so I went to investigate," I said.

"Can you believe they had a monster suit, though? It's *Deep Dish Disaster* all over again," Jenna said, shaking her head.

"You know, it's always the ones you least expect," TJ said.

Jay pointed his finger at Jenna. "Then I suspect you," he said, smiling at her.

"Me? I write cat mysteries!"

"Precisely! It's the one you least suspect," Jay said. The writers started chattering away and I was only half listening. Although they were joking around and seemed somewhat relieved, it also appeared that they were a bit disappointed that there wasn't more to the mystery. For my part, I was quietly panicking inside. I had to talk to Sheriff Hardy as soon as possible.

CHAPTER TWENTY-TWO

Sheriff Hardy was not enjoying the conversation. He sighed down the phone again.

"So they have a monster suit, a bag full of carving tools with wood shavings, and also spray paint," he repeated.

"I'm sorry I have to tell you this," I said.

"I'm not going to ask you how you came upon this information," he said, his voice still somewhat flat. "But if they get caught around town carving or spray painting it means they probably will be blamed for all of the vandalism that's been going on around Harlot Bay and there will be nothing I can do about,".

"I know," I said.

Sheriff Hardy sighed again. I had the feeling he'd been doing a lot more of that since he'd married Aunt Ro and discovered the truth about our family: we were witches and often involved in the strange things that went on around Harlot Bay.

"You know I've had Carter Wilkins in here trying to get me to investigate Rufus and Dawn. He's convinced they're the ones behind all the vandalism, and maybe they *are* behind some of it," he said.

"I don't think Carter has anything serious yet. I sort of agreed to an information sharing thing with him, and I haven't heard anything yet," I said.

"Let's hope no one else gets attacked and that the *Mysterious Mysteries* leave Harlot Bay. It's bad enough we have all the rest of the national media here after Harry Sparkle was attacked drawing attention. If those two get caught doing anything the investigation will roll to one conclusion. I don't want to see two people who are innocent be arrested," Sheriff Hardy said.

He ended the call after thanking me again for telling him about what me and the writers had found. I hung up the phone and continued down the main street, heading to the Harlot Bay Museum. After the break-in, the writers seemed to have been at a loose end, and I think were intending to go to the beach rather than get involved in any more snooping. I had Red drop me off in the middle of town, telling her I would catch a ride home with my cousins and see her tomorrow. There was still a few hours before *Traveler* would close so I thought I'd put it to good use and see if I could find a compass in the museum.

I gradually made my way through the crowd of people entering the museum, paid my fee and then I was in. Although I was still under the influence of the slip power that was desensitizing me to the heat, it still felt nice to be inside where the floors were polished marble and there was a coolness to the air.

The last time I'd been here as a teenager the museum had been full of narrow corridors that had led to larger rooms. In the renovation they'd knocked out a lot of walls making larger rooms that were filled with hundreds of glass cases.

There were cleverly placed walls separating the exhibitions from each other, and tourists wandering everywhere.

I was standing looking at a map of the museum wondering where I would be if *I* were a compass when I felt a finger tap me on the shoulder. It was Aunt Cass wearing an enormous pair of black sunglasses and a cowboy hat that obviously came from her stash at the Chili Challenge.

"Don't you know if you're going to do any snooping for crime you should probably go in disguise? Because after you steal a thing they're going to go back through the security tapes," she said.

I looked her up and down. She was wearing one of her Chili Challenge T-shirts with 'Hot Enough For Ya Sucker?' written on it.

"You're wearing a T-shirt from your business and I'm fairly sure if Sheriff Hardy looks at any security tapes he's going to know it's you," I said.

"Ah right, our man on the inside," Aunt Cass said.

"Man on the inside? I think if we get caught breaking in here Sheriff Hardy is going to have to arrest us," I said.

"He married into the family, he's not going to arrest us," Aunt Cass said.

I wasn't so sure but I wasn't going to get into an argument with her, especially not in the midst of a crowded room full of tourists, some of whom I'm sure would be able to overhear us discussing crime.

I suddenly remembered the other crimes that I'd been talking about with Sheriff Hardy, specifically the spray painting of strange symbols around town.

"Can you tell me why you blackmailed Molly and Luce into spray painting around town? Why are you doing that?" I said in a lowered tone.

"Let's walk and talk. We have a lot of ground to cover,"

Aunt Cass said, pointing a finger towards the display of old whaling equipment.

We headed over, making our way through the hoards of tourists. The exhibition was from an old whaling ship and they were all kinds of cases and boxes, maps, and a gigantic harpoon stuck up against the wall.

"Don't you feel yourself being pushed, a continuous pressure?" Aunt Cass murmured to me as we looked over all the items.

"I guess so," I said. I knew what she meant. Since I'd been told there was a spell cast on me, occasionally I'd felt something, a strange force pushing me. It was hard to know though, because it was subtle. I would think that I should go off to my lair to examine the wall of crazy, and then instead find myself spending the evening on the sofa watching TV or finding some reason to spend more time with Jack. It was hard to know whether that was the spell pushing on me or me being lazy.

"I think the more attention is applied to it the more it weakens. Those symbols appeared around town and some of them I think are from the monster or man. Others are mine and I'm sure those *Mysterious Mysteries* are doing some of their own. But what it means is more attention, more people looking into it, digging into the past and whatever it is, a spell, a curse, it only has so much power. Ollie finding those papers–they were hidden surely by a spell, and then *there they were*, and we discovered something we never knew before! I'm starting to feel like I can finally breathe freely for the first time in decades," Aunt Cass said. We continued moving past the exhibits, looking into each one to see if we could spot a compass or anything that looked like one.

"But *what* are we pushing? What will happen if we get to the other side?" I whispered to Aunt Cass.

"I don't know. But once it breaks then we'll see."

We passed two more exhibitions and continued on our way. There were tourists all around us, but there were still quiet moments in the museum and it seemed Aunt Cass was willing to answer questions so I kept going.

"You said we were going to set a trap... are you still making it?"

"I have some ideas, but these things don't go quick. Wrong trap and it'll slip right out of your hands."

We moved past an exhibition of flags and turned a corner where I was very surprised to see John Smith drifting around. He was doing a ghost thing which can be quite confusing. Sometimes they walk like normal people. Other times they float slightly off the ground, drifting about the place. I was quite surprised to see him in the museum. Given the sheer number of people here I would have thought he would have been bounced out of here long ago. When we turned the corner John saw us and came floating over.

"Hi Harlow, and..." He frowned, struggling to remember.

"Cassandra," Aunt Cass murmured, not paying much attention to him, looking around the room.

"Who's Cassandra?" John asked, confused.

"Never mind. What are you doing here today?" I said.

"Did you see the catapult in the *Weapons of the World Exhibition*? Didn't that belong to your cousin?" John said.

I was surprised again because he never remembered anything. The fact that he'd held on to the memory that the catapult had belonged to Luce was incredible. Before we could talk to him more though a tourist walked straight into him and John shot out of the room at high speed, disappearing through one of the walls. When he didn't return, we continued on our way.

"Have you been keeping track of how many security cameras there are?" Aunt Cass said to me.

"No, I haven't. Do I need to do that?" I asked looking

around. There was at least one security camera in the corner of each room and we were now near the middle of the museum which meant we'd passed by many of them.

"Start counting," Aunt Cass said.

We continued around the museum, eating up another hour and a half, looking through the exhibitions piece by piece. There were enormous glass cases and in each of them there were often up to thirty or forty individual objects, named and numbered, many of them featuring a small plaque with information beneath it. There were also crowds of tourists which made it quite difficult to get close to some of them. We went by the *Weapons of the World Exhibition*, which featured Luce's catapult sitting in the center of a long room. Tourists were posing for photographs in front of it.

We eventually found ourselves in front of an exhibition titled *Wreck of the Appalachia*, a sailing ship from long ago. There were multiple glass cabinets filled with things like old boots, telescopes, a chest, clothing, plates and spoons, the captain's ledger and so on. Aunt Cass and I saw the small compass at the same time. We rushed over and both of us let out a breath at the same time to relax, to sense the magic. Unlike the map, which clearly felt magical, the compass was well shielded. In the swirl of the magic around us, it was barely noticeable. But still, it was clear *this* was the compass the map was referring to. The glass case was locked which wouldn't be a problem considering we could unlock it with a spell. But there was no way we could do that in the middle of the day. In addition to the security cameras in the corner of each room, there were guards moving about the place as well.

"I count at least twelve security cameras we need to get by. I'm going to have to come up with a plan so let's go before we start looking suspicious standing here at the thing that's going to be stolen soon," Aunt Cass said.

I followed Aunt Cass out and she went back to the Chili Challenge. We'd spent far more time in the museum than I'd thought. It was almost getting time for *Traveler* to close so I walked over there feeling that same anxious tension from earlier in the day while plotting breaking and entering with the writers. We witches didn't have such a great track record when it came to breaking into places. Although we'd gotten away with it, many times had been a close call. With the writers on the same track, the *Mysterious Mysteries* in town, the extra media attention, and the sheer number of tourists about the place, I wasn't quite sure how we were going to break into a museum that was in the middle of town.

CHAPTER TWENTY-THREE

*T*hree tense days passed.

The national media was still all over town. They'd come for Harry Sparkle being attacked but now stayed to mock Harlot Bay and make it the joke of the entire country thanks to Rufus and Dawn of the *Mysterious Mysteries*. They'd begun releasing their latest series, *The Mysterious Mysteries of Harlot Bay*. They had a video on the scratches found in the alleyway, another on the mysterious symbols carved into doors around town, and another showing a blurry figure of a monster, leaping across the rooftops, its sharp claws clearly visible. I watched the video and saw immediately that Rufus and Dawn hadn't managed to capture the actual monster at all. It was someone using the monster suit that had been in their holiday rental. To most people it was obvious it was a suit, but the national media in town had hyped it up, attracting attention from all over the country, and the nightly news often featured a reporter barely able to keep the smirk off their face reporting on the latest development in Harlot Bay.

In the blur of work I still found time to talk with the

writers every now and again. They seemed somewhat disappointed that Rufus and Dawn hadn't yet been taken in for questioning or been arrested by Sheriff Hardy. I explained that he needed to gather evidence and that he had them under surveillance, not knowing if that was actually true.

It appeared that since we'd found the suit and carving equipment in their rental property, Red, TJ, Jenna and Jay had considered the mystery solved. They didn't seem too enthused about it however. They seemed quite disappointed that from their view the two attacks and mysterious symbols around town were simply two charlatans putting together a fake documentary.

As for the family and me, well, we knew the truth. There were still wards around the house that the exhausted moms refused to let us help with. Molly and Luce were now staying at home every night so the moms could take the wards off our collective boyfriends' houses. Kira was under a curfew which she wasn't too happy about, but at least she understood why she couldn't go creeping out into the darkness. It was all too easy to look out the window to imagine a monster out in the forest with sharp claws, watching us.

My slip power hadn't resolved itself. I was testing it every now and again, frosting up glasses of water. The stone Aunt Cass had given me infused with the potion was still working well.

On one of the days I'd heard from Red that she'd confronted Markus Hornby, the author who often set up publicity stunts around his books. Despite what Harry Stern had claimed about his cousin being hired by Markus to perform in a publicity stunt to promote his latest book, Marcus denied everything and that was *that*.

Carter Wilkins was still going crazy with his paper, publishing articles every day about the vandalism around town and whom he suspected was behind it. He jumped right on the "monster of Harlot Bay" bandwagon, recognizing it is an excellent opportunity to sell more copies of his newspaper. I think the tourists in town found it all amusing. It certainly didn't hurt business any. The streets were packed every day. Every hotel and motel, and bed and breakfast was sold out, and there were still hoards of vampires and other fans dressed up despite the boiling heat.

I worked every day with Red; her days were packed with writing sessions and we were frequently rushing from one place to another. I was tense and looking forward to the end of Writerpalooza. I'd barely seen Jack as he was too busy with his parents and I was too busy working and then staying home under curfew.

I was at home early one afternoon after Red dropped me off, wandering around the house, thinking that perhaps everything was going to be okay, that the writers would all leave town and then us witches could keep going on about our witchy business in private, when my phone chimed a message from Aunt Cass: *Tonight we take the prize!*

"Oh, great," I grumbled to myself. I was looking at my phone trying to think of some way I could convince Aunt Cass to delay a break-in until at least the media had gone or the writers, when there was a knock at my door.

It was Jack, wearing his work clothes. He grabbed me and kissed me so hard that it left my head spinning. I pulled him inside and closed the door to keep the heat out.

"What are you doing here?" I asked.

"I had to see you, it's been too long," Jack said.

He smelled like sunscreen and wood shavings, which was a delectable combination.

"Have you considered getting out of town? My parents won't mind if I leave. Maybe your whole family can go and the Sterns too," Jack said.

"I considered it but the monster or the man wouldn't

vanish because we did. Maybe that's what happened all those years ago–it couldn't find Stern and Torrent, and so it went on a killing spree," I said.

Jack frowned as he considered this terrible outcome. I could suddenly see why Molly was so upset that we kept talking magic in front of Ollie. Relationships were tough enough without adding magical complications to them.

"Do you think it's going to go on a killing spree?" Jack asked. He was seeming much less small country town builder and much more former policeman with a duty to protect and serve.

"It was saying *killing spree* wasn't it? Brings a few bad images to mind," I said.

"It's not every day that your girlfriend is being hunted by a supernatural monster, is it?" Jack said.

He looked around the house and saw there was no one home except me. Not even Adams was around.

"It's only you here now?" Jack asked, a glint in his eye.

I felt some butterflies start to flutter in my stomach.

"Just me," I said.

"Have you got your magic stone that keeps you warm?" he asked. I pulled it out my pocket and flicked it between my fingers. "Here it is," I said, my voice softening.

"Keep a damn good hold of it," he said before he hefted me over his shoulder and carried me laughing to my bedroom.

CHAPTER TWENTY-FOUR

$\mathscr{I}$t was midnight and the deep and profound relaxation that had come over me after Jack's visit was giving way to the jitters which had three possible causes: one, we were about to engage in some crime; two, the giant coffees me, Molly, Luce and Kira had drunk before coming out; and three, Aunt Cass's driving.

She hit a corner at high speed. I swear the car nearly went up on two wheels. Molly was hanging on for dear life in the front passenger seat. Luce, me and Kira were packed into the back like sardines.

"I'm running a business, I'm engaged, I shouldn't be breaking into museums," Molly wailed.

"Bit anxious are you? I have a potion for that. Take a big gulp and pass it on," Aunt Cass said, pulling out a large silver flask. Molly unscrewed the lid, took a gulp, and winced before passing it on to Luce, who did the same. She gave it to me and I took a huge gulp, hoping it would calm my nerves. The potion burned its way down my throat and into my stomach. I pulled the flask away from my lips and gave it a sniff to be sure. Yup, it was whiskey.

"This isn't a potion. This is whiskey," I said.

"It's a potion if it makes you feel better," Aunt Cass said.

"Harlow, pass it on," Kira said, reaching for the flask. I pulled it away from her, screwed the lid on and passed it back to Molly in the front seat.

"No fair," Kira grumbled.

Thankfully, Aunt Cass had to slow Molly's car down because even at midnight there were still tourists in Harlot Bay. We drove down the main street, took a right and ended up in the street roughly behind where the museum was. Aunt Cass parked behind a building in the shadows. The plan was quite simple: we were going to go into the museum, use concealment spells to cover ourselves from the camera, steal the compass and then get out. Because there were so many cameras, we needed all four of us.

We followed Aunt Cass through the dark towards the museum, heading down a narrow alleyway that adjoined one side of it.

"Good evening witches," a voice said out of the dark. Everyone except for Aunt Cass nearly jumped out of their skins. Thankfully it wasn't the police, but actually a former policeman, Jack, grinning at us as he stepped out of the darkness, carrying a small black bag.

"What are you doing here?" I asked.

"I invited him. He has some useful skills," Aunt Cass said.

"The museum security system is quite good. If you shut off the power it will trigger an alarm, and I'm not sure how many extra cameras they have. But I've seen ones like this before, when I was a police officer. I'm going to help you bypass it," Jack said.

"But you could be arrested!" I said and realized half a second later how absurd that sounded.

"You could be arrested too," Luce murmured.

"It's going to be fine Harlow, besides, this is important. I can't have some supernatural monster stalking my girlfriend and her family and friends and not do anything about it," Jack said.

"You need to *husband* that, pronto," Kira said, pointing at Jack.

"Enough chitchat, let's get moving," Aunt Cass said.

Perhaps Aunt Cass's "potion" had worked because, although I was shocked, I followed along with everyone else until we reached the museum. Jack found a large power box on the outside, which he opened. He removed small wires with clips out of the bag he'd brought and then did some security magic on the box. He turned to us after a moment.

"The cameras aren't recording now. You have about ten minutes," he said.

"This is crazy," Molly said.

"This way," Aunt Cass commanded. We left Jack behind at the power box and went to a small side entrance. Kira used a spell to unlock it and then we crept inside.

In the museum at night the only lights were around some of the exhibits, small glowing pools surrounded by liquid darkness. There were no security guards.

"Let's go," I said as soon as we got inside. Me and Aunt Cass knew the way, so Molly, Luce and Kira followed behind us as we went directly to the *Wreck of the Appalachia* exhibit. It took us about two minutes to get there, another minute for Kira to cast an unlocking spell, and then Aunt Cass to take the compass. She was closing the glass case when we heard whispered voices from the other side of the museum.

"Hide over here," Aunt Cass urged. We bolted away from the light and went to a darkened corner. It was a good thing we moved fast because a moment later four figures emerged out of the darkness, heading towards the *Wreck of the Appalachia* exhibit. Even in the dark it was easy to recognize them thanks to the giant who walked with them. It was the writers. TJ and Jenna split off and vanished into the dark while Red and Jay went to the exhibit.

"What are they doing here?" Luce whispered.

"Obviously after the compass," Aunt Cass said.

"We have to get out of here," I whispered. We moved around the corner as quietly as we could, but then we heard footsteps ahead of us. At the end of the corridor we saw Jenna and TJ creep out of the dark and then stop in place, appearing to have a whispered conversation.

We all froze, pressing ourselves against the wall and waiting in the darkness. Yes, we could have cast a concealment spell over all of us but who knew how much power that would take?

I was standing there with my heart thudding when I felt a small furry shape brush past my legs and then from out of the darkness at our feet Adams spoke.

"I want one extra tin of tuna every day until I die," he said.

"Keep your voice down, this isn't the time to demand food," I whispered.

It was almost impossible to see the small black cat in the dark, but we saw when he flared his claws and scratched them down the side of one of the exhibit stands, setting off small sparks.

"I went into Bella Shade's hotel room and read the next book," Adams said.

"You what!" I whispered.

"I want one extra tin of tuna every day until I die or I'm going to reveal what Carlotta did to Yasmin... and the babies!" he said, dramatically.

I heard Aunt Cass, Molly, Luce and Kira gasp in the darkness.

"No, she wouldn't!" Luce whispered.

"I knew we couldn't trust her," Kira said.

"How many babies?" Molly said.

"Make a deal, Harlow," Aunt Cass said.

"We don't negotiate with terrorists," I whispered.

"I wonder what Andreas thinks of Mitchell stealing the blood ring?" Adams said from the dark, his voice cool and calculating. Molly grabbed me on the arm and squeezed, her fingers digging in.

"Fine, one extra tin of tuna a week for three months and that's it," I whispered.

"Deal. Do you need me to distract those people?" Adams said.

"Go," I said.

Adams vanished off into the darkness. A moment later from the far side of the museum there was a toppling sound of something falling over. It sounded like a thousand tons of metal hitting the ground. TJ and Jenna rushed away and so we made our move. As we reached the exit, Adams appeared out of the dark again.

"Those people are coming!" he said before vanishing again. We went out the door as fast as we could. Jack was outside, closing up the power box and stuffing wires into his bag.

"The silent alarm went off, run!" he urged. He sprinted off into the darkness with us close behind him. We'd barely gotten around the corner when we heard the door to the museum slam open behind us. We didn't stop to see what the writers were doing but continued on our way. Jack said he'd see us later before vanishing off into the dark. The four of us ran to Molly's car, Aunt Cass jumping behind the wheel again. She started it up, hit the gas, and got us out of there as fast as possible. We were two streets away when we heard the police siren. It was hard to tell which direction it was coming from and so there were five very nervous witches as Aunt Cass drove us out of town, thinking that any moment a car with flashing lights was going to come skidding around the corner to pull us over. It was only once we were back at our end of the mansion and safely inside that I felt my heart rate begin to slow.

"We can't keep doing things like that," Molly said, pacing back and forth.

"Why were the writers there? How did they know to go for the compass?" Luce asked.

"I don't know. Maybe they cracked the code on the map and it told them where to go? I'm not sure but it was too close," I said.

"We got what we were looking for. Here, Harlow, you take it, it seemed to work with the map," Aunt Cass said. Everyone held their breath as Aunt Cass passed me the compass but there was no burst of light. Although I could feel a slight tingle of magic, nothing important happened.

"Find monster," I said. The needle didn't move from pointing to true North.

"I need to go to bed," Molly said, rushing off without bothering to say good night. I gave the compass back to Aunt Cass.

"Maybe the compass had nothing to do with all this stuff or it could be broken. Or maybe the spell is worn out," I said.

Aunt Cass tapped a fingernail on the glass and examined it closely.

"This is a witch's compass, it's not going to give up its answers so easily," she said. My phone chimed a message sitting over on the kitchen table (we'd left them at home in case someone tried to call while we were breaking in). It was Jack simply saying he was going to sleep now and he'd see me soon. That helped calm me somewhat but even as I took myself off to bed I couldn't help but think that it had been far too close a call tonight. I also had a lingering worry: what if the writers had seen us? Would they keep quiet? Or would they start to investigate the mysterious Torrent family?

CHAPTER TWENTY-FIVE

"*Y*ou're lucky you're not grounded for that stunt you pulled last night," I told Adams. He didn't say anything but kept purring as he rolled around my feet, giving himself a very thorough dust bath.

I was standing in the front of the mansion waiting for Red and feeling an incredible amount of anxiety. Molly and Luce were already gone to work and had taken Kira with them. If Red or the writers had seen someone last night we didn't want to give them the opportunity to match them to us.

"Did you go into Bella Shade's room?" I asked Adams.

"A cat would never lie," he replied, rolling around.

Aunt Cass had told me to stick to the agreement that we had made—an extra tin of tuna a week for the next three months. I think she was afraid that Adams was going to reveal spoilers about Bella Shade's next book and whether he was lying or not, she admired the cunning of it all.

In the distance I saw the sports car driving up the hill.

"You need to get going in case Red saw you last night," I told Adams. He rolled for a moment more and sat up, licked a shoulder and then paused long enough to tell me that *I couldn't give him instructions* before sauntering off. By the time Red arrived he was gone. I got into the passenger seat and she turned the car around and drove us away from Torrent Mansion. I was tense but it was nothing compared to how Red was obviously feeling. She was gripping her hands on the steering wheel and I think gritting her teeth.

"So are you looking forward to Writerpalooza finishing?" I asked.

I almost cringed when I asked my question. It seemed so obvious I was trying to distract attention from the fact there was something wrong.

Red didn't answer but instead blew out air from between her lips.

"Can I tell you something and trust that it stays private?" she asked.

I knew immediately she was talking about whether I would tell Sheriff Hardy anything she told me.

"I promise it will stay private and I won't tell Sheriff Hardy," I said.

"Last night we went into the Harlot Bay Museum. There was a compass there that, according to our research, possibly had a coded message on it. We'd checked it out earlier that day and then because of the time factor, went to the museum at night to break in and take it. But it was gone and we think someone else was in the museum at the same time we were. Some exhibit got knocked over, an alarm was triggered and we barely escaped before the police arrived," Red said.

I took in a long, slow breath, trying to calm myself. At least it seemed she didn't know it was us, the Torrent witches plus Kira, who had been behind the theft.

"That's quite some story," I said, my voice cracking a little. I cleared my throat and looked out the window, trying to think of what to say.

"There's something very strange going on in Harlot Bay," Red whispered.

"Are you going to be staying after the festival is over?" I asked, trying to keep my voice level.

"Non-fiction isn't my thing... but it is very intriguing," Red said, appearing to be in her own world. We drove the rest of the way to town in silence, heading for Red's first session of the day. I was afraid to speak, lest I give myself away. We arrived at the first session, unloaded the trunk and went inside, only to find Sheriff Hardy waiting for us. He motioned the both of us over.

"Good morning Sheriff," I said, feeling like I wanted to drop the papers and bolt out of there.

Sheriff Hardy didn't even look at me. "I need to speak to Red in private," he said. Red glanced at me and then nodded to Sheriff Hardy.

"Harlow, leave the materials here, I can handle them. You take the rest the day off," she instructed.

I put the papers and books on the ground and then stumbled away in a bit of a daze. Was Sheriff Hardy about to arrest Red? I hadn't even thought to get in contact with him. Should I maybe try to speak with him privately? Tell him the truth that it was *us* breaking in, and we did it for what we thought was a very good reason, to stop whatever this magical monster was that was in Harlot Bay.

I walked down the main street debating with myself over what I should do, heading vaguely in the direction of *Traveler* where I knew I could borrow Molly's car to drive home, seeing as I now had the rest the day off. I wasn't paying much attention, which is why I walked directly into Jack's dad.

"Oh my Goddess I'm sorry," I blurted out before I realized who it was. It was him and Jas, I guess out for a walk. Both of them were smiling at me, oblivious to the turmoil that was churning inside my mind.

"Good to see you Harlow! Not going to run off this time are you?" Jon said.

Jas whacked him on the arm and I gave both of them an embarrassed smile.

"I'm not planning on running away this time," I said.

"We were hoping we could have another dinner with you before we left. What do you think?" Jas asked me.

In the distance over their shoulders I noticed Rufus and Dawn out on the street holding a newspaper. Even from here I could tell it was a copy of *The Harlot Bay Times*. Dawn was shaking it and talking to Rufus as though she was angry, and then they both looked in my direction. Dawn pointed and then they came barreling down the sidewalk towards me.

"Um… sure, that would be great," I said. I had a sudden strong desire to run again but no matter what, not even if there was an angry bull bearing down on me, was I going to run away from Jack's parents again and have them think that I was crazy.

"Are you working at Writerpalooza today?" Jon asked.

"Today I actually have the day off," I said, trying to think of a way to carefully disengage myself from the situation before Rufus and Dawn could get to me. But they were moving too fast and I realized with a sinking stomach that whatever was going to happen was going to happen right in front of Jack's parents.

Dawn came up brandishing the newspaper like a weapon. "We know you're behind this!" she yelled at me. She held the newspaper up so I could read the headline. It said: 'Mysterious Mysteries Fake Monster Suit!' It was written by Carter and at a brief glance, I could see that he claimed to have evidence that they had a fake monster suit and that he'd seen someone wearing it.

"Don't you have anything to say?" Rufus demanded.

I wasn't quite sure what I was going to say but before any

words could leave my mouth, both Jon and Jas stepped forward.

"You need to back off right now," Jon growled. He looked the vision of Jack, strong and tall and not to be messed with. A moment later I realized this was nothing compared to Jas.

"She's a journalist and you're some two-bit con artists. She can report on you if she wants!" she said, breathing fire. She stomped on Rufus's foot and he fell over with a squawk. It all happened so fast I didn't know quite what to do. Suddenly, she was nose to nose with Dawn.

"She's *family*. Do you want to start something because I'm feeling a little hot and being hot makes me *crazy*," Jas said in an undertone.

Dawn went from belligerent anger to clear panic in a second flat. She dropped the newspaper, hauled Rufus up from the ground and then pulled him away down the street, him hobbling to keep up with her. Jas turned towards me, her eyes still slightly wild.

"Sorry about that, we're not going to let anyone harass our family members," she said.

"Come on Jas, they're girlfriend and boyfriend, let's not make it *that* serious," Jon said, trying to make a joke to calm everyone down.

Jas turned to him, "You come on! Have you seen the way Jack looks at her? Oh, and the way Jonas looks at Peta? We're going to have two new daughters-in-law any day now, I guarantee it," she said.

"Um... what?" I croaked.

"We have to get going, time for breakfast, gotta go. Hopefully we'll see you soon," Jon said, pulling Jas away with him.

"It's true love, Harlow, I've seen it before!" Jas called out as she was hauled away.

Sheriff Hardy questioning Red had certainly knocked me off balance, but this had made me feel the entire planet had been knocked off its axis. I renewed my walk down the street, this time speeding up, rushing to get to *Traveler* so I could borrow Molly's car and get home where I could stay in the peace and quiet and hope nothing else happened to me today.

Part of the family? It was simultaneously a terrifying and lovely idea.

CHAPTER TWENTY-SIX

$\mathcal{I}$ stood up from my hard wooden chair, feeling my back protesting, and glared at the wall of crazy.

It sat there looking crazy and... complicated.

After I'd come home on my unexpected day off I'd soon found myself pacing between the lounge and kitchen wondering what was going to happen to Red. Would she be arrested? What if someone had seen her or the other writers entering or leaving the museum? There were hundreds of exhibits at the Harlot Bay Museum so perhaps it was possible the theft of the compass would slip by, but perhaps it hadn't. Maybe even right now the police were working on the case.

It hadn't taken long before I realized I was going to drive myself crazy so I left our end of the mansion and went to my lair in one of the cottages up in the forest. I hadn't been in there in some weeks but unlike my office in town there wasn't a layer of dust covering everything. There was just the wall of crazy covered in notes and pieces of paper and old articles, the table and chair, and Juliet Stern's journal.

I spent the rest of the morning and a good part of the afternoon going through the journal page by page, looking for any mention of Juliet's husband or Marguerite or her husband. But the journal was the same as it ever was. The mundane recordings of running *The Merchant Arms*, pages of eggs and flour and ingredients for beer being delivered. The rare times that Juliet wrote about something occurring in the town it was minor or on the level of gossip. But I was very aware that this was a magical journal. In the past I'd experienced a memory traveling along with Marguerite Torrent with Juliet Stern, chasing the Shadow Witch and seeing the tragedy that had resulted from that: Juliet's daughter dying and Marguerite almost losing her daughter, Rosetta.

Thanks to Ollie we now knew that Rosetta had had a daughter herself, our grandmother's grandmother and the line had carried on down to us. There were no traces however, of what had happened to Juliet and Marguerite's husbands.

I'd gone through the journal front to back, reading each page and then flipping to random pages, hoping that I would come upon something that might explain the man or the monster that was currently stalking Torrents and Sterns in Harlot Bay. Aunt Cass had said that the magic turning gritty, the feeling of it, was the same as what she'd experienced out on Truer Island when a monster had come out of nowhere and attacked her. That battle had ended in an enormous explosion that created a hole in the ground half a mile across. Was that what was required here? Would we have to hunt down the monster and then detonate a large portion of the countryside? What if the monster tried to attack one of us while we were in town? That outcome seemed bad enough but what was worse was the idea that one of us, or the Sterns, could be attacked. Or if the monster couldn't get at one of us, perhaps it would start killing random tourists.

Despite my urgent desire to find some clue, some piece of information that might lead us to an answer, Juliet's journal refused to help me. It was now late afternoon and I was going between the wall and the journal, perhaps pointlessly, not knowing what else I could do. It was clear at least that there was some connection to me in all of this. The map had lit up in my hands leading us to the compass, but now the compass wouldn't work.

I paced the small cottage, two or three steps in one direction before turning around and heading back again. My mind began to drift onto Jack. Maybe he was right and we should get out of town. Perhaps permanently. I was a Slip witch and so staying in Harlot Bay was good for me because the magical confluence helped calm me. But given how often I'd slipped and how many strange things went on in our town, I was starting to think that living somewhere far less magical might be the better outcome. Of course the last time that had happened I had awoken in the night to the sound of fire alarms, and the apartment I was staying in had burnt to the ground.

I looked out the window, seeing the sun was setting. Soon it would be twilight. Molly and Luce had already messaged me to say that I didn't need to return to pick them up. They would catch a ride home with Aunt Freya, so at least I was off the hook for that. As I looked out the window towards the setting sun I saw shadows hugging the trees in the forest. Was there a man standing in them right now watching me? One perhaps cursed to murder or perhaps willing to do so? I turned away from the window with a shiver.

I picked up Juliet's journal again and flicked to a random page. More supplies for *The Merchant Arms*, eggs and flour. As I held the journal, frost began to climb up over the pages, spreading out from my hands. It had been too long since I'd touched the magical stone that Aunt Cass had given me.

"Argh!" I said and slammed the journal down on the table.

I grabbed the stone and began rubbing it between my fingers, starting up my pacing again.

"Why don't you tell me what happened to your husbands? The man we saw, he thought I was Marguerite so which one is he? Benjamin or Johannes?" I said. I realized I was shouting at the journal, sounding like a crazy person. I glared at the wall again, looking at the various notes I'd put up. It was a convoluted mess and I had the sudden desire to rip it all down and shred it into pieces. I was on the verge of summoning a fireball to do just that when another soft, quieter part of my mind spoke up: *there is a spell on you.*

I shook my head. Aunt Cass was right. There *was* something pushing on us, that persistent force and it was getting weaker. I had never been able to sit up here and look at the wall of crazy for this long before. I'd always get distracted, end up tapping away on my phone, or writing my novel instead. Now I'd been up here for hours, concentrating intensely.

I looked back at the journal and then gave a double blink. I'd slammed it shut when I dropped it on the table but now it was sitting open to a page. The writing on the page had a golden shimmer to it, as though it was living ink. I grabbed the journal and read the single entry on the page.

I was forced to lock the men away. The curse is far too strong, I cannot break it alone. When Torrent returns, we may attempt it, but I fear we will fail. I have hidden them in the deep dark place. Their names will find them.

The moment I read the entry the journal snapped shut, as though it had a life of its own. I immediately grabbed it and flicked through the pages but the journal had reverted to its usual secretive self. I dropped it back onto the table.

Their names will find them.

I knew their names. Johannes Tilson had married Marguerite Torrent and had a daughter Rosetta. Benjamin

Mainer had married Juliet Stern. The names came to me easily and I knew what I needed. I rushed out of the cottage, heading back to our end of the mansion where my phone was. I came bursting in through the door, intent on calling Aunt Cass to tell her to come home so I could have the compass only to find her sitting on our sofa, holding it in her hand. I stopped short when I saw her.

"The strangest thing, the compass started glowing and then spinning. I could feel something was happening over here... so what have you found?" Aunt Cass said.

"Juliet's journal has given me a clue," I said. I took the compass from her and held it in my hand.

"Benjamin Mainer," I whispered to it. The needle didn't move.

"Johannes Tilson," I said.

The surge of magic took us both by surprise. The needle spun and then finally slowed, now pointing in a new direction–directly towards Truer Island.

"My trap is nearly ready. We'll take the family and go tomorrow," Aunt Cass said.

I passed her the compass. "Keep it safe," I said.

I glanced out the window where the lengthening shadows were creeping up to the house. An odd sort of calmness had come over me. The monster or man had been stalking Stern and Torrent but now we would be stalking *it*.

CHAPTER TWENTY-SEVEN

*T*he moms' argument had been at a low simmer all morning and now was threatening to boil over completely.

"It puts the Sheriff, my husband, in a very bad position," Aunt Ro said in clipped tones.

We continued to unload our gear from the trunk of the car. None of us wanted to get dragged into this argument. Aunt Cass pulled the trap out of the trunk and gave it to Molly to carry. It was essentially a hoop made of thorns. Molly was already wearing the gardening gloves Aunt Cass had given her so she could carry it safely.

"We can't let innocent people be arrested for things they didn't do," Mom repeated.

"Which way Harlow?" Aunt Cass said, ignoring the argument.

I checked the compass. It was pointing in a direction through the thick forest.

"We go that way," I said. Aunt Cass nodded at me to lead and so I did, my cousins, Kira and Aunt Cass following behind with the moms bringing up the rear.

"They're not exactly innocent are they? They were found with carving tools and spray paint and also a monster suit. How do we know they didn't attack those two men?" Aunt Ro said.

The publication of Carter's article had sent the national media in town into overdrive and had forced Sheriff Hardy's hand. Carter had captured footage of Dawn and Rufus spray painting one of the strange symbols around town. They were taken in for questioning, their rental searched, and of course the suit, carving equipment and spray paint all found. The law now had everything they needed to nail Rufus and Dawn to the wall. The argument that had been simmering away all morning was whether we, as witches who knew that something supernatural was happening, and as also being behind some of the spray painted symbols in town ourselves, had a responsibility to tell Sheriff Hardy that Rufus and Dawn were innocent.

Sheriff Hardy was aware that something was going on but in typical witchy fashion Aunt Ro hadn't told him everything. It appeared now that she, like Molly, was uncomfortable with the idea of revealing the true depths of our witchy nature to her newly married husband.

"If we give him proof that it wasn't Rufus and Dawn, then surely Sheriff Hardy can use his influence to set them free," Mom said.

"No, you can't do that! Molly was right. Where are *our* husbands? Where are *their* fathers? Gone and for all of the same reason: too much witchiness. If we manage to catch this monster or man or whatever it is today, I'll let him know, but I'm not going to put any pressure on him to change the outcome for the *Mysterious Mysteries*," Aunt Ro said, her voice rising to a yell.

"There are bigger things happening in Harlot Bay than some people being arrested," Aunt Cass snapped. That kept the moms quiet for a few minutes as we marched through the forest, which although it was in deep shadow was still quite warm.

"I don't think it's a good idea that we tell Sheriff Hardy that we were spray painting around town," Molly said.

"That we were *blackmailed* into spray painting around town," Luce said in a dark tone.

"I appreciate the general position that the innocent should not be arrested, but he is my husband, not a pawn to be pushed about. We didn't cause Rufus and Dawn's problems," Aunt Ro said.

We continued marching in silence, Kira tapping away at her phone until the signal dropped out and then shoving it into a pocket. When we'd gone out to Truer Island that morning we hoped we would be able to drive to wherever the compass was taking us, but it soon became evident that there was no road where we wanted to go. We'd driven around, even going past the old Governor's mansion, seeing the compass turn as we went. We finally stopped at a dead-end road and headed off cross country. The plan was simple. Use Aunt Cass's trap to capture the monster or man and then see if we could question it to discover why it had attacked two people with the last name of Stern, and why it had been watching us.

Although the plan appeared simple it didn't mean there wasn't a lot of anxiety amongst us witches. On top of all that, the moms were still tired from working late at the bakery, trying to look after the bed-and-breakfast, and maintaining the wards. They'd finally let those spells go this morning which had helped them recover a small amount of energy, but frankly the three of them were exhausted. Aunt Cass wasn't much better. She'd been up all night finishing the trap and kept yawning into the back of her hand. She was carrying her crowbar, the one with her name inscribed on it, and had a determined expression on her face.

We marched in silence for a while until Mom cleared her throat, obviously getting ready to talk again to Aunt Ro, but Aunt Cass had had enough. She whirled around and glared at everyone.

"I'll take care of it! No one is going to have to reveal anything, okay?" she said.

"What are you going to do? Put the whole town under a spell? There's national media here, so many eyes, and everyone knows what they found where they were staying," Aunt Ro said.

Aunt Cass sighed and shook her head at the moms.

"You want my plan? Fine, here it is. I'm going to make sure that Rufus and Dawn are either locked up or very far away from Harlot Bay and then I'm going to carve that strange symbol into as many doors as I can and paint it all over town. I'm also going to set up a fake monster sighting. It'll muddy the waters. If there are *many* people doing it, then it can't be them. Besides, according to what Harlow said, the monster claws had paint on them, not blood. In the end, this is going to be good for the *Mysterious Mysteries*," Aunt Cass said.

"But that's... okay I guess... that's the best we have," Mom said. Aunt Cass whirled around and pointed the crowbar into the forest.

"Quick march, let's go," she said. We continued through the forest, branches cracking under our feet, leaves rustling, and hearing the occasional bird singing in the distance. The day was only getting hotter and it seemed that every living thing in this area had gone to ground, except of course us who were stupid enough to be trudging towards some kind of supernatural monster.

It was another full hour of trudging before we finally

emerged from the forest into a field that led down into a small valley and a dark opening in the ground.

"Please tell me it's not down that murder hole," Molly said.

"The compass is pointing in that direction," I said. We walked across the field and down the hill, heading towards the dark opening. At Aunt Cass's instruction I took a wide arc around the hole and watched the compass needle move, showing that that was where we needed to go. I returned to the family who were gathered outside the hole, my cousins peering anxiously into the dark and Kira trying to use the light on her phone to see further into the inky black.

"It's where the compass says we should go," I said.

"Molly, give Harlow the trap, I'm going to need you beside me," Aunt Cass said.

Molly handed over the gardening gloves which I slipped on and then picked up the trap. It didn't weigh much but I could feel the buzz of magic within it and the spikes looked sharp and wicked.

"We stick together and we'll be fine. If we see it we must try to catch it first, but if it attacks then we obliterate it," Aunt Cass said.

"I hate this part," Luce said. We followed Aunt Cass down into the cave and into the darkness. As soon as we were inside, we threw glowing balls of light so we could see what we were doing. The cave entrance was dark and cool and we could hear the sound of rushing water somewhere in the distance. The temperature dropped noticeably too, and when we breathed out you could see plumes of condensation coming from our mouths.

Aunt Cass took the lead with Molly close beside her, and then me, and everyone else following behind. The cave was deep and dark, exactly as Juliet's journal had described. The dirt floor underneath was flat and smooth and led down in a gentle gradient. It was almost as though the cave had been designed by someone to make it easy to access and move around. As we descended, the air grew cooler and we began to see black and green moss appearing on the walls. It wasn't long before we saw the deep scratches as well, carved into the stone as if by sharpened claws.

"Wouldn't it be easier if we used a few sticks of dynamite and collapsed this whole thing?" Luce said, running her finger along one of the scratches.

"It would work, but we need to talk to that man. It's important. I can feel it," Aunt Cass said. We continued down until the cave turned and then opened into a large amphitheater with multiple dark passageways heading off in every direction. Under our feet it grew wet. There were puddles everywhere and the constant sound of dripping in time with the rushing water in the distance.

"Compass check Harlow," Aunt Cass whispered. I checked the compass then stepped out in front of Aunt Cass and Molly, taking the lead. A moment later I realized what a colossally stupid idea that was when I took a step, and the ground wasn't there. All I saw was a flash of dark as I slipped down a hole and fell. There was the barest of moments of rushing wind in the pitch darkness before I plunged into a deep lake of cold water. Somehow I managed to keep hold of the trap, looking up to see one of the lights follow me down and bubbles of air floating towards the surface. I swam upwards and broke the surface of the water, hearing my family shout over the sound of my own shocked breathing.

"I'm here. I'm okay, I fell into a lake. I still have the trap," I called out.

More balls of light floated down from the hole in the roof. I caught a glimpse of the moms looking down at me. I was in another large amphitheater type cave system, except this one had a deep lake in the middle. Holding onto the trap

I swam over to the side and pulled myself out. There was rocky ground here, but it was still knee deep in water.

"Stay where you are, we'll find a way down to you!" Aunt Cass called out.

"I'm not going anywhere!" I called out and then suddenly wondered whether it was wise to be shouting so loud in a cave that supposedly held a monster. As I listened to the sound of my own voice echo away I heard another voice calling my name.

"Harlow? What's happening?" It was Jack. I saw his face appear at the hole and in the glimmer of the light saw his eyes were gleaming blue.

I heard the moms, Aunt Cass, my cousins, and maybe even Kira, talking with Jack, trying to explain what it was we were doing.

"I'm okay," I called out.

"Are you out of the lake?" Jack yelled back.

"Yes!"

A moment later there was an enormous splash as Jack jumped down the hole and landed in the water. I shot a cold ball of light out over the lake, seeing bubbles fizzing to the top before Jack finally emerged and then swam over to where I was. He pulled himself out of the water and then shivered at the sudden cold. He was wearing his building clothes which meant shorts and a T-shirt plus a pair of boots.

"Maybe next time you go hunting monsters you can tell me and I'll help you," he said before grabbing me in an enormous hug. The hug was brief however. Jack pulled away as lines of frost began to creep up his body. I reached for the stone but it was gone. I must have lost it in the lake. I looked down and saw that ice was beginning to collect around my legs where I was chilling the water down to freezing point. Oh Goddess, the cold had spread outside my hands again.

"Great, I'm going to become an icicle," I complained.

Then I looked back at Jack, who was still watching me with those eyes that hovered on the spot between blue and green. My light, affected by my Slip witch power, was cold, rather than warm yellow and in it his eyes now appeared green. He was watching me, waiting for my answer.

"You're right. The next time I go hunting supernatural monsters I'll make sure to tell you so you can help," I said.

"I was working and I saw two carloads of witches go driving by so I knew something was up," Jack said.

It hadn't even occurred to me that Jack would be at work today when we'd driven past the Governor's mansion.

"Here we are and I think I need to keep moving before I freeze solid," I said.

"Let's go then," Jack said.

I picked up Aunt Cass's trap. I lost one of the gardening gloves but I still had the other. It wasn't going well though. The water that had gotten inside of it had started to freeze against my skin. At least the glove was stopping the ice from spreading out to the trap itself. Goddess knows how it might be affected by that. I sent the ball of light drifting up towards the ceiling and saw only Kira looking down. It appeared the rest of the family had gone rushing off to see if they could find a way down to me.

"Do you know the direction out of here?" Jack asked.

"Oh crap," I said as I realized I didn't have the compass. I looked towards the center of the deep dark lake and knew that it would be somewhere on the bottom.

"Let's pick a direction and keep moving," I said. There were at least five dark cave exits from where we were so I picked the first one at random and followed along behind my cold bobbing light, feeling ice forming around my legs and then breaking off as I sloshed through the water. Jack began rubbing his arms with his hands, trying to keep his body temperature up. If there had been any heat down here I could have possibly pulled it out of whatever it was in and given it to Jack to warm him up, but it was simply freezing underground, wet and cold, dark and damp.

"Is that meant to catch the monster?" Jack said, his teeth beginning to chatter.

"That's what we're hoping," I said. We kept sloshing through the water, slowly heading upwards before dipping again. We entered into another large cavern, this one with some dry areas around the sides. I sent my light floating up to the roof and then gasped aloud at what I saw. The walls were covered in scratches, lines of five, carved in every surface. Someone or something had been down here for a very long time, counting the passing of the years.

"Here take the trap. Throw it if you see anything running at us," I said to Jack. I had to drop it on the ground and then break the ice out of the glove to get it off before Jack could pick it up. Thanks to the Slip witch power of mine I wasn't feeling the temperature much and honestly had no idea whether I'd be able to throw a fireball, but if anything came running at us from the darkness I sure as hell was going to try.

I saw there was a single exit on the other side of the cavern and somewhere far down it I could hear Aunt Cass, my cousins and the moms shouting out to me.

"Let's go that way," I said and then a sudden bitterness filled my mouth as the magic around me turned gritty and sour. A dark shape fell from the roof, landing in front of us. It was so quick, a blur of black.

Both of us jumped back, Jack having the presence of mind to throw the trap and a moment later the monster stepped into it. There was a surge of magic that I could feel was Aunt Cass's, imbued in the trap. A glowing green light lit up the ring of thorns, encasing the monster, weaving up around it like a cage before fading in luminescence. In the jump I tripped and had landed on my butt on the ground along with Jack. Both of us got to our feet, staring at the hideous abomination in front of us. It was a monster covered in dark matted hair, its eyes gleaming yellow, its face some hideous confusion between a wolf and a man. It was as Aunt Cass had described the monster she'd encountered. There was something wrong with it, like it didn't belong here. I found it hard to look at its face, the skin appearing to shift and ripple.

The monster growled from within its cage and clenched its hands, the wickedly sharp claws on the ends of its fingers glinting in the cold light above us. It tried to step out of the circle of thorns, but the cage around it shimmered green light and it could not escape.

"We still need to get out of here in case that trap doesn't hold," I said to Jack.

At the sound of my voice the monster started and then, between one blink and the next there was no longer a monster trapped in the cage, but a man. It was the one Aunt Cass and I had seen in the forest on the night of the dinner. He was wearing ragged clothes not from our time. He had black hair and blue eyes.

"Marguerite?" he asked, peering at me. I stepped closer, bringing the light down from the ceiling so he could see me properly.

"I'm not her. I think I look like her," I said in a quiet voice. "Are you Johannes? Marguerite's husband?" I asked.

The man nodded and then looked me up and down again before glancing at Jack.

"I am but that is my formal name. Those who know me call me –"

"Jack," I finished.

"You have the look of a Torrent about you. Some more of that witchy business I imagine. Tell me, do you have two sisters or two cousins? I've heard the patterns repeat again and again," he said.

"Two cousins," I said.

"I'm Jack too. Are you the monster who has been stalking Stern and Torrent?" Jack asked.

"Yes, I am. Best call me Johannes if there is two of us," he said, his voice grim.

I went to move closer to get a better look at him and realized my feet were stuck to the ground. I hadn't noticed I'd been standing in a puddle which now was frozen solid.

"Why were you hunting us? Why did you attack those men?" I asked, trying to pull my feet free of the ice.

The faint shimmering cage of green around Johannes lit up before fading in luminescence and he brought his hands up to his head as though it was aching.

"Our wives fought the darkness too well and then it fought back, dark witches cursing Benjamin and I to these hideous forms. Cursing us with the desire to kill anyone with the names of Torrent and Stern. Juliet had to lock us away after the deaths on the island," Johannes said through gritted teeth.

"Was Benjamin locked in here too? Did he escape?" I asked.

"He was locked away with me, but then both of us sensed it. There was a Torrent near. We could not help but want to attack and the seal, after all these years, was weak. He managed to escape before it locked tight, but then there was an explosion, something that weakened the seal and I felt his death. Eventually the seal broke and I could finally escape," he said.

The green cage around him shimmered again and this time I saw there were cracks through the light, as though the magic was failing to hold.

"Jack, you need to get my feet free," I said urgently. Jack

grabbed my leg and tried to pull it out of the ice but it was stuck fast.

In the distance I could still hear my family shouting. It was hard to know if they were getting any closer. The green cage around Johannes shimmered again and this time I saw it clearly, a cobweb of cracks spreading out. It was getting weaker.

"Step back. I have an idea," I said to Jack. He moved away and I tried to throw a small fireball at my feet, hoping it would be enough to melt the ice. But no magic came. The mere presence of Johannes had soured it, made it bitter, and possibly my own Slip power was interfering.

"I'm sorry," Johannes moaned, grabbing his head again. He screwed up his face in great pain and crouched down, and began rocking from side to side. I saw his feet were starting to lengthen and grow, his toenails turning into sharpened claws.

"Can you stomp on the ice?" I said to Jack. He did his best, but it was like stomping on an ice-skating rink and expecting it to break under your feet. Johannes looked up at us, his face a mask of pain.

"Why did you curse our children?" he called out.

"Please try to fight it Johannes," I yelled out in panic. The transformation that had begun at his feet was rippling up his body, his clothing merging into his skin.

"Find Marguerite, I feel her presence still," he said to me through clenched teeth. He stood up and hit his hands against the green cage. There was a flash of green light and I saw the cracks in the shimmering bars had almost entirely encircled him.

"I can't get you out Harlow," Jack said.

"You need to kill me. Please," Johannes moaned and then that moan turned into a howl as the transformation consumed him. The monster was back with its sharpened claws and hideous face. The man was gone.

"Family!" I yelled out.

I felt a rush of magic, and Jack was forcefully pushed away from me. In the blur of it I got the sense that it was Mom. Next, a fireball came shooting out the dark, landing directly between my feet and then I was free of the ice. I was burned but in the shock of everything that was happening I barely felt it.

The circle of thorns burst into flame and just like that the trap was gone and the monster dived towards me. I raised my arms and then I Slipped once more. I couldn't grab the magic that was normally around us and so I grabbed the dark that Johannes the monster had caused. A great and powerful burst of cold shot out of my hands and hit the monster as it was diving towards me.

I jumped out of the way and then there was an enormous shattering sound as the frozen monster hit the ground and broke into pieces. I was up on my feet a moment later, gasping and shaking, Jack on one side, Molly and Luce on the other. The room filled with light, every witch throwing up their own ball of light, showing the thousands of scratches spread across the ceiling and down the walls, and the remains of the monster, now little more than fragments of ice. As we watched, despite the cold, they melted away and soon were gone.

"Let's get out of here before you freeze to death," Aunt Cass said. There was no argument from us. I was exhausted and couldn't cast any more magic, but my cousins and the moms helped, flinging up warm balls of light that drifted around us, their glowing nimbus akin to standing near a roaring fire. We followed Aunt Cass back out through the cave and upwards. My legs were still covered in pieces of ice that the fireball had failed to melt, but as we neared the surface the rotating balls of light helped melt them away. Finally we reached Kira in the upper amphitheater.

"That was crazy, what did I feel?" she said, her eyes wide in the dark.

"We found the monster but it's gone now," I said, feeling myself on the edge of exhaustion. Perhaps it was the tiredness that we all felt or maybe we were being reckless, but no one doused their magic lights as we walked out of the cave, straight into the four writers staring at us and the glowing balls of heat floating around our heads.

"What is this?" TJ said. I saw all of them looking at me, their mouths hanging open, shocked out of their minds.

"Harlow?" Red asked.

I felt Aunt Cass's spell moving from behind me. In silent agreement every witch gave it power, and then it shot out towards the four writers like lightning.

"I'm sorry," I said to Red before the spell hit and her face went blank. Aunt Cass was like a surgeon with the memory spell. We doused the rotating balls of light and heat as the writers stood slack-faced, and then marched past them, heading in the direction of our cars. It was only when we were on the edge of the field going back into the forest that Aunt Cass flung back a final spell and the writers continued their way into the cave system.

"But isn't it dangerous? What if they fall down the hole or find all the scratches?" I asked.

"They won't fall down any hole and maybe they'll find something that finally satisfies their curiosity. After all, the more eyes are on this, the weaker it gets," Aunt Cass said.

With Jack, my family and Kira around me as we trudged through the forest, I was riding the manic edge of exhaustion thinking only of what Johannes had said to me. "Why did you curse our children?" he'd asked. He thought I was Marguerite, his wife, Marguerite Torrent our long lost ancestor. The four stones that I had found had a new potential meaning: Johannes his formal name, but everyone called him Jack. *Lost witch took Jack.* Did it mean that Juliet Stern was the Lost witch? After all, she'd locked him and her own husband away. As we trudged through the forest I couldn't speak, but I chewed this over with every step. He'd said he felt Marguerite still. Perhaps like the Shadow Witch she'd managed to extend her life beyond its natural end.

"Did it say anything to you down there?" Aunt Cass asked.

"The man was Johannes, Marguerite Torrent's husband, our ancestor, and this is what he told me ..." I said to my family.

And then I told them.

CHAPTER TWENTY-EIGHT

*B*y the time the writers drove up to the mansion
for their final goodbyes I was *mostly* over my guilt
about helping cast a memory spell on them.

Despite the craziness out at the caves, normality had
reasserted itself... although it had seemed quite strange that I
had to return to work the very next day for the closing ceremony of Writerpalooza. I'd been a bundle of nerves, half
expecting that as soon as Red and the other authors saw me
they'd blurt out "She's a witch! We saw her do magic!" But
nothing of the sort had happened. Aunt Cass's spell had
worked perfectly. Red even told me how they had come to be
out at the caves. Their expert code breaker had indeed
extracted a message from their photograph of the map which
had been a series of instructions on how to find the deep
dark cave. For some reason unknown to us, the creator of
the map, who we assumed was Juliet Stern, had both written
the instructions on it in code and also made the compass,
possibly as a backup. The code had been broken and so the
four writers had come out to Truer Island following the
instructions until it led them to the cave where they'd run

into us. We weren't in their memories however. According to Red they'd entered the caves, explored, but found nothing more than the cavern with the scratches on the roof and the walls. The writers weren't sure what to make of it. Now they considered that perhaps it had been a giant hoax all along. The hidden map, the code, the symbols around town, part of some incredible scheme trying to draw attention to the town.

Aunt Cass was waiting until they were out of town to start up her symbol carving and fake monster sightings that we hoped would clear Rufus and Dawn.

Although I deeply wished I could tell them the truth I simply couldn't, so they were stuck with only half the story and an unsatisfying one at that. Red told me that Sheriff Hardy had questioned her about the museum break in. It had been the same night that Carter had filmed Rufus and Dawn and their fake monster suit. He'd spotted the writers in town. The writers had denied everything, of course, and because Jack had disabled the security system there was no footage showing anyone in the museum.

So the end of Writerpalooza had slipped by, the Town Hall being filled with vampires and other people in costumes, the writers giving their final goodbyes to the massive crowd.

It was now the next day and most of the tourists who had come for Writerpalooza were now leaving town. I was outside the end of our mansion with Kira, who had her suit-case waiting for her grandmother Hattie to pick her up. It wasn't long before TJ's yellow truck was spotted driving up the hill and soon he'd parked it in front of our end of the mansion and all the writers jumped out, rushing over to give me a hug.

"It's been a wild time, Harlow. Thanks for showing us your crazy town," TJ said, squeezing me in his giant arms.

"That's okay," I squeaked from somewhere within his chest. Next was Jenna who was much shorter than me and then I felt I was doing to her what TJ had just done.

"It's been amazing Harlow," she said. "When you finish your book, send it to me," she said.

"No, send it to me. I want to be the one who discovers her," Jay said, laughing. He gave me a hug and then stepped back as Red pulled me away from him and into her arms.

"No, you send it to *me*. You're the one who was working for me and I want to be the one who discovered you," Red said, squeezing me in an enormous hug. I was happy, beaming at them, but I felt a sudden pang of sadness. It had been for a good cause that I, along with my witchy family, had messed with their memories but I wasn't feeling good about it right now. Red must've seen what I was thinking on my face.

"What's the matter darling?" she said.

"I guess I wish you'd found something out at that cave, that there was somehow this made sense for you?" I said.

Red shrugged and smiled at me.

"It's only stories that need to make sense. To have an ending, a direction and meaning. Reality doesn't have to do anything like that. It's full of dead ends and pointless detours, mysteries with no ending. This was one of them. Charlatans in town, a faked monster attack that turned possibly real, and I guess some time in the future we'll hear whether Rufus and Dawn of the *Mysterious Mysteries* were behind it. Was a great adventure while it lasted but not everything is always going to be wrapped up in a neat little package with a bow," she said.

"I guess," I said, smiling back at them.

"See ya Harlow," Kira said from beside me. I realized that Hattie had arrived.

"See you later K-Fresh," I called out, watching the

teenager walk over to her grandmother's car. I felt an urge to go over to talk to Hattie. I remembered that I'd promised her sometime in the past that I'd go out to her farm to work with her. She'd been the one who told me to set up a lair of my own, to examine things, to find the holes and to work on them. I'd promised to go out to see her again and then avoided it for months on end.

"We have to get going now, we've a long drive," Red said. I looked back at the writers and then said my goodbyes, feeling torn in the moment. Aunt Cass had appeared, helped Kira load her luggage into the trunk of the car, and then was next to Hattie's window. I saw Hattie pass back the amulet that Aunt Cass had given her, except now it was blackened as though it had been in a great fire.

"We'll see you some other time Harlow," Red said and gave me a wink. "Harlot Bay has something strange going on. If you're living here, you should write about it," she said.

I said goodbye to the writers and they piled into TJ's yellow truck before driving off down the road, Hattie following close behind them.

"What happened to that amulet?" I called out to Aunt Cass. She brought it over. It was melted and blackened with soot.

"I have no idea. Hattie told me it worked, but she wouldn't tell me what she was doing," Aunt Cass said.

"Typical secretive old witch," I quipped.

Aunt Cass gave me a look as though she was judging whether I was being sarcastic.

"This typical secretive old witch needs to get back to the lab to finish that stone for you, if that's okay," Aunt Cass said and then went marching off back towards the other end of the mansion. I was still frosting things up when I touched them and Aunt Cass had given me a dose of potion to help me but we didn't want a reoccurrence of what had happened last time so she was making me another stone until this frost power wore off.

Suddenly, I was all alone out on the road. Jack was at work. Sometime tonight there was a final dinner with his parents that I *wasn't* going to run away from. My cousins were at work too and so were the moms. And me? I was back to being gainfully unemployed now that Writerpalooza was over.

I was standing on the road wondering what I should do, whether I should return to town and my abandoned office, when Adams brushed past my legs winning himself a thin coat of frost for his trouble. He didn't seem to mind. He threw himself in the dust and began rolling around. I dabbed a small amount of potion on my leg and felt a flush of heat.

"Is it another week yet? Can I have some more tuna?"

"It's not another week," I said. Adams may have been able to blackmail us, but as a cat he was somewhat hazy on what date it was exactly and so if he was going to pull a fast one on us, I decided I'd pull a fast one on him.

"It feels like it has been a week," Adams said, purring and rolling around. I scratched him behind the ears and then wandered off, heading around the end of the mansion and up into the grounds behind it. I soon found myself in my lair, flicking through Juliet's journal. There were still so many questions. Why had the map responded to me? What did Johannes mean when he said "why did you curse our children"?

Last time I'd directly asked the journal a question it had answered. I thought I may as well try it again. I put the journal on the table, opened it to a random page and then addressed it.

"Tell me what happened to Marguerite Torrent," I asked.

I was expecting nothing would happen or, at the very most, the pages would flick open and perhaps I would see a new entry appear. Instead, the journal shot off the table and hit the wall of crazy. As it did, an enormous burst of flame came out of it and by the time the journal fell to the ground the entire wall was ablaze in magical fire. The heat of it washed over me in a wave, along with the jolt of magic. It felt like the magic from standing in that cave, dark and bitter. I reached for the journal but it was too hot, so I dived out the door, tripping on a cobblestone and rolling down the grass. By the time I got to my feet and turned around the entire cottage was ablaze, the heat radiating outwards like I was standing in front of a furnace. The roof caught fire and turned to ash as I watched, stepping back from the intense heat. I heard footsteps and then Aunt Cass was at my side, pulling me away from the heat. A moment later the fire reversed, vanishing as fast as it had come, leaving the stone wall smoking, the roof turned to ashes and everything inside the cottage reduced to dust.

"Was that you? Did you Slip?" Aunt Cass gasped.

"No, it was something else," I said. I walked closer to the cottage, seeing that some of the stones inside were still glowing cherry red from the heat. The table was gone, the journal, the chair too. There was nothing left but the four walls of stone. But as the stones cooled from red to gray, a pale symbol appeared. It was the one that had been carved around town, appearing on doors, the one that Aunt Cass had copied and then spray painted everywhere.

"It's not some *thing* else," Aunt Cass said as the symbol appeared and then faded away.

"It's her, the Lost Witch."

AUTHOR NOTE

Read Lost Witch (Torrent Witches #9) now!

Thanks for reading my book! More witch stories to come. If you'd like an email when a new book is released then you can sign up for my mailing list. I have a strict no spam policy and will only send an email when I have a new release.

I hope you enjoyed my work! If you have time, please write a review. They make all the difference to indie Authors.

In the next book someone lost will be found...

xx Tess

TessLake.com